blaze

(or LOVE IN THE TIME OF SUPERVILLIANS)

blaze

(OR LOVE IN THE TIME OF SUPERVILLIANS)

laurie boyle crompton

 sourcebooks
fire

Published by Sourcebooks Fire, an imprint of Sourcebooks, Inc.
P.O. Box 4410, Naperville, Illinois 60567-4410
(630) 961-3900
Fax: (630) 961-2168
teenfire.sourcebooks.com

Library of Congress Cataloging-in-Publication data is on file with the publisher.

Printed and bound in the United States of America.
VP 10 9 8 7 6 5 4 3 2 1

For Brett, who once told me, "Love is a superpower."
And who continues to prove it is true.

Chapter One

Hear me X-Men! No longer am I the woman you knew!

I am FIRE! And LIFE INCARNATE!

Now and forever... I am PHOENIX!

—JEAN GREY, *THE UNCANNY X-MEN* #138

I am soaring free.

My astonishing future hurtles toward me with supernova force.

The open road ahead is bursting with the promise of *All New Adventures!* and the wind *Whooshes!* with the sound of...

"Fire in the hole!"

"Oh my *God*! A-*jay*!"

The groans hit me a split-second before the stench, and *Bampf!* I remember: *That's right. Soaring free isn't really my thing.*

My thing is driving my thirteen-year-old brother, Josh, and his friends around in a turd-brown minivan. I am the eternal chauffeur to a gang of Soccer Cretins. Make that totally-disgusting Soccer Cretins with reeking emissions issues.

"Dude, you should see a doctor or something," Andrew calls from the back, his voice muffled through the T-shirt held over his nose. "That is totally not normal."

I glance in the rearview mirror and see Ajay look up from his perpetual video game to smile proudly. "You guys like that one?"

Josh sucker punches Ajay, and the two of them start wrestling in the seat behind me. *Bash! Block! Kick!*

Over his T-shirt-mask, Andrew catches my eye in the mirror and we share a look of hopelessness.

Meanwhile, the horny freak to my right is busy ogling my cleavage. Again. I take a hand off the steering wheel to yank up my T-shirt's neckline. "Dylan, if you don't stop staring at my rack you're never sitting shotgun again."

Josh immediately stops his backseat battle with Ajay and leans forward to cuff Dylan's shaved head with his palm. "Dude! That's my sister."

"Ow! I was looking at the dashboard," Dylan lies as he adjusts his glasses. "Just checking how much gas we've used."

Josh, Andrew, Ajay, and I respond with a sarcastic harmony of, "Riiiight," and, "Sure," and, "We believe you."

Dylan scrambles to make his lie more elaborate by blaming all of global warming on the lousy gas mileage of my 2002 Grand Caravan: the mild-mannered minivan also known as the Subatomic Superturd of Steel.

I lean further out the window. The jolt of fresh air is a welcome change from the toxic cloud festering inside the minivan. Plus, it helps erase the sense that I've just been violated by Dylan's vulgar mind. *Please do not let me have a starring role in some near-future wet dream.*

I try imagining a superpower that would reduce my attractiveness to pubescent boys, while inversely making me more alluring to über-hotties like the cretins' coach, Mark. Putting out is likely the missing plutonium to that puzzle. I am, after all, the Amazing Su-per Virgin Girl! Fully flowered! With chastity of steel!

Not that I'm all that virtuous. It's pretty easy to say no when no one's even asking for it. I never took a vow of purity, but I have a nun's reputation anyway. It hasn't done much for my ability to snag a boyfriend, but I don't really want to use all my time and energy working on a sluttier image.

My dad gave me a cool name, Blaze, but my life is so unexciting that my name is more ironic than the soccer ball magnet I stuck on the back of my minivan—my failed attempt to create visual irony. The universal soccer mom badge suits me too well to be ironic.

I finally pull Superturd into the parking lot, where all the other minivans are wearing their soccer-ball magnets in a non-ironic manner. I've barely screeched to a total stop before the boys are evacuating through the sliding doors and thundering toward the field.

In my head, I commission them, *I bid thee, go forth, Mighty Cretins!*

Josh, the Nuclear Dynamo! *Greet your destiny of triumph with your superstar soccer skills. There isn't a twerpy little brother alive that I'd rather be driving all over green creation.*

Dylan, the Colossal Hormone! *May your lewd glances be reciprocated by the sideline MILFs on this fine day.*

Godspeed to you, Andrew, the small but swift Galactic Goalie! *Never has there existed a thirteen-year-old so above the immature fart jokes that surround thee.*

And dear Ajay, the Ozone Destroyer! *What can I say, aside from: Thank God you are clearing the hell outta my minivan before the seats melt.*

As usual, once the Mighty Cretins have cleared, I pull my faded pink beach chair out of Superturd's back end, grab my messenger bag covered in superhero pins, and make my way over to the field. After setting myself up on the sidelines, a bit removed from the cluster of overly aggressive parents, I put on my mirrored sunglasses to scan the field.

I quickly spot Mark, and everything else fades into background.

He strides easily across the field with a net sack filled with yellow soccer balls slung over one shoulder. I focus on the one bouncing playfully against his butt. *Man, how I'd love to be that soccer ball.*

Mark embodies the single wonder in my dismal pseudo-soccer-mom life. His taking over the team last spring was like a wish granted for my seventeenth birthday. A wish that was too fantastic for me to even think it up on my own. He and I go to the same school, but we may as well inhabit separate universes. Our lives are so different, it's like I'm stuck with Batman and Superman in the DC World, while Mark is partying in the Marvel Universe with every other worthwhile character. That's right. I said it: *Make mine Marvel.*

Mark wears a faded blue baseball cap over his dark curly hair and a gray Wolverine team shirt. The odds of him taking that shirt off are lessened by the cooling weather, which is quite tragic considering his spectacular abs.

In private, I've sketched him from every imaginable angle. Looking now at his strong legs, lined with muscles and covered with dark hair, I let myself wonder about what lies further up, under his thin white soccer shorts. Due to my Su-per Virgin Girl! alter-ego, I'm quite unfamiliar with that territory. That is, aside from a traumatizing walk-in on Josh peeing that shall never be mentioned again. To be totally honest, I'm mildly terrified of penises. (*Or would that plural be peni?*) Either way, the lump in Mark's shorts doesn't move as he strides across the even grass to shake hands with the other team's coach. The other coach is cute enough, yet I find I'm not the slightest bit curious what his penis looks like.

TWEEEET! The whistle sounds, signaling the start of the game. With a sigh, I flick my white-blonde ponytail behind one shoulder and pull my sketchpad out of my messenger bag. I take a quick inventory of the vintage comics I packed. There is nothing more awesome than good, old-fashioned, superhero-versus-bad-guy comic books. The classic ones where you can actually read a whole plot in five issues and one sitting. I'm not so into the current darkly stylized ones, and I don't much care for graphic novels or manga, but retro comics really turn me on.

Today, I have two *Iron Man*s, a *Silver Surfer*, and a *Daredevil* packed carefully in their individual Mylar sleeves. I have to take precautions to keep them in mint condition, since they're from the massive collection my dad left when he teleported his life to Manhattan.

My regular soccer sideline routine is to sketch my own comics until the game is nearly over and then lose myself in the super-hero stories. Opening my sketchpad, I flip to an empty page filled with endless possibilities.

"Blaze!" At the sound of my name, I look up and see a soccer ball heading straight for my head. My sketchpad slides off my lap as I instinctively half-stand to catch the ball.

FOOM!

The catch stings my shoulder. Rubbing it, I see Mark jogging lightly toward me. Before I can move, he's directly in front of me, easing the ball out of my hand. His proximity is exhilarating, plus I'm grateful I don't need to demonstrate my awkward ball-throwing technique.

I'm hypnotized by his smiling gray eyes, which are amplified by his gray shirt. "Nice reflexes," he says, and my insides give a twitch.

"You should see me throw." I grin, making a mental note to never let Mark see me throw.

He raises his eyebrows appreciatively, and sonic vibrations run through me. Mark turns to throw the ball gracefully to Josh, but before rejoining the action he gives me another look. Dipping his head, he mouths, "Thanks," in a way that is so hot I have to sit down in my pink folding chair before I lose consciousness. *Eep!*

Mark seems to have some unnamable quality that tunes my whole body to a higher frequency. Like Peter Parker's Spidey Sense, except with a whole different sort of tingling. What can I say? That boy just does it for me.

It takes a few moments before I'm able to refocus my attention back on my sketching, and even then, I draw a few accidental hearts in the margins before calming down enough to get back to work on my comic.

I've always liked doodling, but I didn't start drawing comics of my own until after I read through Dad's entire stash. The collection is stored in six huge boxes in our basement and includes most of the main Marvel characters from their origins up to the tail end of the 1980s. It's almost as if Dad left those boxes of comics behind on purpose. Like he was handing me a message that said he'd never forget about me and would come soaring back if I ever really needed him.

I suppose sketching is my silly way of trying to answer him back. Of letting him know I understand.

This one time, I even mailed a few sheets of my drawings to him in New York. They featured Ice Girl, my first attempt at creating my own superhero. She's a little shy, but seriously kicks butt with her ability to freeze and smash any bad guy that comes her way. I designed her with large breasts, like the super-chicks from the '80s, but I couldn't draw hands yet so Ice Girl flies with her arms behind her back. Which makes it look as if her boobs are her source of power. It probably made Dad wonder about me being gay or something, but I put a lot of time into drawing the comic panels I sent him and I liked how they came out.

Dad usually talks to me and Josh on the phone every few months or so, but he never did say anything about what he thought of *Ice Girl.* I figure he just forgot about it, or else it got lost in the mail. Or maybe she's just so totally lame he didn't want to hurt my feelings. I never bothered bringing it up.

Thankfully, I've moved past creating cheesy superheroes with porn-star breasts, and now most of my comics focus on a character who looks and talks and acts pretty much exactly like I do. Or how I *would* act if I wasn't such a geek, anyway. Plus she has telekinetic powers and mad skills with a dominatrix whip. Oh yes, and she has this ultra-cool hot-pink Mustang that *Zooms!* through the air, instead of a turd-brown soccer mom minivan.

I call her the Blazing Goddess and sometimes Blaze for short because, hey, my life may pretty much suck, but my name is still amazing.

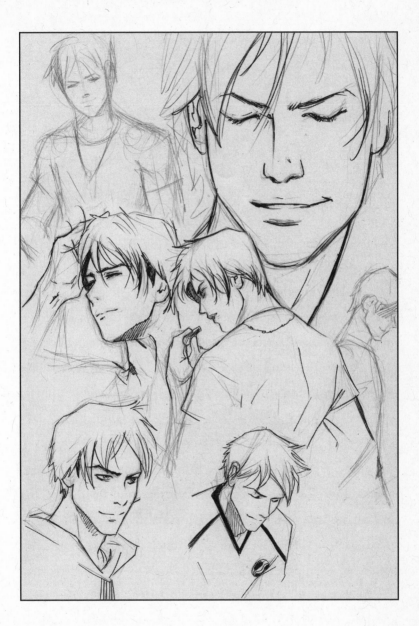

Chapter Two

As usual, I time my sideline activities perfectly. After drawing fourteen new panels of *The Amazing Adventures of the Blazing Goddess*, I start reading the comics I brought. I'm almost finished when I hear the air horn announcing the end of the game, and judging by everyone's expressions, the Wolverines won. I keep *Silver Surfer #51* lying open on my lap as I shift smoothly into Mark-stalking mode. I've built up some super-strong peripheral eye muscles over the course of the season, but with my sunglasses on I can be extra bold with my X-ray visualization.

On the field, the players line up congratulating each other as Mark talks to Josh, probably about how awesome he is at kicking the ball around. Despite the largish portion of my life spent at soccer games, I don't know all that much about the sport. But even I can see that Josh has skills.

I think about what would happen if I stood and walked right up to the two of them. After all, Josh is my brother. It's perfectly natural for me to go over and congratulate him on a game well played. Except that there would be nothing natural about me approaching Mark. I can't even remember how to walk naturally when I get around him. Does it go left foot, left arm? Or left foot, right arm, switch? Just thinking about it makes me feel a little spastic. I look down at my lap.

But then, *what is he doing?* My super peripheral vision notices Josh pointing in my direction. *Oh, God, why is he pointing at me?* I paw at *Silver Surfer #51* in a panic and blindly study Galctus throwing fireballs as my brother leads Mark and that penis of his directly toward me. As they get closer, I try to figure out at what point it'll seem normal for me to glance up and acknowledge them without it being obvious I've been watching them all along.

I peer over the top of my sunglasses, but neither of them is looking at me as they come closer, so I shoot my head back down, hoping Mark didn't see me looking. The next thing I know, they're standing over me. I squint at my comic as if I'm half-blind or something until Josh finally clears his throat. I totally overact, snapping my head up and feigning complete shock at seeing them there. Like they're aliens or things that don't even belong on a soccer field. I regroup after a few mental commands. *Pretend to be normal, Blaze!*

Finally, I manage to spit out a friendly, "Hey there! Good game," delivered to the space between the two of them.

"They really pulled it together in the second half." Mark

bops slightly, as if his body is channeling an inner thumping beat. It's barely noticeable, and yet it's the sexiest motion I've ever seen.

"My sister never really watches the games." Josh totally rats me out. "She's always either drawing or sticking her nose in some stupid comic book."

"Cool." Mark gestures to *Silver Surfer #51* lying open in my lap. "Oh, yeah, what's that dude's name again?"

"Uh, Galactus?" I try.

"No, I mean the silver dude. The one with the flying surfboard?"

"You mean the *Sil-ver Sur-fer?*" There is absolutely no way I can keep the sarcasm out of my voice, but it just makes Mark bop even more. *He's so pretty.*

"I guess that would be a good name for the guy." His smiling eyes draw me in like a tractor beam. The flat, grassy world around us exists only so that I can share this gaze with Mark. The hum of players and parents melts into white noise as I take in his thick dark curls and perfectly shaped face. Even the words on his T-shirt, "Kick Some Grass!", seem like the most clever catchphrase on the planet. The sound of my heartbeat grows so loud its *badda-thump* is all I hear… until Josh clears his throat, making me wish I was an only child.

Pulling out of my surreal Mark-filled moment, I give Josh what he must recognize as my fakest fake smile.

"Easy, sis, no need to get your geek on," he says. "Coach doesn't need to know the origin of the Silver Surfer—he just needs a ride home. I said we could fit him in the van, no problem."

"Yeah, sure," I say casually, as my insides roar at Josh, *No problem? How about huge problem? How about the fact that I drive a freakin' minivan that smells like recycled bologna, and I've been elected to transport the hottest guy to ever put on a pair of soccer shorts?* My apologies to David Beckham.

Mark chivalrously takes my folding chair in one arm, and just like that we're all heading toward Superturd together. Mark and I are about to be thrust together like the first time the DC and Marvel universes collided in 1976 with the oversized *Superman vs. The Amazing Spider-Man: The Battle of the Century.* Our worlds will be overlapping for the entire space of one sweaty forty-minute drive.

We reach the parking lot too soon, and I lunge for the minivan ahead of the gang. Pulling open the driver's door, I start shoving loose Dunkin' Donuts bags under the seat in desperation.

Dylan tries to claim shotgun as Mark tosses my chair and his giant mesh bag of balls in Superturd's butt.

"You're dreamin', horndog," I tell Dylan.

He slinks to the back as Mark climbs into the passenger seat and gives me a comfortable grin. My superhero buttons rattle as I start digging through my bag for my keys. After I find them, I continue rooting around, looking for some non-existent scrap of something that will empower me to seduce Mark and make him my boyfriend over the course of this ride. There is nothing helpful in my messenger bag.

I have no idea what to even talk about with such a fine specimen of male fineness. He's sitting so close I could reach over and touch him. It might be kind of hard to explain, and a little weird, maybe, but still... possible.

At first I'm relieved when he turns in his seat to discuss the game with the boys. Thankfully, there's no pressure to pull off an actual conversation. But as Superturd speeds past farm after farm and his coach-chat turns into a lengthy discussion of the team's "next strategy," I start to feel a bit ignored. It dawns on me that if the entire ride passes without a single interaction between the two of us, it will solidify my nonexistence in Mark's universe. *If I don't do something drastic soon...*

"COWS!" I call out as we pass a field of cattle. "One, two, three, four, five, six, seven!"

"Wha—?" Mark swings around to face me. "Did you just count those cows?"

I grin and call out, "That's twenty-one, plus seven, which gives me twenty-eight. I'm *win-ning.*"

"No fair," whines Dylan, "You have front seat advantage!"

"You lost shotgun rights for ogling my sister's boobs." Josh defends me and humiliates me all at once.

I glance over at Mark and blush. "So," he smiles and gives the bill of his hat a quick lift. "Cows?"

My heart starts *badda-thumping* again.

"It's a stupid thing we do on these long drives. Whoever sees a herd first gets to collect them and add them to their total score."

Ajay chimes in from the third-row seat, "But we've expanded it to include all farm animals. Cows, horses, goats, even chickens." He pauses to slurp one of the orange wedges he scored from Mrs. Schmidt. "Blaze is winning, but Dylan has ten and Josh has thirteen."

"Ajay, that's disgusting!" Andrew yells. "You just spit orange pulp on my arm."

"Yeah, Ajay, don't spit," Dylan says lewdly. "Andrew prefers you swallow."

"Easy, Dylan," Josh pipes in. "Try to keep your pervy fantasies to yourself." Which gets the other boys laughing and teasing Dylan.

Mark gasps, and I'm about to tell him how Dylan's sexual fantasies are just an ongoing joke with us, but Mark is busy pointing. He calls out, "Ooooh! Sheep! I call sheep!" There's a huge flock of them in the field we're passing, and I grimace as Mark starts counting. "One, two, three, four…"

I ease pressure on the gas as he counts faster. "Ten, eleven, twelve…" I urge Superturd to drive faster, "sixteen, seventeen, eighteen…" I glance down and see the needle creeping toward 90 miles per hour as Mark creeps closer and closer to my score, "twentyonetwentytwotwentythree…" The minivan starts shimmying with the effort until, finally, I reach the treeline and Mark has to stop counting his sheep.

"Whew, that's twenty-eight," he says smugly. "How many do you have again?"

"Twenty-eight," I growl. I never lose a game of Cows. Ever.

"All right, coach!" Josh calls out. "My sister never loses."

"I can see why," he laughs. "How fast were you driving?"

"What?" I say innocently. "That's called driver's advantage." I look around desperately for some cows, any cows, even just a single cow to get me back on top. Nothing but massive cornfields whizz by on either side. I shouldn't really mind losing to someone as hot as Mark. I just can't bear to have my ass handed to me in front of the boys.

Mark leans forward in his seat, obviously scanning for a herd of cattle. *I must distract him.* "Sooo, soccer, huh?" I say.

"Yup, love soccer…" His brows pull together as he continues his quest for cows. By now we're both sitting up, our bodies leaning forward in anticipation.

"Team looks good," I try again.

"Yup." My ploy to distract him with a soccer-centric conversation clearly isn't working. He adds, "So, what's the deal with you and the comics?" *As if I can be distracted so easily.*

"Read 'em, draw 'em. Yup, I sure love comics…"

I glance over, and Mark pretends to press his face into the windshield. "Where's the cows? Where's the cows?" he says and grins at me.

We both burst out laughing. I lean back in my seat, and he

shifts his body in my direction and casually raises his left knee, opening his legs toward me. Which only makes the proximity of what lies under his thin shorts seem more undeniable. I focus intently on the road ahead. My mind is no longer thinking of cows.

"Seriously, is 'Blaze' your nickname because you're so into comics, or maybe because you drive so fast?" I glance toward him, and he narrows his eyes. "Or are you a closet pothead?"

"Blaze is her actual name." Josh leans up between the seats, reminding me that Mark and I aren't alone. "Dad was really into *Ghost Rider* as a kid, so he named her after Johnny Blaze. Mom got smart by the time I came along, and that's why I got a normal name."

"Why don't you play your DS?" I suggest kindly, then shoot my head around to emphasize, "Josh!" in my evil older sister voice.

"I'm good." Josh leans his elbow on my backrest. I reach back and knock Josh's elbow so he does a face-plant against my seat.

"Okay, okay." He holds up his hands in surrender. "Ajay's using the outlet back here, I need you to plug me in."

"Fine," I say and wait for Josh to hand me the car adapter for his game.

"I'm playing Sonic Rush," Ajay says. "Wanna sync up?"

I glance in the rearview mirror, and Josh gives me a troubled glance before turning around in his seat to face Ajay. Andrew and Dylan huddle around to watch the rousing DS battle on the teeny-tiny screens. It suddenly feels as if Mark and I are alone, which makes me remember to be nervous all over again.

"So, Blaze, huh?" Mark tips his hat back and bops up and down in a solicitous way. *He is actually flirting with me*, I think as I flip my blonde ponytail off my shoulder. *And more amazing still, I'm flirting back.*

"Yeah, it hardly suits me." I face forward and blush as sweat lubricates my grip on the steering wheel.

"Oh, I don't know," he says. "I imagine there's a burning flame in there somewhere." With my peripheral vision I catch him glancing at my chest. Instead of getting grossed out, like I do when Dylan peeks, I feel a *ka-POW!* surge in my lower belly. Flustered, I squint out the windshield.

"Yes!!" Half the back seat lets out a cheer over something Sonic Rush–related, and Mark turns around. As he's distracted, I allow myself a look of shock over his attention. I blink quickly as my mind screams, *He's totally coming on to me. Doesn't he know about Su-per Virgin Girl? Chastity of Steel? Nobody comes on to me!* By the time he turns back around, I've managed to rearrange my face into a normal expression.

"I used to rock at Sonic." Mark laughs. "So, you never answered me. What's with this great attraction to comics?"

"Oh, well, my dad really got me into them." Without meaning to, I start talking nonstop, telling him all about Dad's prize collection of comics. From there, I launch right into telling him about how he took off to become an actor in New York City.

"Any chance you saw that episode of *Law & Order* where the guy seems all straitlaced, but meanwhile he's killing college girls and throwing them into the Hudson?"

"I'm not sure, maybe?" Mark shrugs. "Sounds familiar."

"Well, anyway, my dad played that guy. He's pretty good. He's been in a bunch of stuff."

"Sounds cool. Much better than my dad, who could probably be the sicko throwing bodies into a river in real life. He's a psycho. But at least he's out of the picture."

Mark says it like it's no big deal, but I feel sad for him. An awkward silence settles around us. *Nothing like bringing up a guy's deadbeat dad to kill the mood.* When I glance back at the boys, I catch Josh give me a look of relief. At least he's happy I'm blowing things with his coach.

"So," Mark says finally, "what superhero would you want for a father?"

Happy for the topic change, I launch into geek-girl mode. "Well, my dad's pretty cool already, but Captain America does have that hyper-honorable thing going on. Then there's the Silver Surfer showing mercy at the cost of his own freedom, not to mention Daredevil and all his charity work…" Mark seems amused by my excitement, but I can't turn it off. My alter ego *Virgin Girl!* won't let me shut up.

I'm working my way through the various incarnations of the X-Men, selecting the most awesome mutant powers, when Mark suddenly interrupts me. "HORSES!" he calls out in triumph. "One, two!"

"*AAAA-aaa!*" I wail and the boys emerge from their Sonic-trance to mock me.

"That's...what is that? Thirrrrrrrty?" Mark sings, "I have thirrrty!"

"And how many do you have, Blaze?" Ajay asks. "Was it tweeenty-eeeight?" The entire minivan is suddenly filled with taunting boys, and I curse myself for allowing Mark to get me distracted.

"Okay, okay, simmer down back there," he says. "The two of us were in the middle of a very serious conversation about superpowers."

Josh says, "Nice strategy, Coach, getting her to talk about comics. But you should know you'll never get her to stop now."

"Aw, Josh, lay off your sis," says Andrew. "And A-*jay*, would you mind controlling your bodily functions?" Groans fill Superturd as the boys pull their T-shirts over their noses, making sweaty cotton gas-masks.

"Man," says Dylan. "I can taste that one!" Ajay smirks proudly, his thumbs still stabbing his DS.

I glance at Mark, sufficiently mortified to have him witness my pathetic world. Adolescent boys, video games, and fart jokes. Add to that my blatant comic book obsession, and you can see a few problems with the whole seduction scene I have happening in my minivan right now.

"So, if you could have any superpower…" Mark says, and I roll my eyes, thinking, *I'd turn back time, wear something a bit more girly today, and maybe ditch the sweaty gang of cretins behind us.*

"Marvel Girl is probably my favorite superhero. You know, the original Jean Grey?" I say. "But if I had to pick one power it would have to be flight. What about you?"

He thinks a moment and says, "I never really followed superheroes. What are some of my choices?"

"Oh, you don't have to pick a particular hero." I forget to hide my inner fangirl. "For instance, Ajay would be sort of like Magneto, with control over electromagnetic radiation to enhance his gaming abilities." Ajay looks up from the DS to grin at me in the rearview mirror. "Dylan would shrink himself into a human fly. Like Ant Man, but without the cybernetic helmet for communicating with insects." I laugh as, behind me, Dylan pretends to style his buzz-cut. "He wouldn't want to get helmet-head."

"Blaze thinks it's so I can spy on the girls' locker room." Dylan leans forward, pushing his glasses up on his nose for emphasis. "But really, it's only to consume fewer of the earth's precious resources. I want to leave a smaller carbon footprint."

"Yeah." Josh laughs. "You'd love to leave your teeny carbon footprints all over Catherine Wiggan's cleavage."

Catherine Wiggan, aka Wiggles, is the school's resident

large-breasted slut, and I need to keep talking so Mark doesn't get lost thinking of her. "Josh would, of course, have super speed," I say. "Like Quicksilver or Flash."

"He almost does already," Mark says, dipping the bill of his hat to Josh.

Josh lifts his chin. "Thanks, Coach."

"Andrew here won't participate because he thinks wishing for superpowers is pointless." I scan for cows as I continue. "Although once, when we were totally lost, he did say he'd like the power to communicate with global positioning satellites."

Mark laughs. "That would be the game against the Timberwolves that we almost had to forfeit?"

"We made it on time." I pout.

"Barely."

"Well, I forgot Ajay's inhaler that day and had to go back for it *just in case*, so we got a late start."

Mark turns around and looks at Ajay. "You need an inhaler?"

Ajay just shrugs as he bows over his DS.

"Ajay!" I shoot. "You never told your coach you have asthma?" Ajay is tall for thirteen, and to look at him you'd never guess he's asthmatic, but he must have a complex or something because he hates when anyone brings it up. I'm pretty furious he hasn't even mentioned his condition to Mark. "What if you had an episode and I wasn't around?"

"Aw, come on, Blaze!" Ajay hunches down further. "I haven't

used the inhaler for almost a year now. Besides, you're always around." He meets my gaze in the rearview mirror. "Where else you gonna be?"

I cringe at that. We're far enough along in the season for Mark to have noticed I don't exactly have a life of my own, but honestly, I don't need Ajay pointing it out. I sigh and tell Mark, "So, *anyway*, that's the gang. You pick and choose whatever superpower suits your needs."

As I wait for Mark's answer, I watch the fields on either side of us thinking, *not even a single stinking chicken.* We're close to home, and the game officially ends at my first drop off, which is Ajay. I can't lose at Cows. Especially when Mark's only been playing for the ride home.

I get the flash of an idea just as he says, "Well, if I had to choose only one superpower I suppose…" I turn to look at him and am startled by how light his gray eyes are, "it would have to be the power to heal."

I swerve a bit and turn my attention back to the road. "Healing? Really?" For the first time, wanting to fly seems like a selfish, self-serving superpower. I want to change my choice to healing too. To help others. But honestly, deep down, I still really want to fly.

Mark shrugs. "Maybe that could free you up from lugging around Ajay's inhaler."

I smile from the inside out as Andrew calls, "Hey, Blaze, where you going? You dropping coach off first or something?"

I see the other boy's heads shoot up collectively. Josh says, "I know exactly what she's doing."

Dylan gives a wolf-whistle. "Looking for a little alone time with the coach, Blaze?" And I make a mental note to murder him later.

Josh leans forward. "Not that." He eyes Mark warily.

"No way," says Ajay as all the boys look out the front windshield. "Coach, you should probably know…"

Pressing my foot on the gas, I coax Superturd to hurry its plump minivan ass up. I strain forward against my seatbelt.

"I can't believe she's resorting to this," Dylan says excitedly.

"What is it?" Mark asks, "Another farm?" He scoots to the front of his seat, ready to claim another herd. "I think I remember someone having emus down this way. Do emus count?"

"No Coach, you gotta listen," Ajay says, but I cut him off.

"What Ajay is trying to say is… GRAVEYARD!" I call out in victory. "Sorry, Mark, your herd is dead."

"What the—" Mark looks at me like I'm crazy.

"Oh, I killed your herd," I explain lightly. "Whoever claims a graveyard first can wipe out someone else's animals. Did I not mention that rule?"

"We tried to warn you, dude," says Ajay. "She's super-competitive."

"Hey, no fair," Mark says. "I didn't even know."

"Take it up with the committee, my friend," I say. "Boys? Can we get a ruling on that play?"

"Blaze wins again," Dylan says. "But you really almost had her, Coach."

"That's the closest anyone's ever come," says Josh, eyeing me skeptically.

Mark laughs. "Okay then, I'd like to declare a rematch." He aims his gray eyes my way. "Any chance I can grab a ride for the Aliquippa game next week? I'm saving up to get a new tranny for my pickup." I can't believe he wants to ride with me again. He goes on, "I caught a ride with Mrs. Schmidt this morning, and I still feel queasy from the smell of all those orange wedges." Mrs. Schmidt takes her role as soccer mom very seriously and is always armed with an orange wedge or a Dixie cup of Gatorade at the slightest hint of parching.

"I'd take oranges over the smell of Ajay's ass any day," says Josh.

"We can drive you," I say, feeling a bit queasy myself. "You guys may manage to whip Aliquippa, but I wouldn't count on you ever beating me at Cows."

"We'll have to see about that." Mark flashes me a grin that gives me tingles, as though Superturd's seat-warmers are suddenly functioning again. Like Mark's super-healing-power wish is already working magic on my minivan.

Chapter Three

"I still think we should host ourselves a little coed soirée," says Josh, pronouncing *soirée* in his fake-snooty voice. "My friends would love to rub shoulders with your friends."

"Ick!" I shudder as I serve dinner for the two of us. "I can imagine Dylan trying to rub more than shoulders. Amanda might think his pathetic boob obsession is cute, but Terri would probably clock him."

"Dylan's a big talker, but you know he's completely intimidated by girls." Josh waggles his eyebrows. "*Especially* seventeen-year-old girls who are totally hot."

"Aaaaand, there's reason number one-hundred-thirty-*seven* why my friends and your friends will never comingle." I stab at the mound of spaghetti on my plate. It's a little mushy, since I was distracted by my social studies homework and overcooked the pasta again. I tried to jazz up the canned sauce with a little oregano and the overall effect is… well, edible anyway. "We are *not* having a party this weekend. Period."

"Come on, Blaze, how often do we get a chance to have an unsupervised par-tay? We could make history among our peers."

I scowl. "We get the chance about every other weekend, and who will care about us making history if Mom comes home from the hospital and murders us? She'd totally know how to make it look like an accident, too, ever think of that?" Mom has an overnight shift twice a month, so Josh and I have this discussion fairly often.

"I'm just saying—you'll be a total hero with the guys if you hook us up with a little face-to-face time with your friends."

"Don't you mean face-to-breast time?" I laugh at my own joke as we hear Mom's Subaru pull into the driveway.

"Very funny," Josh deadpans. "We will discuss these party plans later."

"Or, I could just go ahead and tell Mom your scheme and kill the idea right now," I say. "You know she won't go for it."

"She might. I just think sometimes it's easier to ask for forgiveness than permission." Josh waves his arms and shushes me as Mom turns the doorknob. As if I'd really aggravate her mood right after work by ratting out his plans.

"Hey guys," Mom says with fake chipperness. Her pale-blue hospital scrubs drape from her bowed shoulders. "You made dinner? Aw, Blaze, you're the best." A brief smile fights its way through her weariness, "I don't know…"

"Know what you'd do without me," I finish for her, rolling my eyes. "I know. Why don't you go change, and I'll make you a plate. Then you can tell us all about the lives you saved today." Mom's a physician's assistant and works ridiculous hours in the emergency room. She doesn't talk much about what happens during her shifts, other than to say it isn't at all like those TV shows where everybody on staff is sleeping around with everybody else. *She wishes*. But Josh and I don't need her to say anything to tell she's had a rough day. Judging by the airbags under her eyes, I'd guess somebody died today. Maybe even someone who wasn't all that old or sick.

"Rough shift?" I ask as I serve her spaghetti.

"It was fine. I'm just glad it's over."

The three of us eat in silence a few moments, our mouths cemented shut with starch.

"I saw Dad on television today," Josh reports. "He was playing a corpse on a rerun of one of those *CSI*s. The New York one, I think."

"How nice for him. Playing dead." Mom's smile stays locked behind her mask of weariness. "Sounds like he finally found his true calling. Oh, and Blaze? That reminds me. I got a text from your father the other day asking if you'd take an inventory of those big boxes of comics he… left."

My heart starts beating faster. Does this mean he's coming back to get them? When Dad first *ZAPPED!* off to New York to become an actor, I was Josh's age and Mom promised he'd be back in a month or so. She said Dad would get "all this nonsense" out of his system and come home to his old sales job at Electronics Empire. And to us.

Problem is, he never did.

He hasn't been to the house in almost four years. Not that I can blame him for staying away, what with Mom freaking out and threatening to have him arrested for trespassing the last time he was here.

It seems like a lifetime ago. I was so young. Thirteen. Hadn't even gotten my visit from the booby fairy yet. Dad showed up spontaneously to take us out for goofy golf and ice cream. He drove seven hours and 400 miles from New York to spend a little time with his children. Mom looked so happy. This was back when we were all still hoping he'd give up his acting dreams and come back home to be a salesman again. Dad has sold nearly everything, from cars to fresh preserves to copy paper, and Mom used to say he could sell snow to an Eskimo.

When he invited her to come along that day, it looked like she considered it before shaking her head. "No, maybe next visit. You should spend time with your son and daughter."

Dad grinned at her as he put an arm around each of our shoulders. "Exactly what I plan to do." And Mom actually smiled back. I remember nine-year-old Josh sucking in his breath and privately grabbing my arm in excitement. Because he'd seen what I'd seen. Mom and Dad were getting back together, right there in front of us.

I remember Josh and Dad and I having such a fun afternoon our heads could've exploded. We joked and clowned around so much we got about the worst-ever miniature golf scores. Then, we got big waffle cones of exotic-flavored ice cream from King Cone and sat down to eat them at a nearby picnic table. I even remember Josh taking a big risk by ordering peanut-butter-and-jelly ice cream and Dad letting him toss it for plain vanilla when he got a taste of how bad it was. It was a pretty-darn-near-perfect day with our dad.

Too bad it was the last one.

When he brought us home, he and Mom started off with the friendly talking we'd hoped for, but things took an ugly turn fast. Dad's big mistake was telling Mom that our day had actually been good for his acting career, since he was up for a big role in a sitcom pilot. He'd be playing the father to two children, aged about nine and thirteen.

"They're even a boy and a girl, although in the show, the boy's the oldest," he told Mom happily, not noticing the way the vein in her temple pulsed. "My agent thinks I have a pretty good shot at the role. And then, if the show gets picked up, I'll really be on my way." He seemed so proud, I physically hurt for him since I knew Mom was already twisting the coincidence into something ugly. She was silent for a full three minutes, and I pictured her wrestling with an inner rage. My mind begged her to let it go.

"So you mean to tell me you haven't seen your children for

nearly five months," she started off quiet and grew progressively louder, "and you were finally motivated to take the drive to see them, not because you felt guilty for neglecting them? Or even out of some sense of duty? No!" By that point Mom's neck veins were popping. "This day of playing 'loving dad' was all for research for a *stupid* role for a *stupid* TV show that will be *STUPID*?"

As she shouted her final "stupid" I hustled Josh upstairs and blasted my stereo. But we could still hear scraps of threats delivered in her crazy-Mom voice. ". . . five minutes to disappear… trespassing… never come back…" and finally, "calling the police…" which must've gotten Dad's butt moving, since the next things we heard were the *SLAM!* of the front door and the *VROOM!* of the Oldsmobile he'd borrowed peeling out of the driveway.

That was four years ago. We totally still have a relationship with our dad, talking over the phone here and there and meeting at Mema's house in Ohio that one time, but he has never once come back to take us to eat ice cream and play goofy golf and laugh so hard we can't even hold a club straight.

Shrugging off ghosts of the past, I project fake casualness as I ask Mom, "So, did Dad say why he needs a list of the comics?"

She pauses, chewing her spaghetti slowly, as she gives me that poor-abandoned-girl-with-the-shitty-father look that I hate. I hold up my palm, "Never mind, okay? Just let him know I'll get it done. Mind if I'm excused?"

"Sure, sweetie," Mom says. "I'll clean up when I'm done."

"No, you're tired from your shift." I stand up as Josh studies his plate. "I'm just going up to my room to chat with Terri and Amanda. I'll come back down to clean up in a little while."

Mom gives me a grateful look. "You're the best, sweetie, I just don't know…"

But I'm halfway up the stairs and can't hear the rest of her worn mantra. She really does appreciate all the help I give her. Besides, it's not like I have a ton of social offers waiting for me anyway.

TerriAngel445: Going to game tonight?
AmandaSweetie68: or mall?

Okay, okay. So maybe I have a few social offers. Terri and Amanda are my friends. That is, to the extent that my role as the eternal chauffeur to the gang of Soccer Cretins allows me time for friends. Fortunately, the two of them were locked in before Superturd became my BFF.

Growing up in the country, if you can ride your bike to a girl's house and that girl also happens to be in your grade, *BOOM!* You have yourself a best friend.

The summer before fourth grade, Terri moved into a house about a half-mile away, and even though there are five girls in her family and the odds were in my favor that one of them would be my age, it still felt like a miracle when we met. I finally had somebody I could visit whenever I wanted without begging Mom and Dad for a ride.

Becoming friends with Terri took some adjusting, since she's a little bold. For instance, she's never been shy about asking for my stuff. She'll say in one breath, "Oooh, I love that lipgloss—can I have it?" But then, I suppose living with four sisters makes a girl aggressive with beauty care items in a way the rest of us will never understand. I usually give her what she asks for and figure it's better than a friend who steals stuff behind your back. Plus, like I said, she is just a bike ride away.

Then, later that same year, lightning struck again when Amanda moved in. She's even more of a contrast than Terri: only child, rich overprotective parents, and she lives at the end of a ritzy cul-de-sac. But that ritzy cul-de-sac happens to be halfway between my house and Terri's, so you can see how obviously tight the three of us have been ever since.

We don't actually have tons in common, so our trio grew much less exclusive when we reached high school. But then I got my minivan license and started playing soccer mom, and most of my other friends gave up on hanging out with me all together. Even Amanda and Terri are sick of my excuses. They're not going to be happy I'm staying in again tonight.

TerriAngel445: Blaze? Hello? Earth to Blaze
AmandaSweetie68: i c u online!!

Stalling, I use my index finger to wipe the thin film of dust off my laptop screen. It was a gift from Dad. It's his old one, but it's still in great shape and has plenty of memory and I love it.

TerriAngel445: BLAZE!!!

Blazefire22: No need to shout. Mom needs my help. Sorry can't come out to play

AmandaSweetie68: come on! u never do anything

TerriAngel445: Bet if we were kiddie soccer players, you'd come hang with us.

Blazefire22: I'll have you know, there was a post-pubescent boy riding in my minivan today. A certain coach for the Wolverines :)

AmandaSweetie68: u had mark alone in ur car?

TerriAngel445: !!!

Blazefire22: Well, if you don't count the four boys in the back and call my smelly minivan a car—then, yes, Mark and I were totally alone in my car.

AmandaSweetie68: 4 boys in the back is Wiggles style—lol did u c the latest? http://catherinewigglesisaslut.com

TerriAngel445: that girl has zero shame

AmandaSweetie68: slut

Blazefire22: I saw the link. Nice and skanky. Now can we get back to my gossip?

TerriAngel445: Why would you let Mark the Shark in your van?

AmandaSweetie68: right ter, he's so f-ing hot, how cld she stand it?

TerriAngel445: That boy is such a manwhore

Blazefire22: We actually had a pretty good time.

TerriAngel445: Please don't tell us you played one of those stupid driving games like the time you dragged me to Josh's practice.

I picture the day Terri spent an entire half-hour drive sitting shotgun and growling with annoyance every few minutes as the boys and I played a particularly aggressive round of Alphabet. I don't think she'd approve of my introducing Mark to the exciting and competitive game of Cows.

Blazefire22: Well.... .

AmandaSweetie68: omg you didnt! u r such a geek! it's okay, lol, he prob thought it was cute. u r so lucky u r blonde

TerriAngel445: You didn't go into one of your comic lovin' nerd-fest monologoues did you?

Blazefire22: It's monologues, and I think I hear my Mom calling—gotta go!

AmandaSweetie68: geek!

TerriAngel445: Nerd!

Blazefire22: Peace out—love yas

AmandaSweetie68: xo, gnight.

TerriAngel445: Night Blaze, have sweet dreams about *getting a life*!

I chuckle as I close my browser, throw on PJs, and head back downstairs to finish cleaning up. Josh and Mom have made an attempt, scraping their dishes and putting them into the sink, but there are goops of sauce everywhere and it takes me half an hour to put the kitchen back together.

"Tomorrow's pizza day at school," I call into the den, where Josh is watching TV.

"I'll buy!" Josh calls back, so I stick three singles from the jar on the fridge into his backpack. I love pizza day. Josh always buys on pizza day, and making lunches sucks. Especially since all he ever wants are Fluffernutters and we're completely out of Fluff.

I try to piece my own lunch together from the meager pickings in the fridge. I need to bug Mom to go food shopping. Or even better, I'll just find some time to go, and give her the receipt. Laying out the cash is never really a problem. The Soccer Cretins' parents all insist on paying me gas money even though I have a gas card. Mom says I deserve to keep the extra money for all the help I do, and the cash adds up over the course of the soccer season. Especially since I don't have oodles of free time to run out to the mall. In fact, with birthday money thrown in, I'm up over two hundred bucks right now. Too bad I can't just buy myself a life.

We're out of brown paper bags, so I toss a few crackers, a softening apple, and a hunk of pound cake wrapped in tinfoil into a geeky white plastic shopping bag for myself. As I spin it closed and tuck it into my messenger bag, I think of Mark riding in the passenger seat of Superturd.

He must think I'm so immature, what with all the comics talk and the counting of farm animals. On the other hand, I do have the middle-age-momster wheels and pack of soccer wards to balance out my juvenile behavior. *The girls are right; I'm a freak and Mark will never be my boyfriend.* I'm curious why Terri thinks he fits into the "shark" category. From what I know he doesn't seem to date all that often.

I take out my sketchbook and sit down at the kitchen table to draw a rough picture of Mark cruising the halls as some sort of mutant shark-man. I put gills on either side of his ribcage and sketch a huge mouth filled with rows of razor-sharp teeth. "Instead of the scent of blood," I letter carefully, "*Mark the Shark* frenzies at the sight of an attractive female." In real life, I'm lucky if Mark even sees me as female—forget about "attractive."

Don't get me wrong, I know I'm not a total Mole Man or anything. I'm just stuck in secret identity mode. That is, I'm a terminal Clark Kent/Peter Parker character, lying low as I hang out with my little brother and his horny friends. Pretty much invisible. But not a sexy Susan Storm in blue lycra sort of invisibility. More of a don't-make-eye-contact-with-the-sad-blonde-fangirl-who-is-always-drawing-comics-and-pretending-to-be-a-soccer-mom sort of invisibility.

I do find it interesting there aren't any classic male superheroes whose power is becoming invisible, but it's pretty common with the girls. Heck, Wonder Woman even flies around in an invisible jet. Which would be quite a sight, really. A totally stacked babe, dressed up in a flag, shooting through the air as she moons the whole world with her fabulous blue-and-white starry butt. Boy, wouldn't my brother's perverted little friends love a glimpse of that.

I smile to myself as I pack away my sketchbook. Now that Mark has noticed me, I have a feeling my days of invisibility are finally about to end.

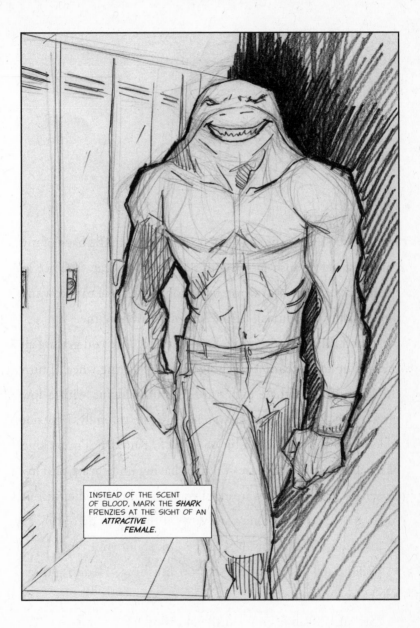

INSTEAD OF THE SCENT OF BLOOD, MARK THE *SHARK* FRENZIES AT THE SIGHT OF AN *ATTRACTIVE FEMALE.*

Chapter Four

In a panic, I rub my honey-glow lip gloss off with the back of my hand just before Josh jumps into the passenger seat. I glance in the minivan's rearview mirror, but I don't have time to throw my loose hair into a ponytail before Josh starts ribbing me.

"Oooh, Blaze," he says in a dreamy voice. "Are you getting all prettied up for Dylan?" Hunching over the steering wheel, I turn the key and accentuate Superturd's starting engine with a low growl. Josh's grin fades as he watches my face carefully. I try not to look nervous, but I'm a bit of a wreck. Knowing I'm picking Mark up is much more stressful than having him thrust into my passenger seat without warning. I've made a mental checklist of topics to avoid, with comics and cows at the top of the list.

Josh says, "Kidding aside, Blaze. Mark is not your type."

I shake my head, trying to stop blushing. "I don't know what you're—"

"Seriously, sis. He's not worth your time."

I roll my eyes. "I don't have a crush on your coach."

"It seems like you do." Josh pulls up a section of my hair and holds it to my face as if anything other than a ponytail is evidence of my crush.

I push his hand from my hair. "You're wrong."

"Why don't we just take a little poll. See what the guys think?"

"You wouldn't…" I envision the mob of cretins mocking me from the back of the minivan. If they say anything in front of Mark I'll be vaporized with embarrassment. My face must betray my fear.

Josh's look of concern is slowly replaced by one of excitement. "I have an idea," he says. "How about we have that coed party I've been talking about? Mom's working her all-nighter this weekend. It'll be perfect."

"No way," I insist as I pull into Dylan's driveway. "Nice try." I'm pretty sure he's bluffing and won't really launch all the boys into teasing me about my crush on Mark.

"Hey, Dylan!" Josh turns in his seat to greet his hormone-laden friend, "Guess what's going on in Blaze's comic book mind?"

The look I shoot him says *You wouldn't!* but his look back says *Oh yes, I would.* I don't know for sure whether or not he'd really tell Dylan about my crush, but I do know I can't risk it.

"We're having a party at the house this weekend!" I announce. *Where the hell did that come from?*

"We?" Dylan leans forward, adjusts his glasses, and turns to Josh to see if it's true. "Will Terri and Amanda be there?" He can't hide the naked hope in his voice.

"Of course," Josh answers before I can undo what I've started.

Flaring my nostrils, I start damage-control. "*But* absolutely no booze! And I don't even know if my friends will agree to come. *And* this is only happening if you boys promise to behave, plus take care of all the details. Dylan, you can bring corn chips."

As we pick up each team member they're greeted with the party announcement and assigned snack items, so by the time I stop for Mark it's all they can talk about.

Josh begrudgingly surrenders shotgun when I get to his house.

Dylan leans forward as Mark climbs in beside me. "Josh and Blaze are throwing a par-tay this weekend."

"No we're not!" I say, "I mean, we are, but it's no big thing. No alcohol, just the boys and a few of my friends."

Mark gives me a smirk that melts my insides to radioactive sludge. "Hmm," he says in a deep voice. "House party? When is it?"

Oh, God. He cannot be thinking of coming.

"Our mom has the overnight shift on Saturday," I say, then shoot over my shoulder to the boys, "which means she'll be home by 6:30 Sunday morning, and the house must be spotless."

Dylan and Josh are so excited I can almost see radiation waves emanating from their bodies. Even Ajay is paying attention instead of focusing on his DS. Only Andrew seems to take the whole thing in stride. He says, "I can't stay too late. I've got church Sunday morning with my mom."

As the others are distracted with calling Andrew "Choir Boy" and butting him with fake finger-horns held to their heads, I steal a glance at Mark. He's watching me with that sly smile of his, and I get so flustered I nearly crash the minivan. "I'd love to come hang out Saturday, if that's cool with you."

I cannot believe the cretins' tawdry adolescent fantasy has just morphed into an opportunity to spend time with Mark beyond the smelly bowels of Superturd. Plus, I see a way to entice Terri and Amanda to actually show up.

"Sounds good." I shrug, hoping Mark can't hear my wild heartbeat. "It's casual. You can bring a friend or two if you like."

Mark nods happily, and I realize I should clarify that I don't need him to bring a date to my house. I glance from the road back to him, trying to gauge whether he'd really use our party to hook up with some slut. Like for instance 'Wiggles' of catherinewigglesisaslut.com fame—the diseased girl at our school with a whole website devoted to her slutty exploits.

I add, "You can bring some extra pop if you do decide to come."

His grin doesn't falter, and I feel reasonably reassured he's not using our soirée for a cheap date. *No matter what happens*, I tell myself, *nobody had better even consider having sex on my mother's bed.* I try to picture Dylan, with his shaved head and glasses, managing to seduce Amanda or Terri and nearly laugh out loud at that possibility. I have a pretty good imagination but still can't work up an image that bizarro.

"DUCKS!" Mark yells at the top of his lungs.

I curse myself for daydreaming. "Ducks don't count," I say.

Ajay chimes in, "They do when they're big white ones hanging out on a farm."

"Those ducks are clearly farm ducks," says Dylan.

"Here we go again," says Andrew as Mark speed-counts the cluster of ducks and I push my Subatomic Sweatmobile of Fate to fly as fast as she can.

• • •

"I cannot believe you talked us into this," Terri says as she and Amanda walk through my front door that Saturday night. Terri is wearing tight jeans and a fitted black shirt that betrays her hope that Mark will bring along someone interesting. Preferably male. The possibility of making time with some of Mark's friends finally convinced the two of them to gamble on the more likely scenario of a gang of adolescents drooling on their cleavage in-between rounds of Wii sports.

Terri has this whole pretty, petite, pixy-thing happening with her short dark hair and freckles and a laugh that makes guys want to take care of her. And Amanda is just gorgeous in the truest sense of the word. Her figure is more female superhero than anorexic supermodel, but let me tell you, human boys go gaga for her juicier physique. Looking down at my green striped Adidas T-shirt, I realize that if I wanted to impress Mark, I really should have uglier friends.

"Is Mark here yet? Did he bring any hot guys?" Amanda asks breathlessly as she hands me a pillow-sized bag of generic potato chips. "This is the biggest bag I could find."

"Um. Hello to you too." I usher the two of them into the house, where the boys are already huddled around the television in the den. Our main floor has two bedrooms in the back. One of those is my mom's, which I've had the foresight to lock before any of the guys arrived, effectively dashing Dylan's unimaginable fantasies. The other has been converted into a den and has the huge flat screen Dad won for being the top salesman at Electronics Empire just before he left. Mirrors on the walls give the illusion the room is a nice big den, rather than the lame converted bedroom it is. Josh and I each have rooms upstairs, but they're barely bigger than the twin-sized beds they hold. Plus, they have low sloping ceilings angled with the roof of the house. Those ceilings are constantly doling out blinding-white head whacks, and I walk a little hunched, even when I'm not in my bedroom.

Amanda gives an exaggerated sigh at the obvious lack of post-pubescent manpower in the den. I head into the kitchen to heat up some pigs-in-blankets and mini pizza bagels. I hid the party snacks from Mom in the back of the freezer, but it was a pretty safe bet she wouldn't poke her head into the world of quickie food preparation anyway. I feel a twinge of guilt as I think of her working so hard. There's actually a small chance she would've let us have this little get-together if I'd asked, but then she'd be worrying about it, and she really doesn't need the extra stress while she's at work. Plus, there's the chance she would've said no, and then I may have been caught with a stupid bag of mini pizza bagels because I couldn't go back on my word with the boys. I guess Josh is right about forgiveness being easier than permission, but I seriously hope I never have to ask for Mom's forgiveness. She is not the forgiving type.

When I enter the den, the boys have Terri and Amanda surrounded as they explain the nuances of Lego Star Wars. I can tell we're all in trouble by the way Amanda flips her smooth dark hair at them. She naturally flirts with everyone—I'm talking all ages as well as both sexes. She flirts without even meaning to. But flirting with these boys is playing with nuclear fission. They don't need encouragement to fall completely in life-long love with her.

About ten minutes later I open my front door to see Mark standing there in a white button-down surf shirt. I'm relieved he doesn't have a slutty date on his arm. Instead he has two bottles of pop and Stuart, a buddy from the varsity soccer team. Stuart is one of only three black students in our school, which makes him a semi-celebrity. I feel somewhat hip and urban having him here at my house. I mentally kick myself for not inviting more people our own age but don't even know who else I could've asked.

When the guys step into the den, there's a palpable shift in the room's energy. The four younger boys wilt at seeing better matches for all females present. Fantasy time is over. As always,

Andrew is a sport and right away takes the opportunity to pump Stu and Mark for soccer tips. Then, just leave it to Dylan to turn a nice casual gathering into something awkward.

Stu is explaining how he manages to consistently pull off some difficult soccer play as he stands in front of the television, twisting his body to demonstrate.

"Forget how you move on the field," Dylan interrupts. "What's your best-scoring move with the *lay-dees*?"

I give Dylan an involuntary parental-type stare-down, and he blocks it with his hands. "What? I'm just looking for a little advice for a loooove connection."

"Dude!" Ajay laughs. "You can go ahead and drop the macho routine. Everybody here knows you're gay."

"Hey, Ajay," Dylan shoots back. "I've got a little something I've been holding for you." He stuffs his hand into his front jean pocket and when he pulls it out he's flipping Ajay the bird.

"Oh, yeah?" Ajay holds up both his middle fingers. "And here's your change." Flipping each other off is sort of an ongoing thing, but I can tell by the look on Terri and Amanda's faces that the boys aren't exactly racking up bonus points.

I grab a guitar. "Who's ready for Rock Band?" I thank the video game gods for creating a game that makes me seem cool for spending all my free time playing Wii with my little brother. We take turns rocking out for the next half-hour.

It seems like everyone is actually having a halfway decent time.

That is, everyone except Amanda, who is tightly tucked into the corner of the couch. I don't blame her for seeming put out. She's been trying to engage the entire mass of testosterone into a seven-way flirting extravaganza, and now she's being upstaged by a video game. Not to mention crude hand motions and politically incorrect gender-preference taunts. I'm pretty sure the younger boys consider their moves flirting with her, but Amanda isn't aiming for the drooling thirteen-year-olds. She has her sights on Mark's friend, Stu. *And Mark, apparently*, I think as I watch her lean over and whisper in his ear.

He gives her a small half-smile, and she bursts into hysterics. I can't imagine what she could've said to him, but it's probably not something promoting me as his future girlfriend. I try to wave at Amanda, to indicate in some way that I need her to cease and desist all flirting behavior immediately. She lightly touches the small of Mark's back. My target is quickly moving out of range.

Standing up, I dump the rest of the Tostitos into a bowl and ask if anyone wants more salsa. There's a smattering response of "yes" and "sure," as most everyone stays focused on the television screen. From across the room, Mark smiles at me with one side of his mouth. My heart starts freaking out as I crumple the empty Tostitos bag, grab the salsa bowl off the coffee table, and flee from the den. Terri catches up to me in the kitchen.

"Remind me again why I agreed to come here?" she says. I

climb on the counter, rummaging through the top cupboard for the salsa I hid way in the back.

"You needed a break from your sisters, for one thing," I say. "Plus, two of the males in that room are hot. Oh, yes, and also, I begged you. And you love me."

I grab the unopened jar of salsa and swing around to sit on the counter. Terri crosses her arms and leans her butt against the cabinet beside me. "So, did Amanda get carried away with the tooth-whitening strips again or what?" she says.

I laugh. "I'm pretty sure her teeth would glow in the dark if I hit the lights."

"And what's the deal with her and Mark?" Terri goes on. "I thought you liked him."

I shrug and kick my heels lightly against the lower cabinets. "I dunno."

Terri reaches up and grabs me by the shoulders. "You cannot let her keep doing this to you!" Terri does have a point. Amanda has a long history of becoming suddenly and glowingly interested in the boys I like. It happened so many times I tried to set her up once by acting as if I liked Ryan Bruchner. Honestly, it was a bit too much to pull off, seeing as how I'm not all that great at acting. Plus, no human being, or synthetic humanoid for that matter, could ever have a crush on the guy. He's not horribly deformed or anything, it's just that everything about him is *wrong*. For instance, when he walks he keeps his entire upper body stiff and tilted forward. It looks even stranger than it sounds, and kids imitate him all the time. I didn't fool Amanda, so all that ended up happening is Ryan now thinks he and I are friends. I've never had the heart to set him straight. After a year and a half of the charade, I suppose we're pretty much friends by default anyway.

Terri pulls me off the counter and spins me toward the den. "You need to get in there and do something!" she commands.

I turn to her, tuck my head into the space between us, and whisper, "I have no idea what I'm doing." Terri's eyes are soft, and I wonder for a moment why she's never had a boyfriend. Probably a feminist thing. I look down at the floor tiles.

She sticks one finger under my chin and tickles it softly for a moment, before stabbing it with her nail, making my head snap up to meet her gaze. Without blinking, she calls into the den, "Hey, Mark!" At his distant "Yeah?" she sings out, "Would you mind coming in here and opening this jar for Blaze?"

With that, she snatches the jar of salsa off the counter and drops it calmly into my hands. "Guys love playing rescuer," she whispers into my neck. *So much for the feminist theory.* She pulls back and winks as she moves toward the den.

Oh, my god, he's going to think I'm a total spaz. I look at the jar. *A total spaz with weak muscle tone.* With that, I start tightening the lid as hard as I possibly can.

"Well, now." Mark's voice is suddenly right beside me. "The fact that you're turning that lid the wrong way could be part of the problem." He surprises me so much, I actually drop the jar I've been sabotaging. I watch it fall in some weird slow-motion-flipping action. Our floor tiles are ceramic, which means that if a glass jar of gooshey salsa taps it with the slightest force, I'm looking at a huge mess. I flinch, preparing for the sound of shattering glass, but inches above the floor, Mark's hand closes in on the spiraling jar.

"Easy there," he says, smoothly opening the jar and handing it back to me. With my heart pounding, I pour the salsa into the bowl and wonder what I should do next. I ask myself that ultimate flirting question: *What Would Amanda Do?*

"You want me to bring in the—"

"Would you like to see my dad's—"

We're interrupting each other. *Lovely.*

"So, what's with the—"

"*X-Men* Spectacular number four—"

"Okay. You've obviously got something interesting to share." Mark smiles beautifully. "Out with it, Blaze."

Oh God, this is all wrong, is all I can think. "Oh, nothing, it's silly," is all I can say. And then I can only stand there, shuffling my feet as I look with scorn at the bowl of salsa in my hands.

Finally Mark says, "All righty then…" *He's leaving already,* I think. *I totally missed my window.* "How's about you show me that collection of comics you told me about?" he asks. "It's here, right?" And just like that, everything shifts back on track.

"You sure?" I ask, squinting up at him.

"Sure, I'm sure." He bops smoothly. "Where are they?"

I point to the basement door. "Down there, but I think the light's burned out."

He stands, looking at me and bopping gently.

"Give me a minute. I'll fetch a flashlight."

As soon as my back is turned, I have to let out the giant geeky grin I've been holding in. This is obvious, clear confirmation that Mark is interested in me. As I drop off the dish of salsa in the den I catch Amanda's eye and put up a mental force field to avoid melting from her death-ray glare. *Sheesh, if anyone should have dibs on Mark it's me.* I'm the one who's been minivanning his cute ass back and forth to games with a third of his team.

I find the flashlight in the closet, click the rubber button, and am relieved when it lights up. Mark grins, takes the light from me, and holds it under his chin, giving his face a sinister look. He laughs maniacally, "Mwa-ha-ha-ha."

"Creepy," I compliment. Taking back the flashlight, I lead the way down the stairs. The darkness swallows all but the reedy beam emanating from my fist.

"This place is huge." Mark takes control of the flashlight and waves it from corner to corner. It's also pretty ghastly. I never come down here at night. Even with Mark shining the light all around, there's so much darkness, I have to shake off the urge to hang onto him. Then I realize that's probably exactly what Amanda would do and boldly clutch his arm.

"Shine it over here," I tell him, wishing I'd kept control of the flashlight. We make our way past old boxes and a few black garbage bags filled with moth-eaten traces of our childhood. "Here they are."

Mark shines the light on the six large, white file boxes. Dad's comic collection. I bend down and carefully pull the lid off the closest one. I'm pretty familiar with which issues are where and carefully pull out *Silver Surfer* #2 from the 1987 series. The cover is purple and red, with the Surfer watching his former lover Shalla-Bal as her translucent dress blows in the wind. Keeping the comic book encased in its plastic, I hand it to Mark.

He gives me the light and nods appreciatively as he turns the issue over in his hands. We both laugh at the tacky ad for Hostess fruit pies on the back cover. "May, I?" he asks, fingering the plastic flap that's taped shut. A pain shoots through my lip, making me realize I've been biting it. I don't want him to think of me as a total geek, but I can't possibly convey to him the value and importance of these comics.

"We really shouldn't," I say. "They need to stay in mint condition, and it's a little musty down here." *So much for keeping the geek concealed.* "They're more valuable as a complete series, and besides…" I sigh and give him the real reason for my hesitation.

"My dad's coming for them soon, and if he finds out I wasn't careful with them he'll murder me."

Mark looks amused. "Well, now," he says, "you'd certainly leave a fine-looking corpse, wouldn't you?"

I want to tell him he doesn't have to use that sort of line with me, but he moves closer and my heart does a crazy loop-de-loop before I can speak. Holding the comic reverently between his palms he offers it back to me with a shrug. I need to undo his disappointment and get back on track for making him my boyfriend.

"Well..." *what am I saying?* "It *is* one of my favorites." I train the flashlight on the plastic pouch, and he uses one finger to break the tape that seals it against the damaging air of our basement. "Just be careful, it's delicate," I warn. Mark lifts the flap.

He respectfully leafs through the pages as I aim the flashlight on the comic, listening to the gang cheer and groan overhead.

In the 1987 series the Surfer is released from being a prisoner on Earth, and in issue #2 he returns to Zenn-la and his first love, Shalla-Bal. I blush in the darkness as Mark pauses on the spread of the lovers embracing. "Boy, Silver Dude's got all the smooth lines, huh?" With false drama he reads the comic aloud, "So many times the thought of this day is all I had to sustain me." He holds up the panel of Shalla-Bal and the Surfer kissing. "And apparently Silver Dude's smooth lines work too."

I hope Mark can't see how red my face is in the light reflecting off the page as he leafs through the rest of the issue. I'm anxious to get the comic back into its protective plastic home. He turns to a page that has Shalla-bal walking alone in the garden after the Surfer leaves. Mark's voice deepens as he reads, "Man is meant to strive… to yearn." His eyes meet mine intensely for a moment before he continues, "Perhaps the taste of danger is what we need." He moves closer and I have a fleeting moment of full-on excitement as he puts his palm gently on my cheek.

His other hand reaches down to mine and clicks off the flashlight.

We're plunged into darkness and I have a three-second freak-out session inside my head before I feel Mark's hand on my face drawing me toward him. *Nebula Unfolding! Is Mark really about to kiss me here in my crusty basement?* In the pitch black I'm like Daredevil: blind, but able to detect everything around me. I can sense Mark. So near. Our bodies slide closer and his hand moves slowly to the back of my neck. I feel his warm breath on my lips. Everything goes still as I wait for my first kiss. I'm trying not to smile in the darkness. Quickly, I lick my lips. Part them slightly. Blind anticipation…

Over the sound of my heartbeat I hear footsteps thundering in a jumble over our heads and unseeing I tilt my head toward the noise. Mark gives a small groan. I wonder if the boys have taken out the Wii Fit and worry for a moment they'll see my Mii has the fitness level of a 45-year-old.

"BLAZE!" Josh's voice calls from the top of the steps. I have time to decide that Josh is not a very good brother for interrupting this moment. And then I make out what he's saying. "AJAY CAN'T BREATHE! AJAY CAN'T BREATHE!"

"Oh my God," I whisper. "His asthma."

"Are they pranking us?" Mark asks.

Shoving over him I shout, "CALL 911! CALL 911!" I bang my shin on a box, untangle from Mark, and trip up the stairs, willing myself to move faster than humanly possible. My eyes painfully adjust to the light as I find my messenger bag in the kitchen and begin clawing at it.

I fumble, dumping everything on the floor, and finally find Ajay's inhaler. I launch myself toward the den, burst into the room and breathlessly take in the scene.

They are totally pranking us.

Ajay looks up at me in surprise and grins. Clearly his breathing is just fine. Everyone laughs and points at the panicked look on my face as I stand, breathing heavily and holding Ajay's inhaler aimed in the air.

Josh looks at me in an accusing way, and I resist the urge to squirt him in the eyes. "What the hell, Josh?"

"What the hell, yourself." Josh volleys back. "You and Coach looking for something in the basement?"

I widen my eyes at him and look over to see Mark is pretending to not hear what's happening. Which is quite a trick, since the game is on pause and everybody's gawking at Josh and I. Amanda slides closer to Stu as Terri gives me a private thumbs-up sign.

But Andrew is looking at me with a furrowed brow, and Josh is outright scowling.

Stu clears his throat and Ajay laughs uncomfortably. I finally drop my arm holding the inhaler and head back into the kitchen to gather the contents of my messenger bag off the floor. Mark seems unsure whether or not to follow me, but when Josh shoulders past him to help me, he heads back into the den.

"Sorry, sis." Josh doesn't sound sorry at all. "I just panicked when I realized you were in the basement with Coach. You seriously need to—"

"*You* seriously need to mind your own business," I snap. "I am a big girl, Josh. I'm sorry you're not ready for me to have a boyfriend, but trust me. I am ready."

"It's not that—" Josh is cut off by the sound of the front door closing. The two of us freeze.

"Hey, guys!" *Mom's voice.*

Holy shit, Josh mouths as we stay frozen to the kitchen floor.

"Surpri—*Oh.*" Mom must've noticed the crowd of people in our home.

Josh and I unfreeze and race to intervene, but when we get to the den we're surprised to find Mom *not* freaking out. She's standing, holding a pizza box in her hands with a lifeless smile on her face. When she spots us her eyes show fury, but her voice remains sugary-sweet. "Hey, guys. You didn't mention you had friends coming by."

"Um. Sorry, Mom," I say. "What are you doing home?"

With her nostrils flaring she calmly explains that she traded shifts with someone who needed off next weekend. "For a birthday party, I think," she over-explains as everyone in the den listens with polite enduring-other-people's-parents-type attention. I notice Amanda is rubbing her hand slowly up and down Stu's bicep. The syrupiness of Mom's voice is really unnerving me, because she should be screaming right now. She finishes by saying, "Sorry, I would've brought more pizza if I'd realized."

Josh actually lets out a laugh before clapping his hand over his mouth.

"That's okay, Stu and I really need to get going." Mark starts the good-byes, so I jump in and let Mom know I was just about to drive the boys home. Everything is hurried and awkward, which is probably why Mark doesn't give me a hug or even a handshake good-bye before heading out the door.

I'm left wondering what my first kiss would've felt like as we all clear out of the house before Mom even takes her coat off.

I envy everyone who doesn't have to come back here to face her the way Josh and I do. *Too bad asking Mark if I can sleep over would be considered a little too forward.*

Chapter Five

Superturd is crawling sadly along at under 20 miles per hour. "Ask for forgiveness, not permission," I mock my brother as we head back toward our doom. Everyone knows the oldest child bears the burden of blame in these situations. Never mind the fact that this was *all Josh's idea*. So unfair.

"She's never come home early," Josh defends. "It's like she has some sort of weird spidey-Mom-sense or something." He's trying to butter me up with a Spider-Man reference. It's not working. "I am honestly sorry, Blaze."

"And what the hell was with freaking me out over Ajay's asthma?"

Josh gives a sigh and sinks down into his seat. "Trust me. I was desperate. Mark is not who you think he is."

"Never mind who I think he is." I pull into the driveway and cut the minivan's engine. "You need to butt out." I don't need my little brother sabotaging my love life on top of everything else I have working against it.

We're quiet for a moment, both procrastinating. "You think she's going to kill us?" Josh asks.

"You'd think so. But she didn't seem too upset when she caught us."

"Yeah. She actually seemed kind of cool with the party."

Turns out, Mom was Not. Cool. With the party.

The moment the two of us walk in the door she launches into a tirade about how embarrassing and offensive it was to enter her own home and be slapped by such dishonesty.

"I try to do something nice, and what happens?" She's close to hysterics, and I glance around at the den to confirm that the place isn't trashed. It actually looks a little neater than usual, since Josh and I straightened up before everyone got here.

After we've endured her verbal wrath for a time, Mom sends Josh upstairs to bed so she can "talk to Blaze alone." *Told you so.*

Josh mouths *I'm sorry* on his way up the stairs.

As soon as he's gone, she announces, "You, young lady, are grounded! You're to go nowhere other than driving your brother around. Got it?"

She glares at me, and it's as if my anger has been flipped on by a switch. I cannot take her treating me like all I ever do is give her grief. I've never been any trouble, and she's acting like I have nothing to do with the fact that she and Josh and I are even functioning as a family.

"You can't do that," I tell her. "You can't ground me and

still have me continue to do your job for you. If I'm grounded, then fine, but you can't still make me drive Josh and the guys around."

Her mouth opens and closes with shock, and I'm immediately ashamed. But I can't turn my anger switch back off. *This must be what becoming The Incredible Hulk feels like.*

"Blaze, why are you making this about me?" Mom asks quietly. "You're the one who lied."

Hulk say, "Because I deserve to have a *life*, Mom. I'm not supposed to be the soccer mom! You are!"

It's as if everything I've been holding back is being released at once. Like my lips are still mad about not getting to kiss Mark, and they're lashing out at Mom.

"Blaze! If anybody stuck you in this role, it's your father with his selfishness." She doesn't realize she's just making *Hulk more angry* as she goes on, "Chasing his stupid acting dreams at forty? I mean, who the hell does that?"

Of course, from there it's only a short segue to Mom pacing around the room giving a dramatic rendition of *"I'm an ACTOR now! I can't possibly be bothered with supporting my family. I'm an AC-TOR!"*

Finally, I cannot take it. *Hulk Smash!* I stand in her path.

"*You* are the one who made the decision to leave your boring nine-to-five desk job working for Dr. Lang so you could have this big exciting adventure working all hours at the hospital."

"Adventure, sure," she says. "Left alone in the middle of nowhere, single mother with two kids and no help."

"*I've* been helping you," I practically screech. "ME! Your daughter! Can't you see how much I've sacrificed for you and Josh?"

Mom blinks at me, finally noticing her offspring has turned into an enormous green monster. "I know you've sacrificed. I tell you all the time how much I appreciate your help."

"I know, I know, you don't know what you'd do without me. But Mom, I've seriously got to get a life."

She stares at me a moment before her face crumples. "I'm so sorry, Blaze." She starts crying, and I instantly go from big and green to small and guilty.

"It's fine, Mom, honestly. You know I love Josh. And I know you need my help. I was just thinking, I don't know. Maybe it would be nice to get a part-time job at the mall or something."

"Haven't the guys been giving you money? I know it's only fair for you to get paid for your time." Mom searches my face with her teary eyes. "Do you need me to call their parents?"

"It's not about the money, Mom," I say. "It's about the fact that I need to get out of that smelly minivan and away from the adolescent freak show a few days a week. Maybe hang out with some people my own age. People who have discovered the wonder of deodorant."

"Blaze," Mom chides.

"Oh come on. Don't tell me you've never smelled them after a game."

A moment passes. Mom's frown gives way to the smallest chuckle, and the two of us are on our way to a truce. She tells me she's going to see what she can do about getting more regular hours, and I promise not to do anything devious behind her back again. The two of us start cleaning up the chips and drinks together and by the time I head up to bed, *Hulk happy*.

• • •

That Monday, the story of Mark and I canoodling in my basement spreads through our small school at supersonic speed.

When I see Terri in the hallway she says, "So, I hear you and Mark may have started a little something over the weekend?"

"You're the one spreading that rumor?"

She nods, and I smile at her. "Thanks, Ter." I look around. "You haven't seen him today, have you? I'd kind of like to know where we stand."

"Oh, God, please do not do the whole Amanda, 'Where do we stand?' needy thing," she says. "You, of all people, cannot go turning into some girlie girlfriend with mush-brain."

I laugh and hold up my palm. "Scout's honor. But I would like to know if I'm a friend that happens to be a girl, or if I'm heading toward 'girlfriend.'" *Or if last night was just some limited edition saga that my little brother canceled permanently.*

"Hey, guys." Amanda walks up and blows superficial kisses to each of us. "That was some party Saturday, huh?"

"Gee, Mandy," Terri says. "Aren't you worried that Stu may not realize you want him? I don't think you were quite obvious enough."

Amanda ignores Terri and confronts me. "Speaking of obvious, Blaze. What is *up* with you and Mark?"

I shrug as we move down the hall together. "I told you I liked him." I turn to face her for emphasis. "Remember?"

Amanda appears to be trying to remember, but it actually looks like she's trying way harder than someone who's forgotten something would look. Terri and I exchange glances. Amanda doesn't *try* to channel Evil Empress behavior, but she could maybe use a sibling or two to straighten her ass out. Nothing puts you in your place faster than having to share your house, your parents, and all of your stuff with another kid. Although I have no idea how Terri deals with four sisters. One time I was over at her house and the screaming that went on over a beat-up old hairbrush was enough to make me grateful Josh is a boy.

"Your Mom is way cooler than I remember her." Amanda changes the subject.

I roll my eyes. "All an act. She tried to ground me after everyone left."

"Tried?" Amanda asks.

I shrug. "She needs me to play soccer mom too much to ground me. The two of us are working things out."

"But why did she even care that you had that lame party?" Terri asks. "You were doing all the work and clean-up. My mom doesn't care if we have people over the house when she's not home, as long as we don't trash the place."

Amanda says, "That's because with all those sisters of yours running around, nobody ever wants to come to your house."

"Very funny," says Terri.

"I just want the scoop with Mark." Amanda pulls on my shoulder. "Are you guys, like, going out or something?" She can't hide her eagerness. "I'm just asking because Stu and I got along really well and we could, you know, maybe double date or something sometime."

With a smile I start telling the two of them about my trip to the basement with Mark, but when I get to the part when I showed him the *Silver Surfer* #2 and start explaining about Shalla-Bal the two of them groan and change the subject to the latest slutty exploits of Catherine Wiggan. *I probably should've led with Mark almost kissing me in the dark*, I think. *Even comic books show the climax of each issue right there on the cover.* Of course, our cover would be too dark to even see what was happening. Plus, technically I suppose nothing happened. An *almost* kiss doesn't exactly count. My heart flutters thinking about Mark's hand on the back of my neck.

His breath on my mouth.

That wasn't nothing.

I jolt at the sound of a male voice calling my name. *Mark! He went out of his way to find me.* Except that it isn't Mark. It's Ryan, the guy who serves as my reminder to never double-cross Amanda again.

"Welp, gotta dash," says Terri. "See you in the caf."

"Have fun talking to your *real* boyfriend." Amanda flashes a blue-white smile and hurries after her. The two of them get immeasurable joy out of my hostage-friendship situation and constantly tell me to just be mean to the guy, already.

Looking at Ryan's hopeful face, half covered by his straight black bangs, I know I'll never have it in me to be mean to him. I'll just have to ride things out until graduation. "Hey there, Ryan," I say without enthusiasm.

"Hey, Blaze," he says.

After an awkward silence I turn to go, and Ryan walks alongside me, his feet slapping the hallway floor the whole way to my locker. As I exchange my books for my next class, he lets out a loud and phony-sounding "Oh, yeah!" As if he suddenly just remembered something he's been meaning to tell me. It's obviously rehearsed. Since I rarely encourage a two-way conversation, he usually shows up with material ready. Ryan knows lots of odd trivia that can be mildly interesting if you happen to care about whatever topic he's spouting. He just hasn't mastered the art of casually working tidbits and facts into normal conversations.

"Did you know your body is creating and killing fifteen million red blood cells per second?"

"Wow." I try to be polite without encouraging him. Hiding my interest isn't too difficult.

"Heh heh, yeah. Oops, there go thirty million more." He chuckles. I shut my locker with a sigh.

"Good luck with that." I start moving away.

"Oh, wait!" Ryan flips his backpack off his wide back and starts rummaging through it.

Oh, goody, and today he's brought props. Finally, he pulls out a small stack of comics. "I'm finished reading these if you're interested."

He holds up current-looking issues of *Daredevil* and *Silver Surfer*. He knows these are two of my favorite characters but doesn't get the fact that I prefer vintage issues. I'm a total Stan Lee devotee, love everything he ever worked on. 'Nuff said.

Ryan fans out the assortment of comics like a plump magician doing some cheesy giant card trick. I really don't want to encourage him, but it won't exactly kill me to check out what's new and happening in comics these days. *Maybe just to inform my own sketches.* Looking at the offerings displayed in Ryan's thick hand, I carefully select two of them. I don't want to act too enthusiastic, but having the comics in my hand inspires a warmer-than-intended smile that makes Ryan blush. I quickly hand him back one of the comics, and it's as if I've thrown cold water in his face. *Better to not lead him on.* I tell him, "Thank you," for the lone *Daredevil* comic I'm clutching. "I'll get this back to you soon."

He starts to protest, but then shrugs, probably realizing that returning the comic will at least mean I'll have to talk to him again. "Yeah, it'll be cool to hear what you think of it."

A few weeks into our awkward friendship, Ryan stumbled upon the fact that if he can get me talking about comics I'll go into geek mode and prattle on without meaning to. For some reason, just having me talk at him makes him pathetically happy. He's gotten more and more knowledgeable over time and actually has pretty good taste in artwork. Or maybe I just think that because he likes *my* artwork. He happened to see my sketchbook one day, and he fawned over my drawings in a way that wasn't just sucking up. Or at least I don't think it was. Well, who am I kidding, he was probably sucking up, but it was nice to have somebody appreciate my talent.

Not that I think my drawings are anything special. It's just something that keeps me from poking my eyes out with boredom during soccer mom duty. I must admit, though, I've gotten a bit attached to drawing *The Blazing Goddess*.

Her newest shtick is a spray that acts as a physical truth serum, revealing people's authentic selves. I got the idea one night when Josh and I saw this cheesy commercial for some perfume that claimed spraying it on your skin would reveal your "inner goddess." Josh teased me that I should go to the store and steal a squirt to see if it made my boobs grow bigger. Of course, I gave him a dead arm with my middle knuckle. But then I got to thinking about how cool it would be if the goddess-spray stuff really worked.

I drew a version of *The Blazing Goddess* with a holster for holding a magic perfume bottle that acts as a spray-on makeover. Now she goes around all the time spraying nerdy kids to reveal their inner gods and goddesses and turn them hot and save their lives. I know, I know, total chick comic. But I like doing it and, as I said, it does prevent me poking my eyes out.

Looking over, I realize Ryan is still walking beside me and is practically hyperventilating trying to think of something to say. I wonder for a moment if I should give him Ajay's inhaler.

"Okay, well thanks, Ryan." I wave *Daredevil* at him, and he blushes back at me.

"Uh, okay, so bye, Blaze." He flicks his chins toward me. "See you later in the lot."

I give a tense nod and pick up my pace to get to class *and away from him*. Just to clarify, Ryan and I do *not* have a standing date to meet and talk in the parking lot after school every day. But since Josh is just too darn popular to leave the middle school grounds across the street without saying good-bye to about a million people and my friends either have over-protective parents who don't trust any drivers under the age of 21 (Amanda) or have track practice daily after school (Terri), I've become Ryan's personal captive audience in the parking lot every day. Let me tell you, it has not helped the whole non-image I've got going on.

The rest of the afternoon buzzes past my brain in a blur of monotone lectures, a quiet whisper or two about Mark and I, and a little covert scribbling of *The Blazing Goddess* in awesome action poses. The one time I glimpse Mark between classes, he gives me a completely unreadable nod. What I'd really love is a super-awesome new identity as Mark's Girlfriend. *I wonder how I can upgrade the whispers Terri started into a full-on rumor we're dating.*

Finally, the school day ends with me sitting sideways in Superturd with my door open to the student lot. I'm working on my sketchpad, waiting for my popularity's arch-nemesis, Ryan, to pounce.

"Blaze!"

My head shoots up in surprise. Besides the voice being too deep to be Ryan's, it isn't at all the way he usually greets me. Ryan always approaches Superturd slowly from the front and waits for me to look up and catch his eye. Then he'll look fake-surprised at seeing me, as if I don't sit here waiting for my brother every day. But today, Ryan's approach is completely different because today it isn't Ryan approaching me.

It's Mark.

By Thor's Mighty Hammer! I think, as the cutest boy in the universe walks directly toward my minivan with a big grin on his face.

"Fun night Saturday," he says, placing himself just inside Superturd's door. "I liked the private party you and I were starting in your basement before your little brother shot me down."

I smile as.my heart *badda-thumps*. "Josh can be a little protective of me."

"I get that." Mark moves his face closer and bops his head slightly. "Guess we'll just need to keep *us* on the down-low."

I nearly black out at Mark's use of the word "us." With my peripheral vision, I spot Ryan, on his usual approach trajectory, except that he is frozen mid-stride and staring directly at me and Mark. *POW!* Guilt hits my stomach like a sucker punch, but when I look back into Mark's eyes my mind is swiped clean. *I never agreed to be Ryan's buddy.* Mandy and Terri have been telling me to ditch him. Maybe they're right.

Mark's eyes drop to my sketchbook, and his eyebrows jump nearly to his hairline. "Hey, you draw?"

Looking down at my hand holding my pencil mid-stroke, I think again, *He's so pretty.* I cover my drawing with both hands and claim, "No, not really. Just a little." Never mind the fact that I've been sketching on the sidelines for an eternity and he never noticed. He is noticing me now.

I glance back up and see that Ryan is gone, which makes me feel both glad and lousy at the same time. As Mark leafs through my sketchbook, he gives appreciative "hmms" at my drawings until I can't even picture what Ryan looks like. Not that I really want to, or honestly try all that hard. I just float in my blissful state of *Mark really likes my sketches*, until Josh interrupts us with an accusatory, "Hey *guys!*"

"So, you mind if I catch a ride with you Saturday?" Mark asks as Josh climbs into the seat next to me. *Saturday? Did he not plan on speaking to me for the rest of the week?* I know our schedules don't exactly include a convenient bumping-into-each-other place, and we are keeping 'us' on the down-low, but with a little effort, I'm sure we could connect at some point before Saturday. And then I realize he's probably just acting aloof to throw Josh off our scent.

"Sure," I say casually while Josh eyes me suspiciously. Mark moves out of the way and I pull Superturd's door shut. His face stays in the window for a moment, smiling at me, before he turns toward Stuart's vintage "cuck," which is what the girls and I call those half-car-half-trucks that guys in this town are in love with. I spot Stu making his way toward the parking lot, and Amanda is notably not with him. She told Terri and I that she fully planned to ride home with him today. "I'll just tell my mom I missed the bus," she said while applying mascara in the bathroom mirror before last period. I wonder if he even talked to her today. If he did, I doubt she let things end without knowing where she stood with him. The way I just did with Mark.

"Did I interrupt anything back there?" Josh gives me a hard look.

"Nope." I keep my face blank as I pull out of the lot. "You didn't interrupt a thing."

Chapter Six

"Did your grandmother call yet?" Mom asks as she walks through the door two hours earlier than usual. She's been trying to work more regular hours since our little gamma-ray-blasted show-down, but that's not why she's home early today.

On top of Christmas and Easter, Mema Sissy usually calls the first day of every month, plus on our "name days." Name days are the Catholic feast days for the saints we're supposedly named after. Mema acts like they're better than birthdays. Nevermind that my true namesake is a motorcycle-riding comic book super-hero with a flaming skull for a head. Mema still calls me every February third for the feast of St. Blaise, some kooky dead monk who talked to animals and apparently healed people's throats. As if my dad would name me after *that* guy.

Trust me, Mom didn't pick "Josh" to commemorate some ancient holy guy either, but the phone still rings for him every September first so Mema can wish him a happy Feast of St. Joshua. He gets annoyed by her phone calls, but I figure at least she's happy to do most of the talking. And besides, it's better than driving in the car for four hours to Ohio to visit her in person. We used to drive to Ohio nearly once a month, but since Dad's been gone we only go once a year. Our annual Let's Listen to Mom and Mema Bash on Dad Extravaganza. This year's visit is coming up soon, and I'm dreading it.

Mema is always insisting we should force Dad to drive us to her house the next time he visits. I always tell her we will, but I don't want to get her ranting by pointing out that he never visits anymore. I will say it's pretty convenient that she doesn't realize I'm driving now, or she'd probably start pressuring me to come more often. I put enough miles on the minivan rushing around to Josh's games without volunteering for an eight-hour round trip odyssey into Old Lady Land, where everybody's named after saints and arguing with your little brother will get you doused with a bottle of holy water. (True story.)

They're no longer in-laws, but Mom totally got Mema Sissy in the divorce. I think having his mother on her side makes Mom feel like she's somehow winning the ongoing battle with her arch-nemesis, my father. I just wish they'd all call a truce already, because I'd honestly like to have a real relationship with my dad.

Mom steps in to set the table with glasses of water and tidies randomly, but she can't help but run her fingertips across the surface of the phone each time she passes it. When it finally gives a smooth *BRIIIING!* Mom freezes and holds up a finger, as if Josh and I are scrambling to answer it. After the phone has sounded twice, she pounces on it and pretends to be all casual as she says, "Oh, Sissy, what a surprise. Is it really a new month already?"

Josh rolls his eyes and flings his hands over his chest in mock excitement. I can't help but laugh. Behind Mema's back we make fun of her for being so religious, but she's fairly sharp for an old person, and she's always so tickled to talk to us that it's impossible to really dislike her. Except, that is, when she starts harping about Dad. I have no trouble disliking her then.

Mom is telling Mema about some random quiz that I forgot I even took that I got a one hundred on. "And Josh is doing so well in soccer," she brags. "They're heading into the playoffs already." You see, that's the other reason I kinda don't mind when Mema calls. It's nice to hear Mom recite all our positive qualities and actions, edited for her ex-mother-in-law's sake. I pretend that, deep down, it's how Mom really thinks of us.

Finally, she calls to me, "Blaze, your turn to talk to Mema." She hands me the phone, and Mema launches into one of our usual one-sided conversations.

She begins by asking how I'm doing, and before I can answer she says, "I understand you've finally begun to find your voice." She carefully explains the reason finding my voice is so significant. Which I already know. She's explained it to me before. Several times.

"Your namesake, Saint Blaise, performed a miracle and saved

a boy's life," she tells me. *Again.* "The boy was choking on a fish bone and Saint Blaise came along and healed him, although I suppose he was just Blaise at that point since he wouldn't have been canonized without performing the miracle first, or *dying*, for that matter…"

"Mema." I cut her off. "I've told you before. I cannot sing. I think you've got the wrong Blaze."

"Very funny, child, but I'm not talking about singing anymore!" She sounds excited to have something new to add. "You just need to find your voice. I mean your viewpoint." She pauses. "Blaze. Voice is associated with the throat, but it can be so much more. You do have opinions don't you?"

"Um, yes?"

"Oh, pshaw. Not '*yes?*'" She mimics my voice in an unflattering way. "Tell me you will work hard at finding your voice."

I croak, "I'll try, Mema."

"Your mother tells me you're learning to speak up for yourself." I glance at my mother, but her back is turned to me as she sifts innocently through the mail. "She told me you're showing real strength of character. Unction. Lord knows you did not inherit that from my son…"

And that's my cue to tune her out. My Mema can rant on about my dad as harshly as my mom does, except it's one thing for an ex-wife to hate a guy, but his own mother? Particularly his bible-wielding, saint-loving mother.

You wouldn't expect her to have a mean bone in her body, but trust me, when the topic of my degenerate father comes up, she has a whole adamantium skeleton of mean bones that Wolverine would envy. Then again, she is rather fond of gossiping in general. I smile as I picture her at some spa in Ohio, her hair up in silver rollers as she dishes about everyone. All of a sudden she ducks out from underneath the hair dryer and delivers Wolverine's classic line, "I'm the best there is at what I do. But what I do best isn't very nice." It sends a little shiver up my spine, and I'm glad Mema's rant is winding down when I tune back in.

"Becoming a father is the only worthwhile thing he's done his whole life," she says. "You and Josh represent the best of that man." Dad doesn't talk to Mema all that much since he "let everyone down" by "chasing his wild dreams," but she's still way harsh for a mom, if you want my opinion. "Speaking of Josh, is he around?" she asks, and I'm finally released.

Josh is in the den watching some *Disastrous Crashes Caught on Video* show and tries to wave me off as I hand him the phone. He refuses to take it from my hand until I hold it up over my head, wielding it like I'm about to pummel him with it. When he instinctively puts up his hands to protect his face, I slap the phone into his open palm. Defeated, he takes the phone and gives a half-hearted "Hey there, Mema" as he slumps into the living room.

Checking the clock, I figure I have enough time to read my

email before the Tater Tot casserole I flung together from *The 4-Ingredient Cookbook* finishes cooking. "Take the food out of the oven when the buzzer goes off," I call to Mom as I take the steps three at a time up to my room.

Ducking my head, I hit the power button on Dad's old laptop. I don't dare hope that Mark would've actually gotten my email address somehow and written to me. But I realize I'm sort of dreaming that could happen when I feel disappointed by my empty inbox. That is, empty aside from an ad for improving body parts I don't even own plus four forwards from Mema Sissy. I could murder the person who taught that woman how to forward emails. Most of them are so lame I don't even bother looking anymore, but every now and then I'll be bored enough to read one of the cheesy stories and find myself tearing up over an angel stopping a guy from killing himself or some stupid cat surviving a fire.

I'm not even finished deleting my crappy emails when I hear the chime of my IM box popping up. I swear, Amanda must just sit and stare at her computer from the minute she gets home.

AmandaSweetie68: blaze! waiting to hear bout u and mark! terri says her sis saw u 2 talking aft school (!!!)

I sigh, realizing I'd love to hear about me and Mark too. As in, could somebody *please* tell me if there even *is* a "me and Mark."

Blazefire22: Nothing interesting to report. What's up with you and Stu?

AmandaSweetie68: lol I'm hoping mark says sometng 2 u! stu and i talked a few x today + he snuck bhind n tickled me once. think he likes me?

Blazefire22: Ummmm let me think... of course he likes you!

AmandaSweetie68: n mark likes u!! wheee! we can doubledate!

Blazefire22: Easy there, Down, Girl! Mark wasn't hitting on me—just asking about a ride to soccer.

AmandaSweetie68: ouch!

Blazefire22: But he is being really nice too. I don't know. He says he'll see me Saturday.

AmandaSweetie68: but thats 5 days away!!

Blazefire22: Yeah, I know. *sigh* But then, we don't run into each other during the day like you and Stu. Our schedules are totally different.

AmandaSweetie68: blaze, there are 150 kids in our grad class. u can c him if u try

Blazefire22: *deeper sigh* Thanks

AmandaSweetie68: sorry! who knows? things may work out for u 2! maybe hes just acting shy?

Blazefire22: Right. Mark the Shark is secretly shy.

AmandaSweetie68: well it cld mean he really really likes u

Blazefire22: Doubtful.

AmandaSweetie68: well, u no i'm pulling for u. i never dated the friend of a friend's boyfriend… fun!

Blazefire22: Well, I hope Mark and I work out for YOUR sake then

AmandaSweetie68: lol

Blazefire22: Where's Terri?

AmandaSweetie68: oh, god, she and I were im-ing and her stupid sis had 2 hog the comp 4 homework. i don't no how she lives with those people.

Blazefire22: Speaking of living with people, time for dinner. Gotta dash xxoo

AmandaSweetie68: fine, u can abandon me 2 xo

I laugh as I sign off, picturing Amanda waiting for one of her other friends to sign online. Of the three of us, Amanda is the one with the largest supply of other friends. I wouldn't even say Terri and I are her closest friends, but she's still ours. At least Terri understands the concept of family duties eating into social time. I glide downstairs to turn off the incessant timer, put on the oven mitts, and picture Terri's house with all those girls gathered around the table. *At least two of her sisters love to cook*, I think as I pull dinner out of the oven and let it slam onto the stovetop. It's the second time in a week I've made a meal prominently featuring Tater Tots.

"Don't worry, I got the food out," I call sarcastically. I've been trying to force some changes around here, and one way is to delegate more work, but I'd rather not eat burnt casserole just to make my point. It tastes bad enough when it's cooked perfectly.

I've just crossed the kitchen to call Josh and Mom to come and eat when the phone gives a fresh *BRIIIING!* Josh is re-perched in front of the television, so I naturally accuse, "Did you hang up on Mema again?"

He shrugs, making me suspect the worst. I answer the phone with a repentant, "Sorry about that, Mema." Mom and I have cell phones, plus Josh and I talk to our friends mostly online, and that means Mema and the school are about the only ones who call the landline. Well, and Dad, I suppose, but he just called two weeks ago. So Mema is the only person who could be ringing us. Except that she isn't.

"Hello? You're sorry about what, and who's Mema?" I'm shocked when a male answers. It takes my mind a minute to place the voice, but my heart must recognize it right away, since it starts palpitating like crazy. My mind finally catches on and starts screaming *Mark! Mark! It's Mark calling me!* like my brain is some sort of hysterical woman.

I mentally shove my hysteria into the refrigerator and approximate calm, "Oh, hey Mark, how's it going?" Then realization dawns. "You looking for Josh?" I can't believe I got all excited over Mark calling our house when meanwhile the stupid soccer-phone-chain is set to the home number. He obviously wants to speak to his star player. I'm just the idiot sister who answered the phone and called him Mema. "Hang on. I'll get him for you."

I head toward Josh, but I don't make it to the den before Mark cuts in with, "Uh, actually, Blaze? I'm calling to talk to you."

Mark! Mark called me! And there goes that hysterical woman brain all over again. The only sound my throat can manage to generate is an insubstantial, "Oh." That "Oh" dangles on our connection for a few moments before it gets swallowed up by a nice awkward silence.

"You don't have to sound so excited." Mark laughs. "I mean, I know you were expecting a call from this Mema-somebody…"

I cut him off, "Oh, no! I'm excited." I cringe at my enthusiasm. "What I mean is, um… hey, what's up?"

"You are a strange girl, Blaze."

Is strange good? "Mema's just my grandmother," I blurt out. "On my Dad's side." *Strange cannot be good.*

"I thought your dad moved to New York," Mark says.

"Yeah, but his mom took my mom's side when they split up," I explain, wondering why I can't seem to steer the topic away from my Mema.

"Wow, his own mother, huh? He must be a real jerk."

"Not really," I say quickly. "My Mema is kind of a gossipy bitch is all."

It's his turn to say, "Oh," and leave it dangling awkwardly in the air.

Then we both start saying something at the same time, which is just obnoxious, and then he says, "No, it's okay, you go ahead." Except that I completely forgot what I was about to say—if anything—and he insists I go first since he's going to change the topic anyway, and by now there's such a build-up to whatever is going to be said next that I honestly can't say anything at all. "Really, really, I mean it, please go ahead," I insist firmly enough to finally penetrate his pretty head.

"Anyway." He finally reboots our conversation. "I got your number off the soccer phone list and was just calling to see if you maybe wanted to exchange email addresses? We can IM or text or something."

"That would be great!" I say, overdoing the excitement again. I hate the phone. I'll probably have a far better chance with Mark if our communication shifts online.

"Now, what were *you* going to say?" he puts me back on the spot.

"Oh, nothing," I claw about my mind for something interesting to talk about.

"Come on, Blaze," Mark teases, "your turn to share."

His tone is flirtatious, but I just can't phone flirt back. I consider using Josh's trick with Mema where he starts saying something and then hangs up in the middle of a sentence so she thinks they got disconnected, but I probably couldn't pull it off. I finally grumble something about needing to call my Mema back,

84

so Mark and I exchange information and I give an awkward, "Okay, um, well… Bye now."

"Bye, Blaze," Mark says, and I hang up before I can act any weirder. I hope I can redeem myself via email, but I doubt he'll even bother writing after I acted like such a spaz on the phone. *I am so not a phone person.*

I try to keep my mind off my laptop all through dinner and clean-up, but as soon as the kitchen is put back together I take the steps three at a time to my little mouse room to see if Mark has emailed me yet.

There are zero new emails in my inbox, which makes me feel really super stupid for envisioning a nice, long flirty letter from Mark waiting for me. *There is nothing more depressing than an empty inbox.*

I open my IM to see if Amanda's online—which, unless she's peeing, she probably is. Even then, she once wrote me that she was using her laptop and we were "having a pisser together." I signed off right away, which probably didn't stop Amanda from using her laptop on the bowl, but at least it stopped her from sharing about it. I'm surprised to see she's offline.

Terri is offline too, and I wonder if she and her sisters can maybe work out some sort of computer schedule so Amanda and I will know when she's online. But then, Terri's home isn't exactly super organized, and her family members aren't the scheduling sort. The intergalactic battle between order and chaos has clearly been decided in Terri's household. Chaos won.

Just then, my IM notifier bleeps and a new screen name pops up.

Soccergod: Blaze? You there?

Oh my god, it's Mark! Mark is trying to contact me! I just sit there, grinning like an idiot at my screen for a few moments before I realize that if I don't reply he'll think I'm ignoring him.

Blazefire22: Hey there. Soccergod—nice screen name btw
Soccergod: Are you implying I'm not a soccer god?
Blazefire22: You kick the ball around just fine with the kiddies, but I've never seen you play against somebody your own size.
Soccergod: We must fix that rite away. U doing anything Thurs nite?

See that, I'm much better online.

Blazefire22: Why? You guys have a game Thursday?
Soccergod: Why is it that nobody ever follows the soccer schedule? I'll bet if I was on football team you'd know if there was a game on Thurs.
Blazefire22: I still don't know if that's a yes or no
Soccergod: Yes! We have a home game Thurs night, K? It starts at six and I'm thinking we can grab a slice after. You mind driving?

Blazefire22: Sounds like fun. You need me to pick you up?

Soccergod: Just a ride home, thanx

Blazefire22: K – guess I'll see you there

Soccergod: I'll be the guy on the field who's awesome

Blazefire22: I'm expecting god-like

Soccergod: Lol! Wow, your tough

Blazefire22: I just hope you're better at soccer than you are at counting cows

Soccergod: I promise I will do my best to wow you

Blazefire22: And I promise I'll be merciless if you don't

Soccergod: I'd better go practice, then. C U, Blaze.

Blazefire22: K See you—bye

I wait, but Mark doesn't type a final "bye." I feel pretty confident it doesn't matter because, *Wheeeee!!!* I scream inside my head. *I have a date with Mark Thursday night!*

Once my overwhelming happiness fades a smidge I get a head start on panicking. I have no idea what the heck to wear to a school soccer game, and more importantly, I realize I'll be sitting all alone in the bleachers for a large portion of our "date."

Right away, I send messages to Amanda and Terri begging them to come to the game portion of my date with Mark on Thursday. *And then please disappear into thin air immediately afterward*, I don't add. I wonder if I'll know anyone in the stands, but besides the fact that my friends list is severely limited, our school's soccer team is not exactly known for drawing huge crowds.

And how sad is it that I can't imagine myself showing up at a soccer game without my little brother and the horny gang of cretins with me?

Chapter Seven

I hit the mall to finally spend a bit of my accumulated fundage on a new pair of jeans for my date. Between the upcoming rendezvous with Mark and Mom trying to give me time to myself, things are definitely looking up. Even my butt got a nice lift from the new jeans swinging inside my shopping bag. They ride up in the crotch a little, but it's totally worth it for how great they make my ass look.

As I walk past the mall's comic book store, I'm drawn toward the yawning arched doorway with a vague notion that I could apply for some part-time work. I'm also thinking I might find a replacement for the 1987 *Silver Surfer* #2 that Mark and I were reading together. When I'd gone back down to tidy up in the daylight, I saw the cover was a little loose at the staples. I doubt it's something my dad would even notice, but it can't hurt to replace it with a mint copy if I find one. Dad has been bugging Mom to have me do the inventory, so he must be coming by at some point to pick up the comics. I've really been missing him, so that's another part of my life that's looking up.

The comic book store has been completely remodeled since I saw it last, with a giant talking comic bubble hanging in the center that exclaims *SECTOR COMICS!* My dad and I visited it together only one time, and Dad walked through the place pointing out which comics were overpriced as he gave me a quick superhero education. I remember him getting into a heated Spider-Man-related argument with the guy behind the counter and I feel the tension of that interaction all over again. It's silly, I know. I was only twelve years old; no way would anyone recognize me. Plus, I'm willing to bet they've had some significant staff changes over the past five years. Nonetheless, I suspend the employment idea and dart quickly in and out of the stacks, feeling like I don't belong.

I see there's somebody new behind the counter, and I imagine the other guy left in shame after my dad clearly bested him. Even though I'd felt bad for that guy, I remember being extra-proud to be Dad's daughter that day. Their showdown had even attracted an audience, including a young kid around my age who'd turned to me at one point to state the obvious—"Wow, your dad is awesome." Squinting at the guy behind the counter I realize something.

He isn't a kid anymore.

Five years can really change a person, but I'm certain I recognize him. He's by a rack labeled with a talk bubble that shouts *Just In!* and he's conversing with a portly customer wearing an oversized orange T-shirt. The crazy thing is, hanging around a comic book store all this time has somehow turned the scrawny kid with bad skin I remember into a fit and not at all bad-looking young man. His hair's a little messy, but who could've imagined that underneath all that acne was a well-structured face? This is *not* your average Comic Book Guy.

"If you honestly think Thor could've led the Avengers better than Captain America, I have a stack of nap-wipes in mint condition I'd love to sell you."

Then again…

As he continues berating orange T-shirt guy, I scan the display case for a copy of the *Silver Surfer* issue Mark and I marred. There are a number of issues in the glass case that I recognize from my dad's oldest comics, but that series must be kept someplace else, since I don't see any on display.

"Can I help you?" The aggressive tone catches me by surprise and sends me reeling backward into the glass case. I look up and see that Comic Book Guy has succeeded in running off the other customer and is set on making me regret entering his store. He may have adored my father, but I doubt he'll even recognize me.

"No, I'm fine." I back away, my bag clutched to my side. "Just looking."

His flashing brown eyes slice me in half. He sniffs the air as if my breathing is turning all the comics yellow, and I move quickly to a bin labeled "$2."

"Do I know you?" he asks the back of my head.

I shake it no, not looking at him, and mumble, "Never been here before."

Thankfully, a mother with a young boy dares to enter the store at that moment. Comic Book Guy's frustration at seeing an actual child looking at the comics takes up all his attention.

I leaf through the bin, just killing time until I can leave gracefully without seeming like I'm fleeing. My eye is drawn to a black cover punctuated with flames. *Ghost Rider*. My namesake. I quickly leaf through and pick out all the *Ghost Rider*s I can find. Adding them up, I count nine, so I grab an old *X-Men* just to make it an even twenty dollar's worth.

Fortunately, as I pay, Comic Book Guy is so distracted calling out, "Ma'am *please* do *not* let him touch that," over and over that he doesn't get the chance to draw me into a debate of any sort. I shove the comics into my bag and walk back through the archway, happily noting that the mother gives no sign of leaving the store any time soon. When Comic Book Guy practically shouts, "Those are *not* meant for *children*!" I think I even see her give a slight smile.

• • •

Walking across the grass toward the soccer field's rusty bleachers, I feel as if the whole world can tell that my jeans are riding uncomfortably up my crotch. There's seriously no way to unobtrusively remove a vagina wedgie. I take a few bowlegged steps before accepting the fact that I'm in for a rough evening, crotch-wise.

There are only about twenty-odd fans spread out over the small set of rusty soccer field bleachers, which means they all turn to look at me as I step onto a creaky metal beam. I'm heading for the nice, empty spot about four rows up, but I lose my nerve and redirect my fine-looking butt to the closest empty space. Thankfully, I've timed my arrival so the game has already started, and the other fans quickly turn their attention back to the field.

My special skill of stalking Mark helps me spot him right away, but I don't want to be ogling him when he looks in my direction so I peruse the fans hoping I'll know somebody. Terri turned down my invite with a "No way. I promised myself I'd never watch soccer with you again." But Amanda still has her sights on Stu, so she agreed to come, except she'll be half an hour late. I debated waiting and coming with her, but I don't want Mark to think I'm not interested. I mean, he did ask me out, and this is, after all, our first date.

I curse myself for not bringing my sketchpad so I'd at least have an interesting prop. Mark still hasn't caught my eye, and I want to be doing something when he finally sees me. It would be too awkward to stand up and walk all the way back to Superturd to get my *Ghost Rider*s, especially considering the denim douche I have happening.. Finally, I remember Ryan's *Daredevil* and fish it out of my bag. I'm horrified to see I've rumpled the cover, but it's still in 'near mint' condition. I'm pretty sure Ryan doesn't know the difference anyway—he only started buying comics so he'd have something to talk to me about. There are too many gaps in his knowledge to believe he's totally into superheroes, but right now I'm pretty darn happy for his charade. As well as his *Daredevil*.

Opening the comic book, I stare at it blindly while listening for a referee whistle. I've been to enough soccer games to know there's always a regrouping after a whistle, and it's a good time to look up and casually catch Mark's eye. It takes a few tries:

Tweet! *casual glance* *Mark's not looking*, *duck behind comic*

Tweet! *casual glance* *Mark's not looking*, *duck behind comic*

Tweet! *casual glance* *Mark's not looking*, *duck behind comic*

Finally, after a particularly long *Tweeeeet!* when I give my *casual glance* Mark happens to be looking toward the stands. I lower my comic shield to my lap and am rewarded when he smiles and waves at me. I wave back and say "Hey there! Hello!" half to myself, since he is much too far away to really hear me. Then, with a horrible thought, I turn and look behind me, expecting to see a big-bosomed sex kitten like Catherine Wiggan sitting there.

But the seats behind me are empty. When I turn back, Mark is talking to a teammate, but his greeting stays with me long after Amanda comes and wedges herself beside me to watch Stu. She tries to stalk casually but lacks my extensive sideline experience and ends up flirting aggressively from the stands, which comes off as a little desperate. She flips her hair, crosses and uncrosses her legs, raises her arms, and fake laughs in Stu's direction. She's so "on" for so long I notice a few players glancing our way between plays. Finally I have to say something.

"Stu knows you're here," I hiss. "Now, the trick is to act so casual he wonders about you."

"What are you talking about?" Amanda gives me a fake smile. I just hold her gaze until she concedes, "Okay, okay." She squints. "Am I *that* obvious?"

I mimic one of her fake laughs, flipping my hair and crossing my legs, which gets her laughing, which then gets me laughing. I mime her outrageous flirting some more to keep the funny coming, and she lets out a hoot in appreciation. We marvel over the fact that *I'm* giving *her* flirting advice, which sends the two of us into genuine hysterics and…

"Something funny?"

We both stop laughing.

It's Mark. Apparently, as the two of us were busy negotiating how we should act as potential soccer-player-girlfriends-in-the-stands, the actual game played itself out, and the players are already leaving the field. Mark walked right up to us without our noticing.

"Oh!" my face goes hot, and Amanda starts scanning the field for Stu.

"You still up for grabbing a slice?" Mark asks, but before I reply he adds, "Just give me a few seconds to jump in the shower." His sweaty hair sticks to his head in beautiful tufts, and his full-on grin gives me reassurance that we will be having an actual *date-date* from this point on.

Mark takes two strides toward the school, turns back and throws over his shoulder, "You can come too, Amanda, if you want. I'll just catch a ride with one of the guys and meet you two at Pizza Shack." He gives me a nod and jogs away.

Amanda and I face each other. It's my disappointment versus her clear excitement.

"That must mean it's a group hang-out sort of thing," she says happily.

"That means it's not really a date," I say unhappily.

"Oh, come on, please be excited for me." Amanda digs a mirror out of her purse so she can watch herself doing quick little baby-primps with her fingertips and check her over-bleached teeth. "I'll bet Stu told him to invite me."

Looking over her shoulder, I see Stu shoot an open-palmed wave to a petite girl from another school, who rewards him with a flash of her dimples. *I wouldn't bet on it.* But I can see Amanda's mind is made up. She's sure she's just been invited to come along as Stu's date, and all I'll end up with is a whole lot of grief if I try to convince her otherwise. Amanda is definitely a hate-the-friend-who-is-just-trying-to-help kind of girl. I decide to spare myself but hope the cute brunette with the dimples isn't coming along for pizza.

• • •

"*So*, how long have you and Stu been dating?"

The brunette answers my question with a shrug as she giggles and puts her hand possessively on Stu's back. We're sharing a booth at Pizza Shack, and the two of them snuggle across from me as Amanda sulks beside me—probably plotting her vengeance. Stu is only partially present, leaning deeply toward the long table filled with the rest of the soccer team. The players celebrate their win as Mark laughs heartily from the head of that table.

Amanda and I had decided to undo her obnoxious flirting with our casually-uninterested-coming-to-Pizza-Shack-late-act. But we ended up arriving too late to fit at the large, rowdy table. We claimed the closest possible booth, and it wasn't so horrible until Stu and his cute brunette showed up and sat with us. Stu is more involved in his teammates' conversation than ours, but his cute brunette keeps a hand perched on his arm at all times. She seems to be reveling in Amanda's beams of hatred.

At least Mark smiles over at me from time to time. Forty minutes into our "date," he calls out, "Hey, Stu, how'd you end up with all the pretty girls?" Which inspires his cute brunette girlfriend to launch herself onto Stu's back and hold firm like a darling little backpack. Stu opens his arms and leans back as if all three of us belong to him.

"Don't get any ideas, Buddy," Mark says. "Blaze is coming home with me." His public acknowledgement of our date feels like a radioactive nip of happiness. The only thing that keeps me from flying to him is Amanda's crestfallen face. I doubt I'd look like a sweet backpack on Mark, anyway. More like a gangly alien attacking an unfortunate host.

I lean toward Amanda. "Don't any of them catch your eye?" I whisper. "If Tony stopped shaving his head he'd actually be kind of cute."

She squints at the brutish-looking junior. "I don't know," she says. "It's hard to picture him with hair. Besides I don't date younger men."

"I'm not saying you should date him," I soothe. "Just that he could be someone interesting to talk to tonight." *So I can start enjoying my date.*

I finally convince Amanda she needs a diversion from Stu and his gloating brunette appendage. The two of us migrate over to the main table, where we squat and kneel until Amanda finally pulls a chair next to Tony. I work my way over to where Mark is giving a play-by-play account of the victory goal. "So I'm looking around and Stu is, I don't know, waving to the stands or something." He pauses to pull me casually onto his lap and continues his story over my left shoulder. "So, I see it's up to me to move the ball downfield." I shift on Mark's lap, before my wicked wedgie becomes permanent. I feel embarrassed and thrilled at the same time and I don't know where to look. It would be weird for me to twist my head to watch Mark talking, since he's only two inches from my face, so I'm stuck looking out toward Mark's staring audience. Everyone's undivided attention is making me nervous, so I reach for the glass of water in front of me just for the sake of something to do.

The water goes down the wrong pipe, which always happens when I'm nervous, but I don't want to start coughing and choking with everyone watching me. I'm nearly crying from the growing tickle intensity, but refuse to give a single cough. If I start I won't be able to stop.

As I struggle to breathe, I notice Amanda palming Tony's shoulder. It looks unnatural, like she's trying to absorb his life-force through her hand, and I wonder if Tony is going to reject her too. As hot as she is, most of the guys at school have become just a little terrified of her clear commitment needs. Her reputation for being high-maintenance seems to have diluted the potency of her flirting.

Mark's story ends with him shouting, ". . . so I caught the ball with the back of my heel, and SCORE!" As everyone cheers and claps, I finally cough until I can breathe again. A Pizza Shack drone comes over to ask if we mind keeping it down. To my mortification, the gang laughs, completely unfazed. They continue on loudly until the middle-aged manager has to come over to kick us out.

The table starts grumbling, and I get nervous that we're about to stage a huge protest scene right here in Pizza Shack, but Mark gives my waist a firm squeeze. "I've gotta get on with my date, anyway, guys. Let's call this thing done." At his command, everyone starts throwing wadded-up bills on the table and giving high-five-good-byes. Chairs scrape tile as we stand up, and I see Tony turn his back toward Amanda, openly dissing her. *Ouch.* She gives me a sad nod, and I wave back empathetically.

Getting turned down by a junior who shaves his head cannot be a good experience. As Amanda turns and flees to her car, I feel a pang of guilt, followed by a shiver of certainty that she will be taking this out on me later.

As I wait for everyone to say good-bye to Mark, I gather the wadded singles and fives scattered around the table and smooth them together, glad to have a purpose. When I add everything up and glance at the bill, I see there's a nearly seven-dollar deficit. And that's before a tip—not that putting pizza on a table and asking us to shut up warrants a huge gratuity, but still. I've already put in my own five bucks, which more than covers the breadsticks I ate.

The table's nearly empty, and it doesn't look like anybody is adding more cash. Stu and Mark talk as the brunette glides her hands up and down Stu's back. Stalling, I go ahead and line the bills up neatly beside Mark's plate with the check on top. Taking a more careful sip of water from my choking glass, I glance about the Shack and try to relax about my impending date.

"Hey, Blaze," Mark calls over, "mind bringing that up to the register?" He indicates the insufficient funds beside his plate.

He gives me a wink and goes back to talking with Stu and I'm forced to pull a ten out of my wallet to cover the difference. At least carrying the cash over to the register by the door gives me something to do. I also get to waste a pathetic amount of sweetness trying to win over the manager who rings me out. His stony expression doesn't soften. I'm pretty sure the three-dollar tip I place back on the table won't make the pizza drone fall in love with us either, but I'm not going any deeper than fifteen bucks for my greasy breadsticks.

I wrestle over whether to bring up my generous contribution to the pizza fund as Mark and I head toward the minivan for our date. As Mark gallantly opens my door, I decide to just let it go. If he mentions the bill I'll let him pay me back, but I don't want to seem cheap by bringing it up. Besides, it's getting late, and I'm curious to see what he has planned for our date.

It really doesn't matter what we do, as long as we're together. Which is a good thing, since he directs, "How about we head to my house?" as soon as he climbs into Superturd.

"Yeah, sure. Let's do that," I say. "Sounds great."

• • •

When we arrive at Mark's house, his parents are in their bedroom, but we're greeted by his big, fat tabby cat, Pelé. As soon as I reach down to give Pelé a little pat he starts purring like crazy.

"Did you know cats never purr when they're alone?" Mark smiles. "Pele is telling you he's happy." Which I have to say is the sweetest bit of cat trivia I've ever heard.

Curled up on the couch in the basement media room, I decide it's actually pretty cool that Mark invited me back to his house. We're already friends and past needing a formal date at the stupid movies or something. In fact, if I could, I'd give a few purrs myself as I snuggle into him.

It doesn't even matter that we end up watching some boring soccer movie based on what must've been an even more boring true story. "The Game of Their Lives?" I mock when Mark shows me the cover. "Seriously? It sounds like a bad soap opera."

"It's my favorite movie," he insists as he puts it in the player. "You'll like it." Which I suppose is nice that he wants to share his favorite movie with me. Seeing as how I've reached the home stretch to becoming his girlfriend and all.

I try to focus on the film, which is about some big soccer rivalry with Britain that took place in the 1950s, but all I can think is, *when will he kiss me?* We fit together so close and comfortable, me leaning into him on the couch, it's like we're meant to be together. I try to focus on the boring sports movie, but Mark's proximity is too much to ignore. I wonder if he's actually absorbed in the movie or if he's as aware of me as I am of him.

I start to grow concerned that we aren't going to kiss at all, which will solidify us a "buds" and nullify any chance of me becoming his girlfriend. Mark must finally pick up on my tele-pathetic signals because he hits pause, turns toward me, and narrows his eyes.

I look at him expectantly, afraid he's about to quiz me on the movie and discover I haven't been paying attention. Then I think maybe he's remembered to ask about the pizza bill. Without saying a word, he slowly closes the gap of space between our lips. As our mouths connect, I physically feel the sentiment, *now this is more like it.*

My first kiss.

His tongue gently prods my lips, and as soon as I part them slightly, the tip of it dips into my mouth. It's warm and soft as it explores, feeling surreal in its moistness. It drives deeper. Excites me.

It's silly that Mark asked for the power to heal, since he clearly has a super power already. It's kissing. *And I'm fully under his lips' control.* Mark's kiss intensifies, and it's as if I can taste how turned on he is. I feel a thrill until he leans further over me and suddenly I'm not just tasting how turned on he is—I'm feeling it too. The evidence of his swollen crotch against my wedgied one is unignorable and reminds me I have this penis-phobia that I haven't quite worked through yet.

I realize in a panic that I've been holding my breath this whole time. I need to breathe. Desperately. As Mark's tongue continues its caress, I focus on exhaling slowly through my nose without blowing a puff of nose-air onto his cheek. I'm hoping he doesn't notice.

Mark's hand slides down to my breast and starts moving

around. It's not unpleasant, but I'm consumed with wondering what the outside of my T-shirt and form-fitting bra feel like to his fingers. And what it means for our relationship that I'm allowing over-the-clothes caresses so soon and if this means I will have to touch his...

Without thinking, I slide my elbow up and around to block his right hand from my chest. I silently curse Su-per Virgin Girl! and her need to be in complete control of the situation. Mark counters by moving his hand to the bottom of my shirt so he can stroke my waist while our mouths remain hotly fused together. Slowly, the hand at the bottom of my shirt begins to travel underneath and upward toward my bra as the other hand gains ground, caressing my other breast from the outside.

A quick assessment determines that the hand underneath my shirt poses the greatest threat, and I quickly press my arm down to my side, effectively pinning Mark's hand. Bra security has been enforced. Virgin Girl is happy.

We continue kissing, and I try to tell myself to relax already. There's really no reason to block every move Mark makes, it's just—

I clamp down on the bottom of my T-shirt a moment before Mark can raise it above chest level.

Undaunted, he shifts his weight, lets my shirt stay on, but plunges both hands underneath it, grasping my bra cups with both hands. *Well played*, I think as my body responds to his massages against my will. It feels so good Virgin Girl is nearly unconscious. We remain like that for a time, kissing and massaging and floating an inch above the couch.

I try to keep my body completely still and just receive the pleasure bolts coming from Mark's touch. But then I feel a finger breach the elastic band of my bra and the next thing I know Mark is cupping my left breast underneath my bra and T-shirt. We have skin-to-skin contact. He is fondling my bare boob, and Virgin Girl is wide awake and wondering how far Mark thinks I'll go on a first date.

The wondering is interrupted by how good it feels to have Mark's hand on my breast, and I manage to convince Virgin Girl he won't try to go any further. She relaxes. Right up until he starts slowly grinding his crotch into my thigh. She takes control and I sit upright, easing Mark's hands out from underneath my shirt. I do manage to continue kissing him, but once the hand-to-hand combat has played itself out, it's only a minute before Mark pulls away and hits play on the movie.

Both disappointed and relieved, I put my head on his shoulder and our breathing slowly returns to normal. My face feels raw from kissing, and I'm glad the lights are low so Mark can't see what I look like. I wasn't really watching before, but there's no way I can focus on the movie now. I sit, daydreaming about how well our names will fit together when we get married.

At one point, the movie shows some crazy-intense game being

played, which makes me think that although the Wolverines are pretty awesome, they have a long way to go. Which then makes me think of star-player-slash-little-brother-extraordinaire, Josh, who was suspicious about me going out tonight. And that thought leads to home and Mom and…

Oh, my God. Mom. Looking at my cell phone, I see it's nearly midnight. She hasn't called, probably because she doesn't want to disturb my date, but she'll be waiting up for me. "I need to call my mom and let her know I haven't been kidnapped," I tell Mark. He nods and continues watching until I elbow his chest. "Umph," he grunts and holds his side, making me think I've hurt him until he starts laughing. He pauses the movie right on a shot of some sweaty guy head-butting a soccer ball. Mark imitates the strained look on the guy's face with a snarl and makes me laugh.

As I dial my phone he says, "Tell her you got arrested and you need her to come and bail you out."

"I am *not* telling my mother I'm in jail." I give him a playful shove as the phone rings on the other end.

"Come on," he urges. "It'll be hilarious!"

I raise an eyebrow, but when I hear my mother's sleepy voice on the other end, "Wha—? Blaze? What's wrong?" it's too perfect a set up to not go for it.

"Hey, Mom." I grin at Mark. "I got arrested. I need you to come and bail me out of jail."

"YOU WHAT?" Mom shouts, suddenly awake. Mark must be able to hear her because his big grin shrinks down to a small letter O.

"Just kidding, Mom." I suddenly remember that the two of us do not have this joking sort of relationship. "Totally kidding. I'm fine. Um… I just wanted to let you know I'll be home late."

"My *God*, Blaze!" Mom is pissed. "I have to be at the hospital early tomorrow! It's a school night! Are you kidding me?"

"Sorry, Mom. No. I mean yes. I'm just… kidding. Sorry." I focus on the couch's armrest as tears threaten to well up in my eyes. I cannot believe I screwed up so bad, but Mark's watching. I need to hold it together. "I'll be home soon, 'kay?" I manage to end on a light*ish* note and hang up.

My face tingles with the combination of post-make-out skin burn and the shame of freaking my mother out. Mark gives me a squeeze. "Guess that didn't go over so well." He shrugs. "Parents, huh?" As if he has any clue about my parental situation. But then he leans in and kisses me with such certainty, I'm convinced Mark knows everything there is to know about everything.

We make out a little more before a stray hand inspires yet another lightning-quick block with my elbow. Make that Virgin Girl's elbow, but Mark just laughs and restarts the movie, stroking my hair absentmindedly as we watch. By the time we get to the feel-good ending, I must say, I'm actually back to feeling pretty good.

"I'll have to rent this for Josh," I say.

Mark hits eject, puts the disk in the case, and hands it to me. "I think you can be trusted," he says.

"With your favorite movie?" I feign adoration. "I'll guard it with my life."

We kiss on the couch a moment longer until Pelé interrupts us—leaping onto the arm of the sofa, right by our heads. After a quick scream of surprise, I say, "And now what is your cat communicating?"

"Jealousy," says Mark, and we laugh as he scratches Pelé under his chin. Finally, I break the bad news, "I'd better head home."

"I'll walk you out." Mark groans like an old man as he stands up, then leans on me so heavily we laugh as we nearly topple over. Once he's mobile, Mark steers me into the kitchen and stops, pretending to prop me against the counter before opening the fridge. He pulls out a plastic pitcher and empties it into a tinted glass. After gulping less than half of it, he dumps the rest down the drain and gives the cup a spin before dropping it noisily into the sink.

I wonder if the flurry of little face-kisses he gives me at the door will become our special after-date good-bye custom. On my way back to Superturd I rub my face and marvel over how well the night went. *One thing's for sure*, I think as I climb into the driver's seat, *I've set my sights on a really super guy.*

Chapter Eight

"What a giant ass," says Terri. She and Amanda have dragged me to the mall practically against my will, and I'm resisting the urge to check my cell phone yet again for a text from Mark.

"Oh, I don't know that he's a *giant* ass," I defend. "Maybe he just hasn't had a chance to text me yet." I look down at my cell phone to confirm that, no, he hasn't had a chance to text me yet.

"God, Blaze, not everything is about Mark," says Amanda. Ever since getting rejected by both Stu and Tony in one night, she's quick to lash out.

"I just want to know where we stand," I whine.

Terri shakes her head and points to the "giant ass" she's actually referring to. It's a two-story high, black-and-white poster in the window of Lucy's Lucky Lingerie. The photo shows a model wearing lingerie that is so sexy-looking Dylan would probably set up a mini altar to worship in front of it. I feel a sharp pang of guilt for leaving Josh home alone on a Saturday night, but Mom will be home from work soon and promised to take him out to eat. I've sworn to never prank her in the middle of the night again but still didn't get invited to dinner.

"Take my picture!" Amanda twists, mimicking the model's pose as she gives a sultry glare over her shoulder. She is an expert at modeling, thanks to a boxed DVD set of nine seasons of the reality show *Model Makers*.

Terri and I laugh, and I snap Amanda's picture with my cell phone.

"Too bad you don't have access to that chick's airbrusher," says Terri. "See how smooth her elbow is? She couldn't even bend it in real life, it would crack right open."

"Who the hell is looking at her elbows?" Amanda gestures like a game show hostess to the model's bulbous breasts.

"Good point." Terri's mom is always harping about how the skinny models with fake boobs are wrecking all our self-esteem, but Terri and her sisters sneak fashion magazines into the house anyway. Still, her mom must have her half-brainwashed or something, because Terri is always pointing out when models are too skinny or when airbrushers go overboard.

The Lucy's Lucky Lingerie model's airbrusher has definitely gone overboard—but then, a girl can use a little help when her ass is blown up to the size of small planet.

I say, "I should get back—"

"Get back to what?" Terri cuts me off. "Sitting at home, obsessively checking your emails?"

"Why don't you just text him?" Amanda asks.

"No way. I can't seem desperate." I quickly check my phone, since a whole minute has passed since I last looked at it. Terri gives me an accusing glare, and I defend, "I didn't say I can't *be* desperate. Just that I can't *seem* desperate."

"Oh, you're desperate all right," she says. "You need to chill out."

"You guys are ridiculous," says Amanda. "It's perfectly acceptable for a girl to make a move when she likes a guy."

I totally blame Virgin Girl for Mark's silent treatment. I just need to reassure him my powers of chastity are not completely impenetrable. He probably doesn't even realize how much I truly like him. My chest clenches and I feel the sensation that I'm being watched.

Looking around, I catch Comic Book Guy staring at me as he strides through the mall. He doesn't avert his eyes when he sees I've caught him looking. In fact, he twists his body as he passes so he can continue gawking at me.

Creeper, I think, mortified that he caught me checking out a lingerie window. I glance again, and his eyes narrow as if he's trying to place me. I want to tell him he doesn't have to worry—I'm not planning to come breathe all over his comics today.

Amanda doesn't seem to notice our stalker as she grabs my arm. "Come on!" I get a final glimpse of Comic Book Guy still staring as she drags me through the wide entrance to Lucy's Lucky Lingerie. We're hit with a wall of powdery-smelling fragrance. Brightly colored bras line the pink walls, and racks of lace teddies crowd around us. Amanda grabs a satin hanger dripping with scraps of pale pink lace and flings it into my chest.

I hold up a twisted strap. "There is no way I am putting this on my body," I say. "It won't even cover my bits."

"That's the idea," says Amanda. "It's supposed to show off your bits."

"Well, I'm game," says Terri. "My bits are bitty enough." She selects a black satin teddy and heads toward the back, where the words "Get Lucky" are painted in gold on the wall with an arrow pointing to the try-on rooms.

"Ooooh, this is stunning," Amanda holds up a tangle of white satin that will probably look incredible on her. "Come on," she commands as she heads after Terri. With a glance at my phone, I drag myself and my pale pink bands of lace to join them in the plush try-on rooms. *Maybe I will "Get Lucky,"* I think as I pass under the sign, *and get a text from Mark.*

As I undress, I think about everything I did wrong in Mark's basement to make him not like me. On top of my Virgin Girl display, I know I didn't seem interested enough in his soccer movie. *Why couldn't we have watched some superhero movie, like* Iron Man *or* Spider-Man? I think. I could've pointed out the little insider nods the filmmakers put in for comic enthusiasts. Not that displaying my inner-geek will win me Mark's love. Once I have on the pale pink number I check my phone one more time as I head out of the changing room. No messages.

Terri looks adorable, but her teddy covers her bits a little too well. She pulls the saggy material at her chest into two points. "Whadda ya think girls? Is it the new me?"

Amanda laughs. "Catherine Wiggan is the only chick big enough to fill out that teddy."

"And the only girl slutty enough to wear it," adds Terri.

"Did you hear about her latest conquest?" Amanda asks in a scandalous tone.

"According to the status updates of everybody on FriendsPlace that's conquest*sss*, plural," Terri says. I tune them out as I adjust the straps to my "lucky" lingerie.

Amanda strikes a seductive pose in her white satin sexy wear. She looks like she belongs in one of the ads. That is, if they airbrush away any softness from her belly and thighs. She looks fantastic, but her chest is the only part of her that matches the models. Amanda rolls her shoulders forward so that her upper arms smoosh her boobs into massive cleavage. "How do I look?" she asks.

"Better than I do," I laugh. Amanda must've handed me an extra small, because my bands of lace are way too teeny. And just as I suspected, they don't quite cover my bits. The lace of the bra pulls tightly over my breasts, and leaves nothing to the imagination. The back of the undies run up my butt and look ridiculous with my saggy briefs poking out from underneath. But even if it hadn't been too small, the outfit still would've been X-rated.

I imagine how Mark would react to this look as I automatically duck my head into my changing stall and pick up my phone. I frown as I register the still-empty text icon. This is awful. I am literally aching for some form of contact from him.

"Oh, for Christ's sake," Amanda says. Before I can stop her, she grabs my phone and takes a step back, aiming the camera in my direction.

"Don't you dare." I give her my most evil grimace, holding my hands over my chest as Terri laughs hysterically behind me.

"Aw, come on, you look cute," Amanda coaxes, but I'm not budging. I hold one arm over my pink lacy bits as I grope for my phone with my free hand.

"Come on, guys, let's make our own ad." Terri laughs.

"Not unless they airbrush out my nipples," I say, pushing out my chest to show Terri just how see-through my bra is.

Amanda twists her butt in our direction. "I'll take a little cellulite smoothing," she says. "Not to mention a tummy tuck."

"I could obviously use a boob job." Terri pulls up her shoulder-straps. "But my mom would kill me for even thinking such a thing, let alone saying it out loud. 'Boob jobs are for masochistic bubble heads,'" she recites robotically.

"I'd just love underwear that doesn't ride halfway up my butt." I aim my lace wedgie in her direction. "Plus, I really need my cell phone back, Amanda."

"Yes, Amanda," says Terri. "Blaze has not checked her phone

for a text from Mark for a whole entire minute." She opens her eyes wide in mock-panic.

Amanda laughs and glances at my phone's screen. She flings her mouth open in shock. "Oh, my God! You got a text!" she practically shouts and dangles the phone just out of my reach as I lunge for it. "And it's from Mark!"

My heart races as I feel excitement rush to my face. "What did he say?"

Amanda's look suddenly turns hard as she twists my phone in her hand and I hear a solid *cla-chick*. It takes me a moment to realize she's just taken my picture. "What the… ?" *Maybe he wrote something bad.* I feel beyond confused and just want to know what the hell Mark finally wrote to me. I start to panic as Amanda punches madly at my phone's text keys.

"Amanda!" I practically shout. "What are you doing? What did Mark say?"

With a blue-white grin she tosses my phone to me. "He didn't say anything yet. But I guarantee he will now."

I catch my phone in one hand. "He didn't…" I look at the empty icon and realize Mark hasn't written to me at all. My heart deflates. Then it starts flinging itself around inside my ribcage as I realize what Amanda has just done. *No, No, No!*

"Oh my God, you didn't!" I turn to Terri for help. "She just sent Mark a picture of me." I wave a hand up and down my body and shout, "Half! Naked!"

"Amanda!" Terri springs to my side. "What the hell were you thinking?" She tries to take the phone from me, but I hold it in a double-handed death grip as I scroll to find the photo.

"What? It's no big deal," says Amanda. "I did it with a boyfriend once, and he *loved* it."

"Mark isn't her boyfriend," says Terri. "And now he's going to think she's a slut!"

"She's not even topless," Amanda says.

"She may as well be!" Terri gestures to my lacy boobs for emphasis, and I nod in agreement, keeping my eyes glued to my phone as I search for the photo. "He'll think it's an invite to hook up!" she says.

"Well, maybe that's not a bad thing for him to think!" says Amanda. "You can see how hot she is for the guy."

"Blaze, were you planning on hooking up with Mark?" Terri asks me.

I glance up from my phone. "I don't know," I say truthfully. "I just really want to be his girlfriend."

The two of them continue arguing over the nightmare I've just entered, but they fade to background as the ringing in my ears grows louder and louder. I've finally found the photo. And it's worse than I imagined.

I feel like I'm drowning in my own heartbeat.

I stare at the image that is, at this very moment, winging its way though cell towers and satellites toward Mark's cell phone.

Feeling desperately out of control, I telekinetically command his phone to self-destruct wherever it is. I imagine myself having the power to zoom after it and delete it before it reaches him. Never before have I wanted to fly so desperately.

I cannot believe Amanda sent Mark this picture.

In the photo, my expression shows open excitement, and the way my left arm reaches forward out of frame makes it seem like I may have actually taken the picture myself. It only shows from the waist up, so my bulging granny panties aren't in the shot, but that doesn't make up for the very worst part. My breasts are front and center and completely exposed through the sheer lace bra. Everything, including the small brown beauty mark beside my right nipple, is clearly visible and in perfect focus. My face is the teensiest bit blurry, but I'm still completely recognizable, so the fuzziness just adds to the overall pornographic effect. I can't believe it's me in the picture. I haven't been photographed naked since I turned four and stopped taking baths with my little brother. Back then I obviously didn't look this slutty.

"You look so hot!" Amanda admires her photography skills. "Really, he's gonna love it."

As my consciousness kicks back to the world around me, I realize Terri is rubbing my back. "It'll be okay," she soothes. "He might not even notice your nipples are showing."

Except that I know there's no way he won't notice my nipples are showing. Boys notice nipples. It is an indisputable law of the universe. Much too late, I cup my hands protectively over my breasts. I want nothing to do with that photo, and now that Mark has it I feel an odd sensation of just wanting him to disappear too. I certainly want nothing at all to do with the scraps of lace still biting into my sides. "I need to get dressed," I report dully and turn back to my stall.

Terri launches into Amanda. "I can't believe you did that to her!" she shoots, then calls sweetly through the curtain to me, "Hey, Blaze, you want a cinnamon pretzel or something? My treat."

I want to escape the mall and get away from everybody. I wonder if I should call Mark and explain that there was a huge mix-up and he should just ignore any and all photos sent from my number. Maybe I should send an odd picture of the ceiling or my foot and he'll just assume my camera phone is acting crazy. I lay it down on the pink bench cushion and numbly get undressed, hanging the damning strips of pink lace on their satin hanger.

I already have one leg back in my jeans when my phone starts ringing. Not only does it ring, but it rings with the love song I've downloaded especially for Mark's cell phone number. *Mark is calling me!* I freeze, balanced on one leg as the cheesy melody fills the dressing room.

Flinging my head outside the curtain I snap at Amanda and Terri, "It's him! He's calling!" Mid-arguing they turn wide eyes to me until I wail, "What should I do?"

"Answer it!" they both command, and I somehow manage to control my hands enough to pick up my phone and hit the green button a split second before the call goes to voicemail.

"Hello?" I say timidly while hoping the text didn't go through and that this is an amazing coincidence.

"Hi, Blaze." Mark's voice sounds sultry. "I got your text." *Damn!*

"Oh, about that, I…" I look desperately to Amanda and Terri for help. "My phone has been acting sort of wonky—"

"Yeah, I'm sorry I haven't had a chance to call." Mark cuts smoothly through my panic. "I was wondering if you're free tonight."

Everything goes still as my mind whirrs with responses. I need to clarify that the photo was all Amanda's idea. I want to make certain it's not the only reason he called. But really, in the end, there's only one possible way I can respond to Mark asking me out.

"You want me to pick you up?" I ask.

"Seven thirty okay?"

"Um-hmm," I say through the ringing that has started up again in my ears.

"Great! Oh, and Blaze," his voice turns sultry again, "be sure to wear that lace thing from your picture."

"That's not—" But he's already hung up.

• • •

The next thing I know, Mark and I are parked in the middle of a cornfield off Route 8. In my mind I try to retrace the series of events that led to the two of us making out in the front seat of my minivan, but every time I manage to string two thoughts together, they're wiped clear by the intensity of Mark's kisses.

With the part of my brain that is still functioning beyond, *Oh my God, this feels so good,* I recreate the cartoon panels leading up to our liplock.

The first panel features the two of us looking out the minivan's windshield as we pull out of Mark's driveway. Talk bubbles show him telling me how funny it is that he was just about to call me when he got my sext and me trying to tell him the whole thing was an elaborate accident. We see a close-up panel of him seductively rubbing my leg as I drive. A cross-section X-ray illustrates the "lucky" pale-pink permanent-wedgie underwear hiding underneath my clothes, worn at Amanda's insistence, and a comic panel shows a close-up of my heart beating through my shirt. *Badda-thump. Badda-thump.*

Comic-Mark suddenly points to the left, his arm flung across my chest as he calls out in big, block letters, "*TURN HERE!*"

Superturd swerves a screechy swerve, and lightning letters "*SQUEEEEE*" up from the front tire in the comic version. And let me tell you, my mind is sticking with the comic version, if only to have something to focus on and avoid going to total mush. I already have the same light, tipsy feeling I got the time Amanda snuck a bottle of vodka into her bedroom for our sleepover. Of course, the burning alcohol going down my throat was much less enjoyable than Mark's sweet kisses.

Back in my comic-mind-version of events, Superturd has missed the sudden turn Mark demanded, mostly because I realize right before crashing that there is no actual turn-off. A half-page panel shows that there's nothing but a big, long corn-field running down both sides of the road. "That's okay," says comic-Mark, "there's another spot just ahead." And this time when he calls out, "Right here! Turn!" he simultaneously grabs the wheel and turns it sharply, sending us lurching toward the wall of corn. And this panel of us has to show a row of e's coming out of my mouth, like "*eeeeeeeeeeeeee!*" as I slam on the brakes. By the time the van stops, we're sitting crookedly in a ditch, but my headlights show that there is, indeed, a break in the cornrows ahead of us.

"Sorry I scared you," Mark's talk bubble says. He gives a worried look as he tenderly smooths a hand over my hair.

"I wasn't scared," my talk bubble defends, despite the fact that I screamed. Plus, my hands have little vibration lines because they're shaking from the aftershocks of adrenaline and terror.

From there, to the present, there's just a short transition page showing panels of the van pulling deeper into the corn-field and our faces moving toward each other in a row of shots ending with a full double-paged spread of our epic kiss. The epic kiss has been going on for some time at this point, and the intensity is growing beyond Su-per Virgin Girl's power to control it.

"Let's get in the back," Mark breathes between kisses, but I stay firmly planted in the driver's seat. The back of my minivan is so smelly and disgusting it will dampen every last drop of passion Mark and I have whipped up.

"Do you have one of those pull-down DVD players in this thing?" he asks teasingly. Slipping through the gap between the front seats, he runs his hand along the ceiling as he moves toward the back of the minivan.

"Sorry, no," I say, my lips already feeling cold and lonely. "Nothing back there but empty seats."

Mark climbs past the middle seats and sits in the very back row. When he pats beside him invitingly, I shake my head "no" with the sense we are playing a game and I don't know the rules. Knowing the rules is important. In this same van, I tricked him into losing at Cows that first time.

"What do you want?" my talk bubble teases as a thought bubble rises from my head asking, *What do I want?*

Mark gives a few bops, then disappears as he lies down across the bench. I wrap my hands around the steering wheel, tempted to start Superturd and drive away.

"Oh, Blaze," Mark calls in a sing-song voice, and I know that if I don't join him I'll never hear from him again. I think of how desperate and empty I felt just a few hours ago. I don't want to go back to that. Ever.

I find myself crouch-walking toward him. When I get to the back of the minivan I don't know what to do. I sway a bit, wanting to get back to the kissing, but not sure how to make that happen. Mark looks so perfect in the moonlight beaming through the back windows and without thinking, I call out "Piledriver!" and fling myself, elbow first, on top of him. I instantly remember I'm not some petite little brunette backpack who can just fling her body around flirtatiously. My flinging is a clear act of aggression. Mark lets out a loud grunt as my elbow connects with his ribs.

"Sorry." I bite my lip. "I think I spend too much time hanging out with thirteen-year-old boys."

"No, that was cute," he insists as he wraps his arms up and around me, drawing me to him. We start kissing again, but the position change makes more of a difference than I imagined. Sitting in the front seats, kissing as we leaned over the gap had been hot enough, but lying on top of him must change my body's entire blood flow or something because, *Damn!* Now all I can think of is our private bits. My brain locks onto what would be going on "down there" if we weren't separated by four layers of fabric. That is, four layers assuming Mark has on underwear. I've spent enough time with the male species to know that isn't necessarily a given.

No sooner does the thought of his underwear (or lack thereof) enter my head than Mark slowly starts lifting the bottom of my shirt. Like he has special make-out telepathy or something. After mentally gagging and binding Virgin Girl, I sit up and raise my arms to help him. When my shirt is over my head and out of the way, I draw in a breath at the sight of Mark's expression.

His hands rest on either side of my waist, and he looks up at the transparent pink bra with such intensity, I feel a fresh *KA-BAM!* in my lower belly. His face is so perfect, and I want him to keep looking at me that way, to draw him to me. Without pausing, he reaches behind me and effortlessly undoes the clasp on my bra. With a flick of his wrist, my breasts are revealed to a boy for the very first time. Mark's eyes go almost animalistic at the sight of them. I feel... powerful.

"You are amazing," he tells my boobs. Pulling me closer, he nearly swallows my left breast. I giggle and suppress the urge to point out that he can suck all day, he isn't getting any milk from these puppies. That's when he pulls back and, with shaking restraint, makes small gentle circles around my nipple with his tongue. It's like little pleasure lightning bolts shooting through my chest. I clutch at his thick, dark hair that's the tiniest bit damp and smells like spicy licorice. Mark turns his head. His tongue goes to work on my waiting breast, and it feels so good my mind is completely wiped clear. There is nothing aside from how good this feels. Su-per Virgin Girl lies passed out in the corner.

My eyes closed, I reach above Mark's head to steady myself and better position my chest for more of his tongue's fondling. My hand touches something smooth and cold, tucked into the space behind the armrest. *What the...?* My surprise at the mystery item pulls me from the perfect paradise in my mind to Superturd's moonlit interior. I lift the small smooth package and sit up, straddling Mark and leaving him with such a look of open desire on his face it's nearly comical. One of the hottest guys in school, out of my league, and yet here he is in the back of my minivan, completely under my control. With that thought, I look at the thing I'm holding in my hand and let out a piercing scream.

"Fucking Ajay!" I say as I dive toward the side door.

Mark tries to hold onto me, but I muscle past him, yanking the door open and flinging the disgusting package outside.

"Wha...?" Mark's face looks like he just woke up from a very deep sleep. I can't believe my romantic encounter was just interrupted by a moldy turkey and cheese sandwich in a plastic baggy. I make a quick mental note to assassinate Ajay.

"It's nothing," I tell Mark with false lightness as I rejoin him. I just want to get back to that mind wipe situation with his face in my breasts.

"You okay?" Mark sits up as I reposition myself over him. His eyes scan my bare chest and claim my nipples. I nearly laugh at the way boys apparently don't get any less breast-obsessed between the ages of thirteen and eighteen. It's as if the rest of me is nonexistent.

"It's just some garbage one of your players left behind, that's all." I shrug, and Mark pulls me down to a close embrace. He's wearing his favorite Kick Some Grass! T-shirt, and it's soft against my bare chest, but I long to pull it up and feel his skin against mine. Which is probably why, when Mark asks me if I want to stop, I answer him honestly, "No."

He asks if I'm sure and as I pull back and look into his earnest face, I see everything. The life I want instead of the one I have. I need Mark to be mine. I can't lose him. He's my Zodiac Key.

Except that I don't think I entirely understand what my answering no means. Or, more to the point, I don't know what I've said yes to, because the next thing I know, Mark is asking me when I had my last period.

My first thought is that he wants to tease me about it. "Um, it ended last week I think?" I say non-committally and remind myself Mark is not thirteen and probably doesn't mock girls for using products from the feminine hygiene aisle.

"Perfect, you should be fine," he says, unzipping his jeans. "But I'll be careful just in case." Apparently, his take-charge coaching technique applies off the field as well. He explains that he will tap me on the hip to warn me when it's time for him to pull out and demonstrates by tapping my hip firmly. I'm to shift quickly to my left when he gives the signal.

As I focus on Mark's instructions, Virgin Girl whirrs awake. *Wait a second,* she protests. *How's about a nice blow job, instead?* But picturing that seems degrading and less intimate and, well,

I'm pretty sure I'd suck at it. I laugh nervously at my ridiculous "suck" thought-pun. Mark must take my laugh to mean I'm ready to get down to business, because he responds with a smile as he unfastens my jeans. This is it. Time to show him how I really feel about him. I think of how much I've longed to be this close to him and even though I'm really nervous, I'm glad that we're about to connect in such a meaningful way.

Condom, Condom, CONDOM! screams Virgin Girl.

I stammer, "Uh, c-condom?"

"It's fine," Mark reassures with a convincing moonlit smile.

At least I don't have to wonder anymore about him becoming my boyfriend. *And, hey, that lace wedgie is finally gone,* I think as he pulls down my jeans and panties in one smooth motion. The matching set never would've gotten displayed even if he hadn't already ditched the bra. Which is fine, since there's not exactly tons of room to perform a seductive striptease here in the back of Superturd.

The comic panel version of what happens next would show the words: *Zip! Thwack! Shlurp! Boink!* in giant starbursts. And before Su-per Virgin Girl! can utter another word, the whole thing's over. Mark and I have had sex. I don't even get a good look at his equipment, which I suppose is for the best, what with my fear of penises (*Or is it peni? I'm still not sure*).

I scrounge about and find some loose Burger Palace napkins to clean up the mess. As Mark wipes himself off and fastens his jeans

I can't help but feel vaguely empty, like I swallowed a teeny, tiny marble-sized black hole. How can something that's supposed to be such a momentous big deal be over with so quickly? I wonder if I was any good.

I pull my shirt on and lean back into Mark's arms as he lounges against the freshly fogged window. I can feel him around me. I breathe in his scent and marvel that I just bonded with him so completely. We did it. The big "it." We did *IT*. All of my lusting and hoping for all this time has culminated in this ultimate encounter. No more wondering what sex feels like. Now I know. *What more could I want?* I feel so close to him, I don't want this moment to end.

Mark reaches up and presses the outside of his fist to the rear window, making the shape of a tiny foot in the fog we just created. As he adds little toes with his fingertip I am hit with a wave of insecurity and I wonder if the cute gesture is meant to charm me, or if it is rather like a small, wishful step away from me.

I see no clues in his half-lit expression as he shifts our embrace and groans happily. After a moment he invites, "Wanna go watch another movie at my house?" And since it's too late to drive all the way over to Cinema World, I nod, pull on my lace-enema "lucky" undies and jeans, and get back in the driver's seat. Mark uses a sweet, smooth voice to tell me that what we just did was amazing and that he can't believe it was my first time, and that he's so into me—but every time I glance in my rearview mirror, that tiny, baby footprint chills me.

Chapter Nine

"Are you sure we're going in the right direction?" Josh is stressing out in the passenger seat beside me.

We're on our way to a game and running late because I made a wrong turn earlier. We're deep in Farm County, where one wrong turn can cost you a half-hour or more and land you in deep manure. With the four players surrounding me, I'm responsible for a crucial portion of the team, and we all feel the pressure of running late. Well, aside from Ajay, who is peacefully playing his DS as usual.

Mark fell asleep on the couch in his den as we watched yet another soccer movie, and I had to wake him to let him know I had to go home. It turns out the flurry of small good-bye kisses all over my face isn't going to be "our thing" after all, which is fine since Mark drools when he sleeps. He sent me a text this morning letting me know his truck was back on the road and so he wouldn't need a ride to the game after all. He wrote that he'll see me there since he has a thing to do afterward. It just makes more sense this way.

His text felt a little formal considering the new level of our relationship, not to mention the fact that it was our first exchange since our *ahem* exchange. But then, he did say he'd see me at the game. Plus, text messages are limited to 160 characters, and anyway, it's not like people sign texts with, "I'm your new boyfriend now," so I'm not really all that anxious. It's just bad luck that Mark's truck got fixed right after our Superturd hook-up.

"Oh my God, Blaze!" Dylan calls out from the back, "Is this yours?"

I glance in the rearview mirror and nearly crash the minivan in horror. Dylan's glasses have slid partway down his nose as he holds up my pale-pink "lucky" bra. The other boys turn to see what he's so worked up about. I shift my focus back and forth from the road to the backseat so fast my head must be a blur. It certainly feels like one.

"Blaze!" Ajay accuses with his thumbs paused over his game system. "What is your over-the-shoulder-boulder-holder doing behind the back seat?"

I swear I can see Dylan vibrating with excitement all the way across the minivan as he holds my bra by the straps and waggles it up and down. The others gape at this physical evidence that, on top of being their soccer mom stand-in, I am, in fact, a girl.

"Um, I, er…" I falter. "I had to go to a thing after school the other day and got changed." Josh will know it's a lie, but I have to get Dylan to drop the bra and the subject of how it ended up in the back of the van before I die of embarrassment.

In the rearview mirror, I see Andrew reach back. In one swift motion, he snags the pale-pink lace away from Dylan and cuffs him in the back of his shaved head with the other hand. He leans up and drops the item over my shoulder with a quiet, "Here, Blaze."

As soon as it lands in my lap, I wad up the bra and wedge it into my bag with a vow to burn it when I get the chance. I can't bear to look at Josh, but at least Andrew has seen to it that the subject is dropped. Once my shock at seeing Dylan holding my unmentionables has faded, I'm able to put the whole thing into perspective and see that dying of embarrassment would be a complete overreaction. I decide I'll feel better about the whole thing once I get a chance to see Mark. Maybe he and I will even have a laugh over this later. At least I'll get to gauge what sort of boyfriend he's going to be in the light of day. Probably not super-attentive, I expect, but that's cool and all, since I have a life. I mean, we soccer mom types have pretty full schedules, and I'm fairly sure Terri is still my friend.

"Be ready to roll, boys," I say as we pull into the lot at the exact same moment the game is scheduled to start. At least our late arrival means that the boys will evacuate the van quickly and my "over-the-shoulder-boulder-holder" will be forgotten. Or so I think.

Josh stays in the passenger seat, giving me a parental stare that should be reserved for actual parental figures. Or at least siblings who aren't four years younger than you. "Is there something you'd like to talk about, Blaze?"

I busy myself putting my keys in my bag and opening my door.

"Blaze," he says sharply.

I stop, turn toward him and say, "Josh. Mind your business."

"You are my business, sis," he says. "I know you like Coach, but there are some things I really should've told you."

I flip my hair at him. "Josh, honestly, everything is totally fine. I know what I'm doing."

And thankfully, not because he believes me, but because we are so late, Josh relents. "Thanks for the ride," he says and gives me a quick peck on the cheek. "I hope you do know what you're doing."

Me too, I think as I drag my faded pink chair over toward the sidelines to watch the boys play. *Me too.*

• • •

Mark looks cuter than ever and completely relieved when he sees us, which makes my heart do a little nerdy dance move inside in my chest. But then the game starts before I even manage to get my chair set up. Aside from a small, shy wave that Mark returns with a wide, open palm, we don't exactly get a chance to communicate before the soccer action is in full swing and sucking up all his attention.

Throughout the game I try to look like I'm focusing every-where except for Mark's crotch as I send constant telepathic orders to him to pop over to say hi between plays, or even swoop in with a big embarrassing kiss in front of everybody, or maybe just make eye contact. My lousy telepathy aside, he does look over three separate times, and one of those times he returns my wave despite the ball being in play, which makes me feel pretty good about where we stand. Plus, he gives one raised-chin "hey there" between talking to players during half time.

Thankfully, I manage to resist the urge to prance across the field and throw my arms around him. Most of the sketches I draw during the game have *The Blazing Goddess* making out with a new Studly Shark character. In my pictures, though, the Shark guy has his shirt off, and the two of them embrace in outer-space—enjoying the benefits of zero gravity, rather than canoo-dling in the smelly backseat of a minivan.

I hear a commotion and look up in time to see Josh standing by the bench, lashing out at Mark in fury. Josh is poking Mark in the chest with his finger and gesturing wildly, but they're too far away for me to hear what he's yelling. *Did I miss some sort of disagreement over a play, or is this about me?*

I stand up when it looks as if Josh may haul off and punch my boyfriend. My brother looks over and sees me wringing my hands on the sideline. Tossing a final remark at Mark he jogs back onto the field. Mark glances my way before snatching his clipboard up from the bench, and I sit back down in relief. I watch more carefully, but Josh avoids his coach for the rest of the game.

The Wolverines do not play very well, which is probably why instead of greeting me when the game ends, Mark dawdles and collects the equipment into his giant mesh bag. Finally, I walk over to him, towing my chair and holding my *(closed!)* sketchbook under my arm.

"Hey there. Guess you win some, lose some," I say.

Mark shakes his head in response. He glances over toward Josh as he drops the final ball into the sack. "We totally should've had those guys."

His contradiction hangs in the air between us a moment before he finally stands and gives me a sheepish grin that makes my insides mush. I feel my face crack open in a smile as Mark swings his sack of balls over his shoulder. We stroll slowly toward the parking lot together, where I can see the boys are already piling into Superturd.

"So," he says, "guess I'll be missing a rousing game of Cows?"

"You know it." I bump him with my shoulder, and he laughs. I'm gauging the distance remaining between us and the parking lot and wonder if he's going to give me a kiss good-bye in front of the Soccer Cretins. I don't necessarily want to deal with being teased the entire way home, especially after the recent boulder-holder incident. Not to mention odds seem good Josh will deck his coach if he catches him kissing me, but I'm still up for a liplock with Mark under any circumstances.

I try to guide our path toward a clump of trees and bushes that could provide a win-win situation—liplock with my new boyfriend without lingering adolescent taunts. Mark still seems distracted by the team's loss, which is probably why he doesn't pick up on my plan to get us a little privacy. Instead he guides us directly to the driver-side door of the minivan.

"So, you have that thing, huh?" I linger, looking at his lips and deciding it might be worth all the teasing for one little smoochie-smooch after all. Mark gallantly opens my door for me and offers his hand to help me climb in. With a flourish I accept his hand and climb into the minivan as if Superturd is a chariot. "Why thank you," I say elegantly.

He closes the door for me, nearly taking my foot off in the process. At my surprised gasp he apologizes through the open window. "Sorry about that. I didn't get you, did I?"

I dip my head toward his seductively and whisper, "Oh, you got me all right."

Glancing over my shoulder to where Josh sits glaring at him, Mark understandably hides his grin. He calls back into the van filled with his team members, "That's okay, guys, you'll get 'em next year!"

Amid their half-hearted groans, I stutter, "Wait, what?" I'm beyond flustered. "That was a playoff game?"

Mark chuckles. "You really don't pay much attention to what's happening on the field, do you?"

"Well, um…" *Busted!* I blush. "So the season's really over now? I'm sorry." I mean it.

He gives another glance toward Josh and points his thumb over his shoulder. "Well, I've got that thing." After a grin-and-hanging-palm-combo, he saunters toward his waiting pickup. I watch as he hoists the bag of balls into the truck bed and runs his hand through his dark hair a few times before climbing into the cab. He switches his sunglasses for regular glasses, which surprises me, since I had no idea he needed glasses to drive. They have black frames that look perfect on him. I wait for a final good-bye so I can get the full-frontal view, but first he starts playing with the radio or something inside the car.

"Blaze?" Josh's gruff voice makes me realize I've been staring at his coach for an awkwardly long time. I snap back to the inside of the minivan. Josh looks at me hard.

I reach over to ruffle his sweaty hair. "You okay about losing?"

"I'll be fine." He turns and slumps into his seat. I wonder what his fight with Mark was about. And if maybe the team lost because their star player was distracted over his big sister's bra turning up in the backseat of her minivan.

"Yeah, everything will be fine," I say under my breath as I start the van.

I can't believe I'm actually sorry the soccer season is over. As

I shove Superturd into reverse, I call out with fake cheer, "Okay, so I've got twenty-three in my herd so far, any challengers on the way home?"

But the van stays quiet.

A stop for ice cream at King Cone on the way home helps to cheer up most of the gang, but Josh remains sullen and I still feel a letdown that no chocolate-peanut-butter-crunch waffle-cone can soothe.

• • •

It's another night of Mom working late as Josh begs me to drive him to Ajay's house. I keep on insisting that (a) he should've asked way back when I was dropping Ajay off (b) I think he's lying when he claims his fight with Mark had nothing to do with me and (c) he and Ajay are already playing Halo and talking with their headsets through the Xbox. Driving all the way back over to Ajay's house just so they can smell each other's farts as they play is a super-waste of my time.

Time I need to spend doing some serious decoding. I have to figure out what Mark and I are to each other. I doubt he'd allow my little brother to just chase him off, but now that we aren't going to see each other at soccer anymore I'm fairly desperate to go out with him again. He hasn't called or texted me yet, and I'm pushing away a niggling worry—is Mark honestly busy doing "that thing," or am I getting the major send-off now that the two of us did *that* thing?

I try to distract myself by cyber-whining to the girls as I wait to hear from him.

Blazefire22: He's so great when it's just the two of us.

Blazefire22: They had just lost their playoff game so the season's over early and that totally explains why he's acting weird.

Blazefire22: I don't even know if he's acting weird, I just expected different is all… This waiting to hang out with him is killing me!!!!

Blazefire22: I'm obsessively checking email.

Blazefire22: Nothing but silence.

Blazefire22: Hello?

Blazefire22: You guys there?

TerriAngel445: Sure, just letting you get it all out.

AmandaSweetie68: he shldve called u by now

Blazefire22: I'm starting to regret hooking up with him

AmandaSweetie68: well, there is a diff btween hav sex with a guy youve bn c-ing and hooking up with a guy on the first date.

Blazefire22: SECOND date – sorta. And I totally blame that sext you sent! It made him think I was asking for it!

AmandaSweetie68: u were the 1 acting all obsessed I didnt tell u 2 sleep with the guy.

TerriAngel445: Mandy's right, B, I mean, what were you thinking?

Blazefire22: I was thinking that I want to be Mark's girlfriend!

AmandaSweetie68: gd luck with that now

Blazefire22: Ack! This is your damn fault, Amanda!!

AmandaSweetie68: srously? i tried 2 help u and this is how u act? f u blaze!

Blazefire22: OMG You guys!

Blazefire22: Help! He can't just blow me off!

Blazefire22: I need to fix this!

Blazefire22: Hello??

Blazefire22: WTF!

TerriAngel445: I'm still here. You know Mandy still blames you for the whole Stu debauchale.

Blazefire22: It's 'debacle' and it was totally not my fault.

TerriAngel445: You begged her to go to the soccer match.

Blazefire22: I never promised her Stu!

TerriAngel455: She says you talked her into throwing herself at bald Tony.

Blazefire22: I wanted to enjoy my date with Mark. She was pouting. Do you think she sent Mark that photo just to get even with me?

TerriAngel445: You guys will work things out.

Blazefire22: I can't believe she's really this pissed at me.

TerriAngel445: U know how she is. She'll ignore you for a few days and then get over it.

Blazefire22: Right, but I need her to help me sort this thing out!

TerriAngel445: Maybe she hoped youd get embarrassed the way she did.

Blazefire22: I don't care about embarrassed! I think I'm in love with him Terri.

TerriAngel445: I wouldn't share that with anyone until you know where things stand. Maybe you should worry a little about embarrassed.

Blazefire22: OK. Got it. I'll keep feelings to myself. I've gotta go give Josh a ride.

TerriAngel445: Try not to stress over this whole thing, ok.

Blazefire22: K

Yeah, right. Everything's K.

Josh lucks out because I feel an urgent need to get the hell out of the house and driving him to Ajay's is as good an excuse as any. When we get there he gives me a "Thanks," leaps out, and runs for the front door. I look behind me as I back up Superturd and nearly have a heart-attack when a woman's voice screams out "Wait!"

I slam on the brake, terrified I've run over a pet of some sort. *I'm never giving in to Josh's begging again*, I think, but when I turn, Ajay's Mom is trotting toward me, smiling.

"Blaze!" she says when she gets to my open window. "I keep missing you when you drop Ajay off, and I've been meaning to give you some gas money." She produces a yellow envelope.

"It's fine, really," I tell her. "My mom gave me a gas card so—"

"Well, just think of it as payment for your time, then. It

cannot be fun getting stuck driving your little brother and his friends around all the time."

I swallow and whisper, "Thank you," as I take the money. I back slowly down the driveway, trying not to think of the way Mark was supposed to save me from my miserable soccer mom existence.

I can't help but drive past his house. I ache for him. His truck isn't in front, which is probably for the best. It's not like I can just walk right up and knock on the door. I don't seem to have girlfriend rights, after all.

In comics, it's easy to figure out who the good guys are and who're the bad guys. It would be really helpful if real life could be a little more like that.

• • •

I wander blindly through the mall, just killing time before I pick up Josh. I feel so lost and beaten down. If Mark is blowing me off, I've just wasted my virginity on… nothing.

I pass Sector Comics! and think of the ruined *Silver Surfer* again. I feel a rush of rage wash over me. Who the hell does that Comic Book Guy think he is? He thinks he can intimidate me? I'll bet I know comics better than he does.

Turning back toward the store, I stride courageously through the archway. Comic Book Guy is standing behind the counter, and his automatic default annoyance at anyone invading his dominion shifts to a more neutral sourness when he sees it's me.

"Do you have *Silver Surfer* #2 from the 1987 series?" I ask, feeling my boldness falter as his light brown eyes pierce me.

Comic Book Guy's hair is messy, but not the sort of messy some guys obviously construct on purpose. It's just genuinely, adorably messy. Looking me up and down, he raises one eyebrow at my messenger bag with its superhero buttons. Wordlessly, he walks away, pulls a binder off the shelf, and walks back to me, flipping through plastic sheathes.

"Number two, got her right here." He pulls out a plastic-wrapped mint copy of the comic and places it on the counter between us. "What do you want with it?"

"Um, I'd like to *buy* it," I say sarcastically.

"For your *boyfriend*?" he taunts.

Which is like a trigger word for me right now. "What the hell is wrong with you?" I'm almost happy to have a target for all my misery. "You think girls can't enjoy comics?"

"Fine, then. Who's your favorite superhero?"

"Jean Grey," I counter quickly.

"Okay. So, what's your favorite issue?"

I meet his gaze. "*The Uncanny X-Men* number one-three-eight, from October of 1980."

His forehead jumps, so I go ahead and seal his admiration by quoting, "Hear me X-Men! No longer am I the woman you knew! I am FIRE! And LIFE INCARNATE! Now and forever... I am PHOENIX!"

A smile tugs at his mouth, and I see his hands move toward each other as if they want to applaud. Instead, he folds them calmly over the stack of comics he was organizing. "I'm sort of into classic Marvel," I confess, and he launches into a series of rapid-fire questions, designed to trip me up:

"What was the first comic ever published by Marvel?"

"*Golden Age Human Torch.*"

"What was Wolverine's first appearance?"

"*The Incredible Hulk* #180 includes a cameo of Wolverine on the final page, but issue #181 is generally accepted as his first official appearance."

"Who is the Scarlet Witch's twin brother?"

I feign a yawn and answer, "Quicksilver. Aka Pietro Maximoff."

I'm seriously enjoying myself as I nail answer after answer. I notice that when he talks, Comic Book Guy has a small, disappearing dimple just under the left side of his mouth. Our eye contact is unwavering. Neither of us is getting tired of this game. "Who confronted the Avengers when they were sent back to nineteenth century by Kang?"

"Five Wild West heroes." I smile and add. "Including Ghost Rider who is, *bonus point,* called Night Rider in that series."

"Wow." He grins and actually does give a few claps. I blush and confess, "I feel like I cheated on that bonus point. I'm named after Johnny Blaze."

"Your name is Johnny?"

I shove at him from across the counter, surprised by how naturally playful it feels. He asks what I thought of the *Ghost Rider*s, and I'm shocked he remembers what I bought. He squints. "You look sort of familiar, to be honest."

I'm afraid he might remember the big fight my dad had with the old manager and quickly claim, "I just have that sort of face."

He studies it a moment. "No. You don't."

I dip my head, but my smile sets my cheeks on fire.

By the time I'm ready to leave I've discovered Comic Book Guy is less than a year older than me and taking classes at Butler Community. His actual name is Quentin, although he'll always sort of be Comic Book Guy to me. I've also procured the replacement *Silver Surfer* issue, for a fair price after a bit of haggling, and have received an open invitation to come back and talk comics anytime.

When I tell him I'm interested in some part-time work, he says, "We could really use someone with your knowledge to organize our overstock. I'll talk to the boss." Quentin smiles and I'm drawn in by that mischievous dimple. For a moment. I turn to go, reminding myself that my heart belongs to Mark. And if Mark ends up breaking it, I'm never offering it to anyone else.

But I still get a little thrill when I glance back and see Quentin is watching me walk away.

Chapter Ten

Our annual pilgrimage to Ohio, aka Mema Sissy–land, is coming up next weekend, but I'm still holding out hope that Mark will ask me out. In fact, I'm getting nearly cross-eyed from watching for him to write or call or text me. I've decided I'll feign illness and ditch the trip to Mema's. But I'll need to play it just right, since Mom's a pro, and I must seem to be getting sick but still well enough to go to school, so Mark can actually ask me out.

He's probably just keeping things on the down-low on account of Josh being so against the two of us dating. Or maybe he's just blowing me off now that I let him swipe my V-card.

By Thursday, I'm beginning to suspect the worst.

"Am I visible?" I ask Terri, holding my hand up in front of my face and waggling my fingers just to be sure.

"Of course you are," Terri says. "Otherwise, everyone would be staring at me talking to myself right now." We stand just outside the flow of students switching to their final class for the day.

"Has Amanda given any indication of how long she plans to ignore me?"

"She did ask how you're doing with the whole Mark thing." Terri shifts her backpack to her other arm. "I'm thinking that's a good sign."

"Yeah, great sign." I sigh. "All that means is that Mark ignoring me is so obvious that even though Amanda is also completely ignoring me, she can still tell Mark's ignoring me."

"Maybe he's just been really busy and distracted?" Terri is trying to be helpful, which makes me feel even worse.

"I just lost my virginity to the guy!" I whine. "I can't believe he hasn't spoken to me, let alone asked me out this weekend. I mean, I'll take an email forward at this point."

"It's only Thursday. Maybe he's just waiting until the last minute to make plans with you."

"Yeah, maybe," I say. "But how sad is it to hope that he's a thoughtless procrastinator who assumes I'm such a loser I won't have other plans this weekend?"

"He's a guy." Terri shrugs. "What can you do? Let's just hope it's the procrastination thing."

"Right," I sigh. It's probably my best shot.

• • •

Mark may be a thoughtless procrastinator, but that isn't the reason he didn't ask me out. That is, unless he's put it off for so long that he runs out of time and just assumes it's too late when he gives a wave good-bye from his pickup Friday afternoon. *Right.* That's what happened.

I drop my whole getting sick routine after school on Friday, since going with Josh and Mom to Mema's sounds infinitely less pitiful than sitting around all weekend being ignored by Mark. A part of me still hopes he'll call or text or IM or email, but hoping so hard is wearing me out.

Maybe if I'm not so available he'll assume I'm mysterious and want me that much more. As if he'll even be able to tell the difference between my sitting at home stalking my inboxes or being off in Ohio. Too bad there's no good way of pointing out to a person how aloof you're being.

As usual, we leave for Mema's so early I stay in my pajamas. I let Josh have shotgun as Mom drives so I can stretch out across the back bench seat and sleep. I usually do really well with sleeping in the minivan on long trips. I can nod off almost anywhere and in any position. But this time I'm haunted by what Mark and I did in this very spot. My mind traces over every second of our date, searching for what ruined everything. Things had seemed so perfect. I picture him lying under me, making small circles on my breasts with his tongue.

I spring up and move to the middle row.

Pushing my knapsack against the window as a pillow, I manage to drift into a trance. I'm not sure if I sleep or not, but by the time we get to Mema Sissy's my mouth seems coated with latex. At least I've managed to string together a few moments when my gut didn't ache with emptiness and Mark wasn't fully and completely the only thing on my mind.

• • •

"… and did you see what he did to my poor Blessed Virgin?"

We're sitting around the table at Mema's, and she's giving us a blow-by-blow account of all the transgressions committed by her gardener. "I asked him to please give her a good cleaning, and the next thing I knew, he'd sent her out to be touched up." She lowers her voice. "And they tarted her makeup up like a little whore."

Josh is about to squirt mashed potatoes out his nose as he tries not to laugh. We're gorging on Mema's home cooking, which doesn't include any of my three specialties: burnt, soggy, and tasteless. Josh hisses under his breath, "Mary in the half-shell, that little slut."

Which makes me need to focus on not completely losing it.

Mema's pair of mini dachshunds happily catch the bits of garlicky grilled chicken she drops to them. "Please pass the mashed," she says, and I hand her the ceramic bowl loaded with more potatoes than twelve people could eat in one sitting. She asks, "Now, Blaze, honey, what's new with you?"

Josh coughs to cover up his laughter, but I keep my sniggers under control, "Nothing, really, Mema, I—"

"Oh, Blaze has a new boyfriend," Mom cuts in enthusiastically, which makes me turn my wide-open mouth toward her. "What?" Mom gives me an innocent look. "You're dating Josh's coach, I thought. That night you had your little joke with me on the phone. It sounded like you were having a good time."

You have no idea, I think, but only say, "It was fine, but I don't think that necessarily means he's my boyfriend."

"You can say that again," Josh growls, nearly to himself. I bore holes in him with my electromagnetic mindwaves, but I can't grill him about what he means. The dinner table at Mema's is a confrontation-free-zone. I'm talking, not even my *parents* ever fought at Mema's table, and we had visits during times when all they *did* was fight.

"Well, what's this boy's name, dear?" Mema asks, and instead of disrupting things, I bow my head and answer her. "Mark." Just uttering his name makes the idea of he and I together seem real and impossible at the same time.

Josh gives a deep sigh.

"Oh, well! Mark is a wonderful saint!" Mema starts in about Saint Mark, who is apparently, like, one of Jesus's top guys or something, and I don't have the heart to tell her that there is no way the Mark I went out with is any kind of saint.

And I should know.

I'm more annoyed at Mom than she probably deserves as I watch her kissing up to my Dad's mother. She loves to do this—feeding

Mema little tidbits of gossip as if Mema is a wiggling little wiener dog and our lives are minced up garlicky chicken.

It makes me wish I'd just stayed home and stalked my empty inbox.

• • •

"What the heck do you have against Mark?" I ask Josh as soon as I get him alone in the living room. Mema's dachshunds wiggle around our feet, hoping we'll create laps for them to snuggle into.

"Don't you mean Saint Mark?" Josh holds his palms together and raises his chin in mock reverence.

"Josh, seriously, I—"

"Hey, do we know them?" His eye catches the row of frames standing along a shelf above Mema's boxy television. A few hold photos of me and Josh when we were younger, but the majority show the happy, handsome people who came included with the frames.

"Don't change the subject," I warn. "I want to know what the deal is with your coach. What did you say to him about me?"

Josh says, "Do you think Mema forgets and thinks these people are related to her?" He waves a frame toward me that holds a black-and-white photo showing a mob of children surrounding a woman in a bridal gown. "Clearly they're mini-cannibals, just look how happy they are."

Scooping up an elated dachshund, I tell Josh, "I want to know what's up with Mark."

"I'm not sure that you do, sis." Josh puts the frame back and crosses his arms at me.

I sigh, slump back on the couch, and look up at Mema's yellowed ceiling. "Fine," I say as the dachshund on my lap promptly falls asleep. "How about if in exchange for full disclosure I'll give you a ride to wherever you want on a day when I really don't want to."

Josh looks at me skeptically. "Based on the boulder-holder incident in the van, anything I have to say will just be hurtful at this point."

"I can take it," I say with certainty, but as Josh drops his head and takes a deep breath I realize I'm not so sure. My heart does flips and I absentmindedly stroke the warm wiener dog sleeping on my lap as Josh lays out Mark's character details.

Apparently, Mark already has a super power after all. But it's not healing.

Mark has the power to pick up girls, and he is extra-especially super at picking up blondes. Accepting the stream of human Barbie dolls my brother describes is beyond my mental and emotional capacity. Apparently Mark has a girl at nearly every school the varsity soccer team plays, which is why he didn't invite me to an away game for our date. He's like some mutant strain of hook-up guy. I think of the girls at school who are "known past affiliates." With a shudder I realize that they are, without exception, blondes.

But surely I don't fit into their category of blonde *blondes.* I'm an accidental blonde, and my hair's usually up in a messy ponytail anyway. The girls Mark has hung out with are bottle blondes who wear their hair in actual styles. Still, as things stand, unless Mark has a major character makeover, becoming his main sidekick is starting to seem outside the realm of possibility. According to Josh, Mark's profile looks something like this:

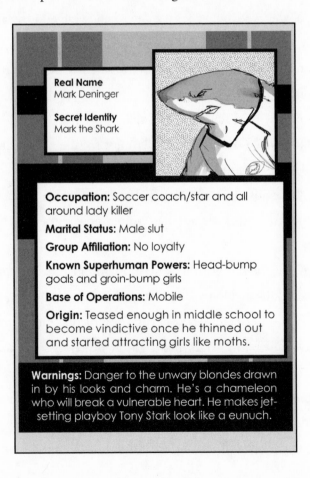

Real Name
Mark Deninger

Secret Identity
Mark the Shark

Occupation: Soccer coach/star and all around lady killer

Marital Status: Male slut

Group Affiliation: No loyalty

Known Superhuman Powers: Head-bump goals and groin-bump girls

Base of Operations: Mobile

Origin: Teased enough in middle school to become vindictive once he thinned out and started attracting girls like moths.

Warnings: Danger to the unwary blondes drawn in by his looks and charm. He's a chameleon who will break a vulnerable heart. He makes jet-setting playboy Tony Stark look like a eunuch.

His profile doesn't exactly draw a promising picture.

I'm having a hard time breathing and my vision is going all wonky and that's when Josh squints at me and makes his final confession. His fight with Mark during the soccer game the other day was about dating me.

"I just couldn't help myself after seeing your bra in the van," he says. "I warned Coach to stay the hell away from you."

"Oh my God! Josh!" I stand up and the surprised wiener dog summersaults awkwardly onto the couch.

"I'm really so sorry, Blaze." Josh clearly means it, but of course I'm still obligated to reach over and give him a knuckle punch in the thigh as hard as I can.

POW!

Josh drops to the carpet with a *Thump!* "Unnnngh."

As he writhes back and forth, holding his dead leg, he concedes, "I did have that one coming."

"Damn straight you had that coming," I hiss, low enough so Mema won't come charging in with a bucket of Holy Water.

Through my blind fury at my brother I recognize a lightning bolt of shining hope. This must be the reason Mark hasn't been in touch. He still really likes me. He's just minding my brainless little brother.

Once Josh is able to sit up he says, "I'm sorry, sis. Mark is just such a dirtbag. I was trying to protect you."

Before I can give him a second dead leg, Mema and Mom

come into the room complaining to each other that they ate too much. Josh and I quickly move to sit side by side on the couch and the dachshunds happily accept the gift of our laps.

At Josh's look of misery I take pity and whisper for him to stop worrying. "I'll get over Mark."

But all I can focus on is the fact that I need to break through that anti-girlfriend force field. When Mark sees how fully committed I am he'll forget all about Josh's outburst and see that we can still be together.

After all, even Tony Stark made a great boyfriend when he was with the right girl.

● ● ●

After everyone has gone to sleep, I find myself peering into the crazy-intense magnifying mirror my grandmother keeps on her bathroom counter. Apparently Mema is half-blind, because I'm looking at my skin at a level of detail nobody should see. I find the beginnings of a small pimple under my chin and alternate a hot water compress with squeezing until a pearl of yellowish cream finally finds its way through my pore. "I knew you had it in you," I say. Which, I know, is not normal, but I don't get all that many zits, so it's totally okay that I talk to them.

I splash my face with cold water to close my pores and am invigorated by the icy slap. Now that I know about Josh's interference I'm feeling pretty hopeful about becoming Mark's girlfriend. I mean, Tony Stark had his Meredith McCall, right? Well, and then he had Pepper Potts, Natasha Romanova, and Madame Masque. But there's also Bethany Cabe, right? Bethany helped Tony overcome his alcoholism. Just like I'm going to help Mark overcome his addiction to blondes. I just need to do a bit of strategizing.

I do have the advantage of spending all that time driving him around in Superturd playing Cows, which means we're already sort of friends. I smile at the image of us laughing together as we competitively searched for farm animals. Cabe and Tony Stark were friends first when she was acting as his bodyguard. I mean, sure, she hated Iron Man, which is technically the same thing as hating Tony, but that's before she realized—I have to stop myself.

Focusing on the fictional romantic lives of comic book characters will in no way help me win Mark. I just have to convince him what I already know in my heart; we're destined to be together. Now I just need a plan of evil genius proportions.

I spend the whole next day floating around Mema's house, smiling at my family members and facilitating dachshund naps while silently constructing my Ultimate Scheme for Total Mark Domination.

The first step of my plan includes a rigorous study regimen that will make me an expert on all things soccer. If Mark loves soccer, *and does he ever*, I will learn to love soccer. Seeing how my brother is a great player, not to mention a gigantic soccer fan, it shouldn't be all that tough. Once Mark realizes all the interests the two of us have in common, it will be smooth sailing in the seduction department.

I also figure that one of the greatest advantages I have in my arsenal is sitting right on top of my head. That being: the Power of Blonde. This is not a power I have ever tapped into, despite having been a blonde all my life. But if there was ever a time to call upon my hair's unique hue supremacy, that time is now.

A new schedule of waking up early to blow-dry, style, and fluff my hair to release its inner Mark-drawing energy will be replacing my current daily routine of sleeping in until the last minute and pulling everything up in an elastic band on my way to school.

Beyond that, there will be no point in *literally* losing sleep over my hairstyle if Mark isn't going to see it. Mark's school schedule doesn't naturally overlap mine, but if I can figure out his daily routine I can make it a point to see him more often. Our senior class is small, but our school building is made up of sprawling, interconnected hallways. Six basic corridors are joined together by Habitrail-like glass enclosures that we all scurry through at the bell's command. Seeing Mark between classes is just a matter of figuring out which Habitrail to run through and when. This is the portion of my plan that might require a bit of assistance. I think of Amanda and Terri.

Based on former pissy-fits, I'm fairly certain Amanda will be finished ignoring me by Monday. It'll be mortifying if the two of them help me with my plan and Mark blows me off anyway, but if I can get him to be my boyfriend it will be worth the risk of utter humiliation. Besides, becoming Mark's girlfriend will officially de-slut-ify me in my friends' eyes once and for all.

I finally make my way to bed, where one of Mema's dachshunds pleads to join me until I lean over and scoop her up. She burrows happily underneath the covers, and I envy her ability to drop immediately off to sleep.

My mind continues racing. It's focused on the way my boring soccer mom life completely changed the moment Mark stepped into Superturd that first time. He needs to know how much he means to me. We belong together. It's the strongest I've ever felt about anything.

It's over an hour later before I finally join the dachshund in dreamland.

• • •

Blazefire22: Hello?
Blazefire22:…
Blazefire22: You in or what?

I've laid out my plan for Terri in an IM, and I chew on my lip while waiting for her to write back. It's perhaps not my smartest move, what with the way people can just ruin lives by cutting and pasting things into FriendsPlace, not to mention forwarding to the entire school's email address book. That happened to Wiggles once. But, hey, it's not like I'm soliciting sexual favors the way she does. I'm just asking for a little help, and I need to start trusting somebody sometime. Also, Terri is currently my only friend not blocking my email.

TerriAngel445: You sure you want do this? Maybe Mark's not the monogomous type.
Blazefire22: It's 'monogamous,' and you don't understand. We have a true connection.

There is a long pause. Finally, I type:

Blazefire22: Pleasepleaseplease?

Pause.

Blazefire22: If we hack into his school account, we can get his schedule and coordinate this the right way.
TerriAngel445: well… since you're so truly connected do you have a guess what his password is?

And that's when I know I have her. With Terri's competitive drive engaged, we are doing this. Operation Total Mark

Domination begins right away. It takes a while, but by trying all the soccer terms I find via Google, we guess Mark's password: nutmeg. It's what they call it when a player puts the ball right between an opponent's legs.

I ignore Terri's "nutmeg = ew," response to his password and tell her to, "call me!!" because Mark's class schedule pops right open.

By cross-referencing both of our schedules with a map of the school, Terri and I figure out a way I can flip my blonde hair in Mark's face at least once between each and every class except second period study hall on Thursdays. Terri will have to meet me with my science book before fourth period since I won't make it to my locker and back in time to see Mark enter room 206. Plus, I'll either be late to gym class or *very* late to gym class, depending on whether or not I can draw Mark into a conversation. Or maybe even a mini-make-out session in the hallway. Which would be the ultimate victory and make all this totally worth it.

Before we hang up the phone Terri says, "You know this is crazy, right?"

"But crazy-romantic, isn't it?"

Terri pauses, "I'm pretty sure it's just plain crazy-crazy, but you never know, Mark may like psychotic stalker girls."

"That's right!" I jump on her tiny bit of positivity. "You never know."

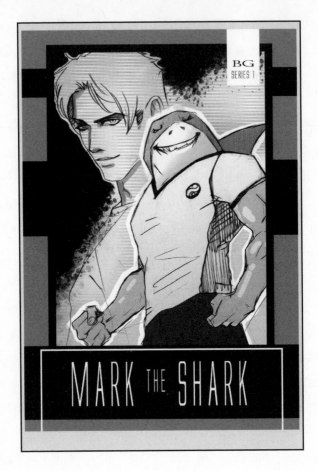

Chapter Eleven

Monday morning I get up at dawn so I can blow-dry my hair to within an inch of its life. I tell Josh I'm heading to school extra-super-early, and he opts to sleep in and take the bus.

"Impressive hair," Terri says when I pick her up. "You're sure about this?"

I nod, and my hair moves independently, making me feel like a bobble-head. "Super-sure," I say.

"Well, I admire your determination. And seriously, if running into Mark every forty minutes doesn't get his attention, that hair certainly will."

"Thanks!" I grin, but I'm getting the sense that as my sidekick, Terri doesn't fully believe in our mission. Mapping out a detailed obstacle course in order to *literally* chase a boy down probably goes against her feminist roots. I mean, her mother made everyone at her tenth birthday party wear buttons that said, "Barbie is a tool of the man." But she doesn't comment, and I'm grateful for her help.

Terri's not half the flirt Amanda is, but she does have all

those sisters, so we have a ceremony wherein she bestows all the wisdom passed on to her in a quick flirting tutorial in the bathroom before school. Her main points are (1) I shouldn't go with my instincts to give Mark my huge, geeky smile and wave each time we pass each other and (2) Honestly, she really means it, *no* on the huge, geeky smile.

With Terri's coaching, I practice looking flirty in the mirror until the first bell rings.

"Let's go, lioness," says Terri patting at my huge blonde mane. "You'll be fine."

For my first Mark encounter, I pretend to be completely unaware of his presence, even though I know exactly when and from what direction he's approaching. At the last possible moment before he passes I dip my chin toward him and look up through my eyelashes the way Terri coached me. I give my head the slightest shake and feel my puffy mane sway back and forth. Mark's eyebrows shoot up, and I'm rewarded with his classic smile-bop combination. He even turns back for a second look.

I geeky-grin to myself as I walk/run back down the hallway toward class, thinking, *this is going to be easy.*

Of course, I'm totally wrong.

I'm late to three classes, since Terri and I severely overestimated how fast I could walk/run through the school's crowded glass Habitrails. A few times, I need to break into all-out sprints, my shoes clacking as my giant puff of blondeness hangs onto my head for dear life. By the end of the day I've gotten two official teacher warnings and numerous dirty looks, plus I've nearly lost an eye colliding with Catherine Wiggan's airbag chest. Mark's casual greetings and one actual warm "Hey, Blaze," (*between periods three and four*) slowly morph into slight puzzlement at my suddenly appearing everywhere. Make that, suddenly appearing everywhere *and* disheveled *and* out-of-breath.

When the final bell sounds, I'm thrown entirely off course when Ryan breaks the unspoken protocol between us and approaches me at my locker instead of waiting to see me in the student lot. My Mark-stalking-mission has no time for Ryan and his annoying random trivia.

"Hey, Blaze, you sure seemed busy today." He is mesmerized by my hair.

"Um, yeah." I need to get out to the lot in zero-point-eight minutes if I want to give Mark a final casual nod before leaving for the day.

"So, have you gotten a chance to look at that *Daredevil* yet?" Ryan is unbelievably present.

"Oh, that!" *Point four minutes.* "I'll get that back to you just as soon as I finish."

"Oh, no need to rush. It's not like I need to read it again right away." Ryan is trying so hard to lure me into a conversation it's painful. "Oh yeah, Blaze? I've been meaning to ask... did you know most dust particles are made up of dead skin?"

He's hopeless. "Sorry, Ryan, I've really got to bolt." I place a hand on his arm, which seems to distract him. "I'll be sure to catch you later, though."

I fling my body into my jacket as I run out the doors of the school, toward the student lot. My feet cycle at top speed until I spot Mark and Stu walking together toward Mark's pickup. I brake hard. They've already passed my minivan. My window for a Mark encounter is closed for the day.

I feel deflated. Although, thanks to all the hair products I used this morning, my hair is still nice and fluffy. I watch Mark and Stu say good-bye, but just before he climbs into his pickup Mark's eyes dart over toward Superturd. My heart starts *ba-bumping* faster. *Is he looking for me?* That glance sparks unthinkable boldness in me. I stand up straight and fast-walk directly to the driver's side door of Mark's pickup. He's putting on his glasses when I tap on the window, startling him.

"Hi, Mark," I shout through the glass, at which point I realize I have no idea what the heck I'm going to say to him. Terri and I should've made plans beyond 'flirty eyes.' He smiles and rolls down his window, too fast for me to get any interesting ideas. *No wonder Ryan always approaches me prepared*, I think as I smile dumbly.

"Hey there, how's it going?" I shake my big hair, hoping to distract him.

"'Kay," Mark shrugs and looks at me through his glasses pleasantly, but expectantly.

Think, Blaze, think. I'm about to repeat Ryan's disgusting trivia about skin-dust when I finally think of something. "Oh yeah!" I nearly shout, resting my hand on the door of Mark's truck. "I just wanted to see what you thought of the World Cup this year?" I Googled enough about soccer to know that the big finals were called the World Cup, but then I'd gotten distracted by pictures of well-muscled players in action, so I don't know a single World Cup detail.

Mark raises one brow. "Um, it's not happening for another two years, so…"

I just laugh and pretend I don't feel like a complete dumbass. "Oh, I just remembered," I say, my mind whirring. "I need to give you back your soccer movie!" *At least it's better than skin-dust.* The big geeky grin Terri warned me against breaks through for a second.

"No worries." Mark smiles. "You can get it back to me whenever. Like I said, I trust you, Blaze." And there it was. That spark of a connection we'd shared in my minivan. For a moment I can almost see little comic love arrows shooting back and forth between us.

"So I talked to my brother," I say, leaning my arm in his open window. "He's sorry for what he said at the soccer game. He was being a jackass, but everything's cool now." Mark's eyelids blink rapidly behind his glasses, and I add seductively, "So, what're you doing now?"

I pull at him with my eyes. Willing him to lean out and start kissing me.

"Hey, Blaze, listen, I'm really sorry." Mark touches my arm, and his window starts climbing slowly, making me leap back. "I've gotta go, but I'll be sure to catch you later."

POP! I stand, absolutely stunned by the same words I just tossed at Ryan. To get rid of him. My face twitches. The flirty look I've been channeling freezes into a sneer.

Mark backs his truck away as I stay paralyzed like I've been hit with a bitter freeze-ray.

For some reason, my mind flashes back to a long-ago summer when I got a job picking strawberries in a field down the road from our house. Instead of enjoying a beautiful summer day playing like every other eleven-year-old, I spent five long hours bent over rows of plants as the sun scorched the back of my neck. When I finally brought my large bucketful of strawberries to the barn, the big boss-man weighed my labor and announced that I'd earned a grand total of $3.45.

The quick, friendly wave Mark turns to give me as he pulls away does nothing to release that haunting sense of regret.

● ● ●

I lie on my back, my body molded to the bottom of the tub, as the shower pummels my chest. I focus on my toes, propped up on the tub wall over the spigot as the hot, pulsing water from the shower numbs my stomach and breasts.

I feel warm on the outside, yet my core remains frozen.

And then all at once my outside is frozen as well.

I scream and jump up from the tub shouting "JOSH!!" I hear him laughing from outside, where he's squirted the icy hose water right through the window-vent. It's an old trick we used to play on each other. "I'm going to murder you!!" I shout, and mean it, although that declaration is actually a regular part of the game. Throwing a towel around my numb midriff, I hear Josh outside, still laughing, and vow revenge.

I move my damaged self-pity-party to my bedroom and sit on my bed, surrounded by my dripping hair. I'm so much worse off than I was before that boy climbed into my minivan. Then I'd just been an invisible nothing. Now Mark's alias makes painful clear sense. I feel like my insides have been attacked by a shark.

I pull my towel closer around my body and try to stop thinking.

Josh knocks on my doorjamb calling, "Hey, sis. Sorry, the hose slipped."

"Very funny."

"It's time to drive me and Ajay to see a movie over by the mall."

"And what makes you think I'm driving you after you just froze me with the hose?"

There's a pause as he gives me time to remember our deal.

Damn!

"Are you forgetting our little…"

"Shut up!" I shoot. "I'll drive you in a little while, okay?"

"T-minus ten minutes and counting," Josh sings. "We have a movie to catch, and a deal's a deal."

And don't I have a brilliant gift for entering deals I didn't bargain for.

One thing's sure—I don't want Josh to know how upset I am over the whole Mark incident. His being right is bad enough, no need for him to know he was right. I'll just erase the whole thing, like the old *Superman* movie when Superman flies against the earth's rotation so he can save Lois. My dad hated that ending, thought it was an insult to comic fans everywhere. But in my imagination, *The Blazing Goddess* is already firing up her flaming Mustang so she can speed through the air against the rotation of the earth.

Twisting my defeated hair into a damp bun, I slap my cheeks a few times and start applying concealer under my dark-rimmed eyes. My memory spins backward, erasing every trace of my episode with Mark. Winding back to before he set a single soccer-cleated foot in my van.

• • •

"Are you okay, Blaze?" Josh eyes me as I focus on the twilit road covered with dead leaves.

"Great," I snap. "I'm doing just… great."

"Is this about my coach?" Josh asks.

"This has nothing to do with him being an asshat; this is about you being annoying."

"Gosh, first you flip out on Mom, and now you're snapping at me." Josh pushes his feet onto the dashboard. "Next you'll be cursing out poor Mema and knocking her tarted-up Virgin Mary in the head with a shovel."

I uncork my wrath. "You *froze* me with the hose, and then forced me to drive you to the mall. And Mom and I are getting along *fine*." I turn on the radio to end the debate. But I do it angrily enough to prove Josh is right. I'm a bit on edge.

"Don't mind Blaze, she's just seething," Josh tells Ajay as he climbs into the van. "Actually, I think I'll just join you back there." He ducks between the seats to escape my burning death look.

"You okay?" Ajay leans forward, cupping my shoulder in his palm.

I think of the over-the-shoulder-boulder-holder comment and remember the moldy sandwich. I turn to launch into him about it, but the look of concern he gives me shuts me up. Without answering I turn up the music and redirect my attention to getting the both of them to the movies. And out of my head.

After dropping them off, I wander aimlessly through the mall. My heart really isn't in it. Everything just feels so pointless. Listlessly, I hit the drugstore to pick up tampons. I won't need them for a few weeks still, but I ran out during my last cycle and had to resort to wadding up toilet paper in my underwear. Not my favorite scenario. As I stand in the checkout line holding a giant box of tampons, I get a one-word text from Terri saying: 'Well???'

My brain is so fogged in, I actually have to think a full minute before figuring out what she's even talking about. I send a text back: "Mission Aborted. I repeat: Mission Aborted."

It had been a stupid plan. I can't believe I honestly thought Mark was only blowing me off to honor Josh's wishes. Like he was suppressing his love for me in order to make my little brother happy. I'm an idiot. After paying for the embarrassing economy-sized blue box of tampons that the poor kid behind the counter seems afraid to touch, I zombie-walk through the mall.

A group of kids wearing blue and gold band jackets from the only other high school in our area are gathered around the pretzel counter. I feel a sad sense of being excluded, even though I don't play a band instrument or even go to their stupid school. I duck past them, careful to avoid eye contact and consumed by the awareness that I'm holding a bag containing tampons.

As I head toward Sector Comics! I quickly stuff the big box of tampons into my messenger bag. They don't quite fit, but I'm determined to avoid a "most embarrassing moment" with Comic Book Guy.

When I walk through the archway, there's a Stan Lee look-alike standing behind the counter. I'm more disappointed than I mean to be when I see Quentin isn't here. When I ask if he's working tonight, Stan's twin tells me, "No," as he eyes the buttons on my bag. "Hey, you're not Blaze, by any chance?"

"Um, yes?"

The older man gives me a huge grin. "Quentin told me all about you. Says you might be looking for a bit of part-time work?"

I nod and shrug.

"Well, he gave me his full recommendation. Said you're a total wiz with the oldies, and I can tell you," he leans in close, "I've known Quentin a long time, and it takes a lot to make an impression on him. You, my dear, have made an impression."

I smile and blush. "He'll be mad he missed you." Stan-alike picks up his phone. Before I know what's happening, he barks, "Got Blaze here for ya," into the receiver and thrusts the phone in my face.

"Um, hello?" I say hesitantly.

"So, you met Stan, huh?"

I give the old man a closer look and falter, "He's not really…"

"Ha, no." Quentin laughs. "We just call him that. What're you doing at the mall?"

I smile quickly at "Stan" and walk away from the counter. "Oh, just dropped my little brother off to see a movie. Thought I'd swing by."

"Sorry I missed you. Copy my number from Stan so you can text me next time. I'm working now, but I would've met you if I'd known."

"Where are you working?" My mood starts picking up as Quentin explains he does a nice side business selling comics online. "I do a lot of trade shows, actually. You'll have to come sometime."

"I'd love to," I say honestly.

"I've stayed pretty local so far. The one in Pittsburgh is the furthest con I've made. San Diego has the biggest, coolest one of all, but I'll be happy to make it to the one in New York sometime. Google Comic-Con, and you'll see how awesome they are."

The two of us talk for a while until Stan gives me a knowing smile, and I start to feel self-conscious and hyper-aware that I'm packing a giant box of tampons. Before saying good-bye, Quentin asks if I've read the *Ghost Rider*s yet. "Um, gotta go." I laugh. "But I promise I'll get to them."

"What is *wrong* with you, girl?" Quentin teases. "He's your frickin' badass namesake! I'd kill to have your coolness factor."

"I know, I know. I'm awesome," I say. "To be honest I've been going through a rough patch. Haven't really been in the mood for comics."

"Blaze, that's when you need them more than ever."

I laugh. "You just might be right, Quentin."

"Of course I'm right. Give it a shot. And text me when you're done. Don't leave me hanging."

I can't help but return Stan's warm smile as I hand him his phone.

"We'll be seeing you around, I hope," Stan Lee says as he

writes down Quentin's number. And he makes my whole week
when he adds, "'Nuff said."

• • •

I nestle into the quiet protection of Superturd as I click on the
dome light and start rooting around for the *Ghost Rider*s. Finally,
I find them under the passenger seat, still in the bag. Putting
them in order, I see I have a few in the teens and then issues 19
through 22 in the 2007 series. Looking at the covers, it's obvious
they made some creative changes as the series progressed, which
is usually not a great sign. At least this series features Johnny
Blaze, since over the years other guys, like Danny Ketch, have
become Ghost Rider. All I can say is, thank goodness Dad didn't
name me Ketch.

I start with the earliest issue in my stack, which is number
four. The cover has Ghost Rider standing in the midst of what
appear to be corpses with horns as his burning skull pleads
toward the heavens.

The first page has the usual recap of what is going on with the
story, which is good since, as I said, I'm looking at issue number
four. It starts out...

*Motorcycle stuntman Johnny Blaze has always had his heart in the
right place... and made all the wrong decisions.*

It goes on to explain how Blaze made a deal with the devil and ended up as the Ghost Rider, a spirit of vengeance who hunts down the guilty. And distributes bloody justice.

The truth of all that pierces my chest. It's me. The heart in the right place. The wrong decisions. I even feel like I made a deal with the devil. In the form of a certain shark. Of course, I already know the origin story of Ghost Rider. It's just that having it written out like that makes it seem so real. So much like a prophecy for a girl named Blaze.

I flip the page to see Ghost Rider in a graveyard, trying to revive some guy he accidentally killed with his penance stare.

As Ghost Rider tries to get the dead guy to "Breathe, dammit, breathe!" a bright light suddenly fills an entire panel. "You have more power than you know, Johnny Blaze!" says a woman with flowing pink hair and white eyes. She actually sort of resembles my sketches of *The Blazing Goddess*, except for the missing pupils. Her name is Numecet. The rest of the comic is just a lot of Numecet telling Johnny about Lucifer's evil plan to escape Hell and walk the earth. I'm a little disappointed in the issue overall, since there isn't really much action, but I'm interested anyway, what with the potential divine personal message and all.

Numecet tells Johnny only Ghost Rider can stop Lucifer, and in the end Johnny Blaze takes off with a *KKRRROOOOMM!* on his Hell Cycle. His mission is to thwart the devil's plans. I smile at how right Quentin is about my namesake. I mean, sure, fighting Juggernaut or Venom is tough, but my guy is taking on freaking Satan himself. How badass is that?

I go on to lose myself between the other glossy covers, each depicting some form of flames or fire. It's strange to be reading comics created this century. I miss the ads for all the junk they have in my dad's really old ones, like joke gum, hand buzzers, and "the insult that made a man out of Mac," promoting Charles Atlas body-building. My favorite though has always been an old Tootsie Roll ad that ran a contest to win a "Jog-a-long Stereo," which according to the picture is basically an enormous iPod with headphones that look like plastic earmuffs. These newer ones have things like Got Milk? ads and video games. Overall, I have to say, the parts that I read have pretty solid storytelling with some nice-looking art and escalating action.

But more than that. They've given me an idea.

Not only am I ready to take vengeance, but reading Blaze's short origin story repeated at the opening of each comic gets me thinking about origins. About a good origin story for *The Blazing Goddess*. And maybe one for me.

It's about time for my real story to begin.

By the time the boys get out of the movies, I'm in such a good mood I take them cruising around back roads until the Walmart closes so we can fling each and every shopping cart one-by-one into the parking lot. The carts look like ridiculous metal cattle bumping into each other and sometimes falling over on their sides.

And here's the best part: On top of getting out any and all aggressive energy you have—no matter how terrifically awful your day has been and even if your plot to score a boyfriend has been thwarted and your life seems stuck in a Gamma Bubble— winging shopping carts into each other makes it impossible to keep from laughing hysterically.

Chapter Twelve

I get to work on my super-secret three-step plan straight away. This plan makes my hairspray and stalking routine seem pathetic.

I tell Terri the whole Mark thing was just a big prank, and she pretends to believe me. And Amanda goes ahead and starts speaking to me again now that I've completely humiliated myself. But I don't tell either of them my new plan.

Everything seems totally back to normal, so the first outward sign that anything is even up with me is my hair. It's sort of hard to miss, seeing as how I dyed it pink using twelve packets of tropical punch Kool-Aid.

Amanda squeals for a straight minute when she sees it, and Terri declares me crazy. But it gets Mark's attention. Because I know his schedule, I realize he's come entirely out of his way when he stops me in the hallway between third and fourth periods.

"Hey, Blaze!" he says. "Cool hair."

I tilt my head at him. "That would be Kool-*Aid* hair, since that's what I used to dye it."

He laughs. "You're joking, right?"

I lean in. "Have a sniff."

He bows his head to smell my hair and when I pull away he gives a few bops. "Mmm, fruity."

"Tropical *punch*," I say pantomiming a big punch in his arm. He gives a sarcastic laugh, but then, before he can say anything else, I waggle my fingers good-bye and walk away. Glancing back over my shoulder, I see he's watching me leave. *I guess maybe pink is the new blonde.*

The biggest unforeseen side effect of my new pink hair is that Ryan stops stalking me entirely. I don't get his aversion to the pink, but I take his sudden rejection as a really good sign.

• • •

"Kickass hair," Quentin says when I walk into Sector Comics! later that day.

"Thanks!" I grin at him. "Stan's not making another cameo?"

"He's not around but has authorized me to officially offer you a position organizing comics after school. Two or three days a week, whenever you're free. Pay's not great, but come on, you belong here."

"Well, gee, won't that mean you and I will—"

He nods slyly. "Yes, we will be caught in our own comic sector. Sentenced to spend time together." I give him a geeky grin, and he goes on. "We can be like Hawk and Dove, playing good guy, bad guy with the customers."

I pull back and wrinkle my nose. "Hawk and Dove?"

"They're DC." Quentin shakes his head. "You really haven't read anything besides vintage Marvel, have you?"

I shrug. "What've you got to show me? These days I'm open to new things."

• • •

Part two of my plan upsets the Soccer Cretins a bit. The season is over, and Mom has gotten much better about pitching in, but I still end up running the weekend shuttles about town and to the mall when she's at work. When I show up at each of the boys' houses to gather them up for a bowling party, one by one they give me the same dumbstruck reaction before climbing into Superturd. Make that the *All New!* Flaming Superturd of Fierceness! The boys each whisper to Josh some form of, "Dude, what's up with your sis?" As if I'm not right there listening from the driver's seat.

I guess I can't blame them. The awesome flame job I hand-painted on the sides of the minivan is so cool they'd probably love it if it wasn't hot pink. Josh just sinks down lower and lower in his seat, shooting me a look that says, *"Really, Blaze? Really?"* It's the same look I got when I dyed my hair.

I wouldn't say he's outright worried about me anymore, but he's definitely watching for signs of a breakdown. Mom reacted with an, "Oh, wow. Um, okay…" before hustling off to the hospital, which makes me glad all the pink is not an actual cry for help.

It takes me a few weeks to get everything set up for step three of my plan. Not that I mind. In fact, I'm enjoying my time organizing the stock at Sector Comics! and hanging out with Quentin. Even Josh gets into poking about the store now and then, although he is drawn to the strangest indie comics. I'm grateful Comic Book Guy is actually really nice to my little brother when he's at the store despite Josh being under the age of fourteen. Of course, Quentin does tease him mercilessly for having such quirky taste, but Josh seems to enjoy the attention.

Finally, I'm ready for step three of my plan. The part where vengeance kicks in. While getting attention for my pink hair and my pink flame job and basically turning into a female version of Comic Book Guy, I've also been working overtime on a new set of sketches. Quentin doesn't fully understand their purpose, but when he first sees my artwork, *KaPow!* I pretty much blow his mind.

"Blaze." His brown eyes flick over the page. "These. Are. Amazing." He starts rattling off a detailed critique that's so positive it's embarrassing. "Your lines are so bold and yet clearly show a feminine point of view."

"Wait a minute. Are you trying to say girls can't draw like boys?" I ready myself for a rousing debate, but this time he just puts his hand on mine and looks me in the eye. "No, Blaze. I'm saying that your style and voice are fresh and unique. And important."

I blush and look away, wishing I could share the meaning

behind this particular project. But I'd be mortified if he ever found out. "When you're ready for a manager, I'm your guy." He smiles. I wonder for a moment whether or not I should see this thing through. I look over and catch Stan Lee watching the two of us with a slight smile. I take a step back.

I can't let myself get distracted by a messy-haired boy with a teasing dimple and great taste in comics. I have to see my plan through. It's what Ghost Rider would want me to do.

Finally, I'm satisfied with the results of all my hard work and ready to show Mark that he messed with the wrong former blonde. I upload my scanned images to Kinkles Kopies at the mall and feel deeply empowered as I flip through the pages of the finished product. It's a comic titled *The Blazing Goddess vs. Mark the Shark*. It's an origin story.

The adventure begins with Blaze as an ordinary girl whose father just so happens to be a mad scientist. Let's face it, what origin story is complete without some form of crazy genius pseudo-science, right? So, anyway, Blaze's dad asks her to drive to his laboratory to deliver a bunch of chemicals but warns her to be careful. If combined, the chemicals could become fatally toxic. The next page shows boring, blonde Blaze loading a bunch of glass beakers filled with rainbow-colored fluids into the back of her black Mustang. Because, cool flame job or not, there is no way my origin story is featuring a turd-brown minivan.

Blaze speeds happily along until she comes upon a handsome

boy wearing soccer shorts who's hitchhiking. She debates, but decides that the road is so long and deserted she might be the boy's only hope of rescue. He's thankful when she stops to pick him up and explains that his truck broke down a few miles back when he made a wrong turn into a cornfield. The boy is a bit awkward and makes Blaze uneasy as they drive along. Suddenly, he leans over and announces he's going to kiss her. Blaze is so shocked, she slams directly into a cow that has wandered onto the road.

The glass vials in the back seat shatter, showering the pair in a dangerous cocktail of noxious chemicals. Everything goes dark for a few panels, and then we see a close-up of Blaze's eye opening. When the scene draws out slowly, panel by panel, it shows that she has transformed into the Blazing Goddess, complete with pink, flaming hair and suddenly exposed cleavage. The hitch-hiker has transformed as well, into a horrible man-shark. With his words muffled through layers of teeth, he announces his new name: Mark the Shark! And an epic battle between the two of them ensues.

The panels with them going at it were the most fun to draw. Blaze puts up the fight I wish I had when Mark the Shark tries to bite her again and again. In the end, she wins of course, with the Shark left in the middle of a mown field, tangled in a large soccer net—squirming like a caught fish.

Blaze soars away in her mustang, which has been completely

transformed with pink flames shooting out all around it. The epilogue explains how the combination of chemicals created a serum that always reveals a person's true inner nature. Blaze's father is able to recreate the formula and concocts a new batch so Blaze can carry around a spray-canister of the serum. So now she can turn back into the Blazing Goddess whenever she wants. Plus, with a simple squirt she can reveal the inner nature of others and thwart all the evil genius plans to destroy the earth and all that good superhero stuff.

Okay, so maybe the random chemical combination is a little lame, but hey, it's tough to come up with an origin story while taking out real-world revenge on a boy you wish you hadn't had sex with. I'm sticking it to him good too, since anybody who knows Mark or even knows *of* Mark will know right away he's the shark guy. Going public with this comic is seriously going to hurt his game, and I'm not talking about soccer either.

It's a vengeance so absolute, Ghost Rider himself would surely be proud.

• • •

My Blazing Goddess comic book starts out as an intimate little mailing. A copy goes to the vapid blonde junior Mark's been pursuing as well as a few other girls he's dated. I also upload the files and post scans of all the pages on a web address I bought for ten bucks: http://blazing-goddess.com. And Quentin absolutely insists on selling physical copies at the store under the talk bubble sign "Up-and-Coming Artists."

Amanda can't believe I actually did all this, and Terri thinks it's the most spectacular thing she's ever seen. "Way better than primping and stalking," she says. It feels really good to shock people who've known you most of your life.

Before I know it, things take off and people I didn't send the comic to are stopping me in the hallway to tell me how much they like it. I didn't bother to put a hit counter on the web page, but I know it has gone big when I catch glimpses of printed-out sheets getting passed around the school. It makes me kind of wonder how people got revenge before the Internet came along.

Finally, the reaction I've looked forward to the most lands directly in my path. I just re-applied more Kool-Aid last night, so I'm particularly pink when Mark walks up to me. He's holding a copy of *The Blazing Goddess vs. Mark the Shark*.

"This is supposed to be funny?" He shakes the comic in my face, and I have to suppress a laugh. I was nervous that Mark might feel flattered in some way when he's supposed to be humiliated. "What the hell, Blaze!"

Or, okay. So anger works too. "What?" I give him my most innocent look. "You don't like my artwork?"

"Why would you make me look like such an idiot?"

"Look like an idiot?" I savor his delicious rage. "I thought I went easy on you."

"Wha—? Easy?"

"I could've made reference to your little guppy guy there." I nod toward his crotch in a direct hit to his ego. If there's one thing I've learned in all the time spent with the boys, knocking the size of a guy's genitalia is the ultimate in low blows.

Mark's jaw drops as he looks around at the gathering gawkers. "Blaze!" He covers his crotch with my comic.

"Oh, come on, I'm kidding," I say. "It's not like I even have anything to compare it to, now do I?"

"I'll have you know I'm above average in that department."

"I'm sure that you believe that you are." I pat the side of his handsome face. "Oh, and Mark?" He still looks bewildered over the way his confrontation is failing. "You really shouldn't fuck with people who helped you out when you needed a ride. It's not very sportsmanlike."

I spin on my heel and stride away. Perfect exit.

I can't believe I actually gave it to Mark that hard core. *Well,* I think, *maybe that will teach him to be nicer to the girls he sees as Shark Bait.*

I'm grateful to be done with any and all association with him.

• • •

"Blaze, what the hell is going on between you and my coach?"

Josh waves a copy of my comic in front of my face as we get into The Flaming Superturd after school. *Oops.*

"Hey there, little brother," I say cheerfully. "How was your day?"

"Do not change the subject, Blaze." Josh grabs my arm and asks earnestly, "Did you actually sleep with him? You only went out, like, one time!"

"Josh!" I can't believe he'd ask me such a thing. *Besides, there was no sleeping involved.* "We had two dates, for your information."

"You see, that's why I'm waiting till I'm married to have sex." Josh shakes his head and slumps into his seat.

"What the heck do you know about sex?" I ask.

"Nothing." He shrugs. "Except that Ajay's older cousin had a girl totally stalking him after they did it. She slashed his tires and everything."

"Well, now, *that's* crazy."

"Yeah." Josh waves the comic pointedly. "And so is distributing a *very* well done yet embarrassing comic that features you beating up the guy you slept with."

"Mark and I did not sleep together. And the comic is just a Blazing Goddess origins story. I've been meaning to write her one."

"Yeah, whatever."

"Well, Mema will be proud of you." I grin. "If you're really waiting for marriage to have sex."

Josh gives me a serious look. "Really, sis. Are you honestly okay?"

I turn my attention back to the road, "Don't worry about me, I'm fine."

"You want me to kick Coach Mark in the balls for you?"

"That won't be necessary."

"Well, are you about finished turning things pink?"

I reach over and give Josh a shove. "I'm done," I promise. And I am.

• • •

Looking at my website, I'm smacked with a wave of happiness that it looks even cooler than I remember. I wonder how many other folks are looking at my work at this very moment. It feels good to think I'm providing such a valuable public health service. I mean, just think of all the innocent virgins who can avoid being harpooned by Mark because of my little exposé!

The phone rings. I have a fleeting fear it's him, calling to ream me out some more, but I can tell by the way Mom's mouth tenses when she checks the caller ID that it's our dad. Mom holds the phone toward me, and I take it into the kitchen so she won't have to hear me talk to "that man."

"Hey, Dad," I say happily.

"Hey, kiddo!" His voice is upbeat. "How goes it?"

"Good! I'm almost done making that comics list for you."

"That's great, Sweetie!"

"Have you ever read any recent *Ghost Riders*? 'Cause I just took a look at a few issues from Volume 5 and I have to say the artwork is…"

"Hey, that's super, Blaze. Listen, I don't have a lot of time to talk, but I wanted to see if I could get you to go ahead and ship those boxes of comics to me here in the city."

What!? "Oh, I, um…"

"I know it'll be expensive, but don't worry. Your mom can lay out the funds, and let her know I'll be getting that right back to her. Save the receipt."

"So you're not coming here to pick them up?"

"Coming there? No, no. I've got lots of stuff happening here. Great stuff. Really big stuff."

I glance at Josh and can tell he's trying to listen in without seeming like he's listening. I tell Dad, "So, I'll just try to get that out to you next week. Um, what's the address?"

"It's the same. One-sixty-two West Sixty-Fourth Street. Apartment four F."

"Right, I remember, like the Fantastic Four," I joke as I wonder again about Ice Girl's fate. It strikes me as funny that her boobs seemed like her source of power, and my boobs were the source of my demise, in a way. Or at least, Virgin Girl!'s demise.

"I really need to have them here A-sap." Dad says. "Do you think you can get them to the post office by early this week?"

"Sure, Dad. And I drew a new comic that's—"

"That's great, Sweetie. You be sure to keep that up. You never know where things might lead. I'd better get going, thanks again for sending those along."

I pause and brace myself. "Do you want to say hi to Josh?"

"Sorry, honey, I'm on my way out, but do give him a hug from me, will you?"

I look over to where Josh is watching me expectantly. I mentally kick myself for asking right in front of him.

"Right, sure. I'll get that out, and we'll talk soon."

I watch Josh's face crumple ever so slightly before he recomposes and we roll our eyes at each other. I hang up with Dad and Josh says, "Yeah, I didn't really want to talk to him either."

We laugh, and Mom looks up from her paperwork. "So, what's going on with your father?" She doesn't sound like she honestly cares.

"Oh, nothing," I say. And because I'm annoyed that Dad made me hurt Josh's feelings, I add, "He wants me to ship him the boxes of comics. He said you'll be okay with laying out the money."

"The hell I am." Mom stands up and storms out of the room, presumably to call Dad and tell him off.

"He is super-busy," I tell Josh. "I feel like I just caught a minute of *The Dad Show*. You okay?"

"Well, I'm not about to go dye my hair pink, if that's what you're afraid of." Josh laughs. When I continue with my patented worried-big-sister look, he adds, "Seriously! I'm fine. But if you want to take me and the guys to the mall, that would totally make up for my shitty relationship with our father."

"Yeah, right," I laugh. Then, because Quentin has been

texting me to come hang out, I add, "You can let the guys know Superturd will be leaving in oh-minus-half-an-hour to shuttle your stinky asses to the mall."

Josh lets out a whoop and scrambles to alert the cretins of their good fortune.

• • •

Once I've steered the boys away from Lucy's Lucky Lingerie I set them free and head toward Sector Comics! It's strange, but I can't seem to shake the odd sense I'm forgetting something really important. Something lingering just outside my conscious thoughts, yet somehow weighing me down. I've tried to focus on what it might be a couple of times, but—

"You left your headlights on."

I blink dumbly at the red-haired girl standing in front of me. I have no idea who she is, and I'm so thrown off that I actually look down to make sure my nipples aren't showing through my T-shirt.

"It's okay." She's smiling. "I turned them off for you. The door was unlocked."

"Wha… ?" I say, "Um, do I know you?"

"You drive the minivan with the pink flame job, right?" She grins.

"Yes?" I glance around, looking for the boys, wondering if they're setting me up in some way.

"Well, I saw your headlights were on, so I tried the driver's side door." She shrugs. "I turned them off for you. Didn't want you to drain the battery."

"Uh, thanks?" I say, and the girl spins and disappears as quickly as she showed up. *Okay, that is weir—*

"Oh, and by the way." She reappears suddenly. "I love your hair."

This time, when she turns to go, I stop her. "Hey, hang on," I say. "Do you even go to my school?"

It turns out she doesn't, which means my hair and my minivan have achieved Small Town Infamy. *Wow*, I think, *I have an honest-to-goodness fan!* Who would've thought putting soft drink mix in my hair would put me and my turd-brown minivan on the A-list? After talking to my fan for a while, I give her the web address for *The Blazing Goddess vs. Mark the Shark*.

"Check it out, you'll like it," I tell her. The girl looks wide-eyed, like she can't wait to take a look at my pages. She'll probably share them, and then Mark won't be able to sucker innocent girls from her school either.

Not that I think he's a total rapist or anything. It's just that I would've appreciated a heads up before canoodling with him in the back of Superturd. Like, maybe seeing a comic drawn by one of his post-canoodling ex-blondes would've helped. So you can just see how important my work to raise Male Slut Awareness is to the community.

"Just sold out of your comic," Quentin greets me at the store. "That's awesome."

"No, your comic is awesome, and you need to work on your next installment."

"Oh, yeah?" I scrunch my nose at him. "Who should the villain be?"

"How about a new ally?" He scrunches his nose back at me. "A certain geeky comic book guy?"

I grin happily. "I thought of you as Comic Book Guy before I knew your name!"

We're interrupted by a man rapping on the glass counter with his keys. He's wearing a gray business suit, and we didn't notice him come in.

Suit Guy is giving off a vibe. He is not one of us.

Quentin shifts back into Comic Book Guy, turns to Suit Guy and gives a sneer. "Can I help you?"

"Actually, I believe I can help you," says Suit Guy. He opens his briefcase with a flourish and produces a comic that I recognize the moment I see it. "I've been sitting on this for a long time, and I am now ready to part with it. That is," he pulls it away as if we'd just lunged for it, "only *if* you make a decent offer."

Comic Book Guy and I look at each other and burst out laughing.

After a full minute of laughter, I ask, "May I?" Quentin gestures toward the very confused-looking Suit Guy as if to say "have at him."

"Well, sir," I start with mock-politeness, "what you have there is a Superman number seventy-five from 1992, otherwise known as 'Death of Superman.'" The man clutches the comic, still sealed in its original black polybag with the red S insignia dripping with blood.

"Yes," he says, "And I'm not some stupid kid, so don't think you can rip me off. I never opened it. Preserved its value. Thing must be worth a fortune by now."

I glance at Quentin and smile evilly. "Problem is, those poly-bags were actually made with cheap, acidic plastic that by now has turned the comic inside an ugly brown. But that doesn't really matter anyway, since so many folks invested in this publicity stunt and also never opened their bags. What you're left with is a rather unremarkable item worth about twenty bucks, if you're lucky."

"Twenty bucks!" Suit Guy's face goes red. "Nice try! It must be worth at least five hundred!"

At that, Quentin and I help ourselves to another fit of laughter. Finally he catches his breath enough to tell Suit Guy, "I wouldn't even give you two bucks for that piece of shit issue. That stupid promotional gimmick pissed off a lot of people and wrecked the comic market. This store was lucky to keep its doors open through the nineties, thanks to that stunt. Lots of stores weren't so fortunate."

I want to hug Quentin, but instead I rest my hands on the counter and watch Suit Guy stammer and sputter. "Nice try," he finally says as he turns to go. "Ripping me off. We'll just see what it's really worth."

"Good luck," Quentin says. "Now get the hell outta here and don't come back."

I. Love. It.

As Suit Guy storms off with his valueless treasure, I ask, "Should we have warned him that Superman came back to life?"

Quentin grins, shaking his head. "Probably the only comic that meathead ever owned, and he never even bothered opening the bag."

By the time I step out of Sector Comics! I've managed to hold my own in a heated discussion over which Wolverine costume was the best. I actually got Quentin to agree that I made a strong case for the old brown and yellow, since it had a different feel to it that separated Wolvie from the other X-Men. Not to mention that it's the suit he wore when he defeated the hell out of Apocalypse. When I'm with Quentin, I remind myself over and over to take things slow, but our debates are almost as titillating as having my breasts massaged. I'm still buzzing from my victory.

As I walk through the mall, I can see my future so clearly. Working at Sector Comics! with Quentin. Flashing my pink hair as I show customers my latest *Blazing Goddess* comics and then laughing shyly as they rave about her awesomeness. Watching Mark fall into a depression for letting me get away. Once and for all losing my identity as eternal chauffeur to the gang of Soccer Cre—

"Oh my God, you guys are so embarrassing!"

I just walked up to the fountain in the center of the mall to find Josh, Ajay, Andrew, and Dylan busy dipping their hands in the water and flicking it on each other.

SPLASH!

Suddenly, one whole side of my shirt is dripping wet. I stand there eying them all as my wet top drools all over my jeans.

Josh holds his palms out toward me as he stammers about it being an accident. The rest of the guys all stare, waiting for me to explode.

"Oh, no, you did not." Before I even think about it, I slam my cupped hand into the cold fountain water. I manage to create a wave that arches up and breaks over Josh's head.

Dylan immediately adds to Josh's soakedness by giving him a few extra swipes of water and then Ajay has to bring it to a new level by sticking his face in the fountain and spewing a stream directly into Dylan's ear. Andrew is the last one to join in, and it takes me practically shoving a wall of water into his face to get him going. The next thing I know, all five of us are laughing and soaking each other along with half the marble tiles around the fountain.

Now, I know that people are always making jokes about mall security guards being cop wannabes, but let me tell you, it is a total matter of reality in small-town malls. The boys and I have had to defend our behavior with the mall cops on more than one occasion. Which is why I quickly shift from one of the hooligans playing in the fountain, to the mostly grown-up adult-type figure yelling at the other hooligans to haul ass outta the mall.

"I'm freezing!" Dylan complains as we drip our way across the mall parking lot. His glasses are streaked with water.

The other boys are all hugging their arms tight across their chests, but that doesn't stop them from jumping all over Dylan's manhood for complaining about being cold. He's harangued with accusations of "wuss" and "poor wittle Dylan chilly?"

Josh is hunched over, walking next to me and calls over his shoulder, "Hey, Dylan! Do you need to borrow one of my sister's tampons to plug up that vagina of yours?"

And I stop. Dead.

My legs go numb as my mind locks onto the something that has been bothering me. I picture the bag of tampons sitting unopened in my closet. I should've needed them by now. *What the... ?* Why haven't I needed them?

BAM! POW! SPLAT! My life just got dropped into a vat of toxic waste.

"Blaze? You okay?" Josh turns back to see why I stopped so suddenly. I try to veil the open terror that must show on my face.

"I'm fine," I lie, "I just slipped a little." I point to my pink converse and try to smile. "Wet shoes."

This cannot be good, is all my mind can say. Over and over. *This cannot be good.* All the way to the van. *This cannot be good.* The soggy group of us pile in. *This cannot be good in any damn way.*

All I want to do is to run back into the mall and buy a pregnancy test from the pharmacy, but I can't very well risk the boys finding out. I can always claim I need a new toothbrush or something, but then I think of the girl who knows me and my minivan by sight. I don't need somebody spotting me with a pregnancy test. And I certainly don't need to be the girl with the pink flame job and the pink hair *and* the pink plus sign on a pregnancy stick.

I try to remember when Flo last came to visit but draw a complete blank. I've never really paid much attention to that before. I didn't realize it was Su-per Virgin Girl's secret strength. No Flo fear. *Think, Blaze, think!* It was definitely before hanging out with Mark.

Leaning forward to start the minivan, I privately grab at my breast and wince at how sore it feels. *That means my period is coming, right?* I flip back through my mind. I remember it came during school, right after third period. We were reviewing the first half of a science unit, so, that would've made it the middle of the month. And that means it was a week before Mark and I hooked up.

One week plus over four weeks is… *five and a half?* Five and a half weeks?

I pull the van over to the side of the road and stare out the windshield until Josh's voice penetrates my steady thought stream of *This is bad! This is really, really bad!*

"Blaze?"

I grab my phone and start texting Terri.

"I'm fine," I lie again "Just almost hit that squirrel. Didn't you see it?"

"Who are you texting?"

"Just Terri." I finally tell him something true.

My text reads:

911 need you to meet me at my house with PG test STAT!!!!

I hit *SEND* and ease the van back onto the road.

"I just asked her to swing by later to watch a movie." I'm back to lying to my little brother. But it isn't like I have options. I never even admitted the truth about having sex with his coach, so I'd best keep the lies flowing.

At least something is flowing out of me.

Chapter Thirteen

"Oh. My. God!" Terri exclaims as soon as I open my front door.

"Did you bring it?" I ask.

"I can't believe you might be P.G."

I shush her, and she whispers, "I got this from my sister's stash." Terri's second oldest sister sleeps around and supposedly buys pregnancy tests in bulk. I always figured Terri was exaggerating about her, but here she is at my door waving a plastic grocery bag wrapped around a wand-shaped item. I take it and ignore her wide-eyed stare as I head for the bathroom.

By the time I come out, the still-developing test is back in the bag clutched in my hand. Terri has moved to the couch, but her shocked look remains the same. I wave for her to follow me up to my room, where she parks her bug-eyed self on my bed.

"I know, I know." I toss the bag containing the test that will determine the rest of my life on the bed beside her. "You don't need to say anything."

"I can't say anything," Terri finally manages to speak.

I look at her. "I can't believe how screwed I am."

"How late are you?"

"Over a week?"

The two of us watch the bag until she finally says, "I think it might be done by now."

"I can't look." My mind chants a new and louder stream of *This could be bad. This could be so bad.*

"Well, I'm not gonna touch something you peed on."

We stare at the bag for another few minutes.

"I can't handle this." Terri finally grabs at it.

"I got it, I got it." I reach in and pull out the small white plastic wand.

Please don't let this be bad. "Okay, so it shows two pink lines. What does that mean?"

I close my eyes and wait for Terri to give me the news.

"Oh, um…" she stammers, and I open one eye to glare at her. "I'm not sure?" Terri waves her arms, her hands flopping uselessly up and down. "There were three tests left in the opened pack," she wails. "I just grabbed one of them and came over."

I resist screaming at the top of my lungs. But just barely.

"We should call Amanda," Terri says. "She'll know what this means."

Amanda doesn't answer her cell phone, and I decide she's officially a lousy friend.

"What'll we do?" I'm scarcely holding it together and my little mouse room is getting smaller by the minute. "Is the second line a minus sign, or does the second line just being pink indicate that my life is officially over?" I examine the little window as closely as possible, but the two pink lines remain meaningless, and finally my hand starts shaking.

"It'll be okay," Terri soothes. "We'll just look it up online."

Jumping onto my laptop, Terri quickly finds the site of the company printed on the side of the test. It doesn't take long for us to get the information we need.

Turns out: two pink lines represent one indicator that the test is working, plus one minus sign that equals two over-joyed teenagers.

Terri and I start jumping up and down and laughing and hugging each other. I cannot believe I've just escaped complete disaster. I'm so elated I feel like I can fly.

Terri pulls back, grinning. "I didn't want tell you in case you really were preggers. But my sister once told me it's pretty common for your cycle to get messed up after you do it for the first time."

I grin back at her. "I could slap you for not telling me that sooner. But I'm just too damned happy to care right now."

"Something like this really puts things into perspective, doesn't it?" Terri picks up the mirrored sunglasses resting on my dresser and asks casually, "Can I have these?"

I nod, just as my phone starts blasting Amanda's perky ringtone.

"And look who's calling five minutes too late to be helpful."

"Typical Amanda," says Terri.

"I'm not complaining," I say. "I'm just grateful for everything right now."

"Hello, negative-pregnancy-test-results-R-us!" I jovially answer Amanda's call.

"Oh-my-god-I'm-so-sorry!" Amanda's voice rushes from my phone.

"Um, I wasn't really trying to get pregnant or anyth—"

"No, not that!" she practically shouts. "Haven't you been on FriendsPlace tonight?"

"You know I don't have time for that stuff," I say, but Amanda's tone is making me nervous. I mouth to Terri, "Sign onto FriendsPlace."

"I'm-so-sorry-I'm-so-sorry-I'm-so-sorry," Amanda keeps babbling, until Terri finally deciphers what she's babbling about.

"Uh, oh," is Terri's assessment.

"What the heck is everyone freaking out about?" I look over Terri's shoulder and scan the threads of ongoing conversations to find the one that has exploded with comments. The thread belongs to Mark.

THWACK! I physically feel the impact of what I see.

There I am. In all my nippled glory in the photo Amanda sent. The amateur-porn-like blurry edges, the inviting expression, the see-through pink lace. The beauty mark underneath my right nipple might as well be giving a wink. The photo is labeled, "Blaze in Heat!" Staring at it, I can practically smell the putrid perfumed air from Lucy's Lucky Lingerie all over again.

"That bastard!" I shout. Which gets Amanda going again with the I'm-so-sorries. "Just shut up, Amanda," I say and hang up on her.

"Oh my god," Terri says. "These comments are horrible."

She tries to block my view, but I can see that the thread is completely wallpapered with the letters S and L and U and T, in that order. Over and over. And usually with exclamation points, like: SLUT! SLUT! SLUT! SLUT!

I imagine the gravelly voice of the Thing from the Fantastic Four grumbling, *What a revoltin' development this is!*

I couldn't agree with the Thing more.

"Hey," says Terri, "it's not all bad. Here's a comment from someone who says 'I don't care, she looks so hot it doesn't matter what sort of—' oh, sorry."

She gives a sheepish grin, and I resist the urge to cuff her in the back of the head with my palm. Barely.

"Out of my way." I knock her aside with my hip and start typing.

"What're you doing?" Terri asks. "You're not leaving a comment, are you?"

"God, no," I tell her. "I'm just letting Mark know I'm going to murder him in cold blood if he doesn't take this photo down immediately."

"You should tell him you're calling your lawyer," Terri encourages. "I've heard about guys getting labeled as sex offenders for this kind of shit."

The thought of actually finding a lawyer makes me feel a little queasy, but I'm pretty sure Mark will take the photo down once he realizes the crazed reaction it's causing. I can't believe all the comments. It's as if there isn't anything else to look at on the Internet.

"This is going to blow over at school, right?" I say, trying not to panic.

"Right!" says Terri. "I don't even recognize half of the people leaving comments."

"Great. So people who never even met me think I'm a slut."

Terri starts to shake her head with a protesting *No!* but has to redirect to a nod, conceding that the FriendsPlace consensus seems to be: *I'm a slut.*

"Well," I say. "At least I'm still not pregnant."

"That's right." Terri brightens, but I don't join in her improvisational no-baby-in-da-belly dance. I don't feel much like celebrating. After a bit of fake cheering, I let her know I'm heading to bed.

"Thanks for these," Terri says, putting on my sunglasses and giving a few model poses before she leaves. I snap my laptop shut, realizing they were my final surviving pair from the summer.

It looks like I'll have to face everyone at school without

mirrored shades to hide behind. Eye contact will not make this easier. I plant my face in my pillow. I'm definitely staying home tomorrow. A day away should give rumors and gossip a chance to die. Once Mark takes the photo down, I hope my nipples' online debut quickly becomes a faded memory. It'll suck if folks at school treat me differently over a stupid photo that I never even sent.

I'm not a slut. I'm sure people who know me will figure out the truth right away. Problem is, even with the attention I've been getting from my pink hair and flaming minivan and my comic circulating through the school, not many people really know me.

I may need to practice going invisible all over again.

• • •

Soccergod: Take down that stupid comic and I'll take down your picture.

Blazefire22: You didn't take it down yet?? What the hell is the matter with you?? People are calling me a slut online.

Soccergod: beats getting called a manwhore

Blazefire22: That's practically a compliment. Besides. I was *just* a virgin and you are a *total* manwhore.

Soccergod: slut

Blazefire22: Seriously, Mark. Take the photo down or I'm calling a lawyer. I'm underage you know.

Soccergod: yeah, well so am I

Blazefire22: That doesn't even make sense. I wrote a parody of our pathetic relationship. You posted a naked picture of me online.

Soccergod: Not totally naked.

After sharing such sharp, stimulating banter with Quentin, this nonsense exchange with Mark makes me feel like my brain is being shoved into a jar.

Blazefire22: Writing to you is making me stupider. Take the fucking picture down, Mark. Or you're going to be sorry.

Soccergod: I already am sorry. Sorry I was ever nice to you. Ever tried to show you a good time.

Blazefire22: Take the picture down NOW you simpleminded asshat. I'm signing off.

He is so *not getting his DVD back.*

• • •

"Hey, Blaze! You in there?"

I open my eyes. I must've fallen asleep at some point, since morning sunlight is slicing through my room. My head feels thick as I heave into a sitting position and yell at Josh to go away. "Just take the bus to school."

"No way!" he whines. "You promised no bus this week."

I scan my heavy brain for a reason why I'd made such a promise. There isn't one.

"Did not!" I shout back.

He's quiet a few minutes, so I know I caught him bluffing.

"Pleeeeeaaaaase!" Begging is always Josh's final option.

I consider a moment. It really wouldn't be a big deal to drive him to school. I can still come straight back to bed and resume the depression I've slotted for today.

Or maybe I should force Josh to stay home with me. We could have a superhero movie marathon. Of course, thinking of that makes me think of Dad and then the fact that I still haven't finished inventorying his comics like he asked, let alone mailed them to him. If I'm treating myself to a day off, I may as well revisit the basement, aka the scene of the almost-kiss that would lead to the untimely death of Su-per Virgin Girl.

"Wanna stay home and help me go through Dad's comics?"

Mom left before five a.m., so as Josh's surrogate guardian I feel it is within my power to demand he keep me company on this miserable day.

Josh asks, "Can we go to the Country Kitchen for breakfast?"

"Lunch," I counter.

"Deal! I'm going back to bed."

"Yeah, me too," I say and roll over.

I can't get back to sleep, so I just lie there in the fetal position thinking about the awful things people were saying about me online. All I wanted to do was send a message that girls shouldn't get taken in by sharks who pose as cute boys. It was my own fault that I lost my virginity to Mark. I'll probably always regret it. But I don't deserve to have the whole Internet think I'm a slut. *This hurts so much*. I just want to disappear.

Finally, I can't stand my thoughts another second and get up. I go downstairs and eat a few handfuls of crackers before heading into the basement with a light bulb borrowed from the living room lamp. Once I get the light working, I start going through Dad's comics. Eventually Josh comes down and sits on a box of stuffed animals that probably houses generations of mice along with our soft childhood friends. He doesn't move to join me as I flip through a batch of *Dr. Strange* issues from the 1970s. I did read through them once, but to be honest, I don't really get Dr. Strange or understand why Dad ever liked him.

It may be that he reminds me too much of a magician, and I've always hated magicians. When I was younger, I'd drive myself crazy trying to figure out how they do their magic tricks, and then I just sort of gave up and decided to ignore the whole magic thing. Yes, I know, Dr. Strange is a sorcerer, not a magician, but still. Not even the fact that he's so tight with Spidey can elevate him in my mind. And maybe that's part of the problem—being able to levitate stuff doesn't make you a superhero. It makes you an entertainer at kids' birthday parties, wearing a silly cape and a ridiculous mustache.

I hand Josh the list. "I'll call them out and you write them down."

Josh growls a little as he takes the pen and notebook. He doesn't have as close a relationship with dad as I do, and I think part of that is because he doesn't appreciate the awesomeness of Dad's comics. Josh tells Mom we should just sell the whole collection and buy a big boat or something with the money. I don't know what the heck we'd do with a boat here in the middle of nowhere with the closest lake 70 miles away, but I think Josh likes the fact that it would drive our dad crazy, since Dad can't even swim.

"I'm thinking of maybe driving these to New York." I lob the grenade and wait for Josh's reaction.

I can see his jaw working for a few minutes before he detonates. "Sure, Blaze, Dad seriously deserves you driving 400 miles to return his precious comics to him. I swear we should tell him the basement flooded, sell them, and go do something really crazy, like take ourselves to Disneyland or something."

"You seriously want to go to Disneyland?"

"No. I just want to blow Dad's stupid comic money on something we can enjoy. We. As in you and me. Remember us? The kids he dissed?"

"Sorry, Josh, I didn't know you were still so…"

"So what?" He flings his hands in the air. "So pissed at him? Yeah, sis, I'm pissed at him, but not because of the reasons you think I'm pissed at him. I don't care that he barely talks to me on the phone. But how could he be so selfish and leave when Mom needed so much help? You got stuck picking up all the slack."

"Things have been better."

"Yeah, I know." He looks at his hands. "I heard the blowout between you and Mom that night after the party. When you confronted her about feeling like a soccer mom?"

"I didn't know you were listening. Sorry." I lean over and rub his arm. "You know I've loved being *your* soccer mom."

He gives my hand a few pats. "I know, sis. But you deserve to have a life. Dad took that from you."

"You're starting to sound like Mom and Mema, bashing him all the time. You don't remember him the way I do because you were younger when he left. He was awesome in a *lot* of ways. If he didn't live so far away, you'd see. He's not so bad."

"Do you want to know the worst thing Dad did?" Josh locks his gaze into mine. "He corrupted any halfway-happy childhood memory we ever had with the shitty way everything turned out. I can't even look at that stupid family portrait Mema has on top of her television."

"You mean her one photo of *actual* family members?" I try to joke him out of this rant. Josh is not the ranting type, and I wonder if maybe we need to find him some sort of physical activity as an outlet off-season.

He rewards me with a half-smile. "Right, well, when I look at that picture I feel like the four of us are lying through our teeth with our smiles. Pretending to be some happy family for the sake of some asshole photographer."

"But Josh, we *were* happy back then—"

"*That's* what I'm talking about. It's as if Dad took all that happiness we ever shared as a family and sucked the guts out of it. He turned it all into lies. Like he packed up all the good stuff and shipped it off to New York. Well, he doesn't deserve to have you ship him his precious comics too, Blaze. And he sure as hell doesn't deserve a special delivery from the Blazing Goddess."

I look with amazement at the young man sitting across from me. I've seen how Dad's leaving made me grow up much quicker than my friends, but I'm blown to bits by Josh's maturity. I think of the stupid, slutty photo of me circulating at that moment. The realization that it might reach Josh and the guys sweeps through me and brings tears to my eyes.

"Oh, come on, Blaze, don't get all sappy."

I lunge across the space between us and he catches my hug tightly. We were the young girl and boy in foot pajamas, snuggled under comforters, eating microwave popcorn and watching videos. We used to take turns picking movies and would generally watch some variation of princess movie / Pixar movie / princess movie / Pixar movie. We trusted that our parents would always protect us from bad things.

"I hated my hair in that picture, anyway," I say with a chuckle. My voice is rough when I add, "And the people in that photo? Their story is still unfolding. Still plenty of time for a happy ending."

"Or a crappy one," Josh counters, and we laugh.

I pull back and look at my brother on the cusp of manhood, ruffle his hair, and ask, "Country Kitchen time?"

"Now you're talking!" He lets out a whoop and bounds toward the stairs. I stand and carefully pack up the issues I've been counting.

"Come on, Blaze, blow that shit off," Josh calls from the steps.

"You know I can't."

"I know you won't."

"I'm almost done anyway." I make my way up the stairs after my brother to go pretend everything's okay. I hope he won't resent me as much as he resents Dad if today's memory gets corrupted by his coach sharing my stupid nipple shot with the whole world. But the best I can do is enjoy a nice, normal meal with my growing-up-too-fast little brother.

I suppose I should maybe attempt a bit of extra maturity myself. Before heading out to Superturd, I stop off in my room, delete my website, and send Mark a text.

I give up.

Chapter Fourteen

TerriAngel445: Where the hell have you been???

Blazefire22: Hey there—went to lunch with Josh

TerriAngel445: On the moon??

Blazefire22: Left phone at home—what's up?

TerriAngel445: I've been trying to call you all day!! That photo of you is everywhere!!

Blazefire22: WTF? I just checked FriendsPlace—Mark took it down

TerriAngel445: Too late! Got posted on some 'hot or not' website. Good news is you're hot. Bad news is that pic is everywhere. People have it on their cellphones, Blaze!! Everyone is asking me where you are! Even Mark asked if you're okay, something about some text he got saying you were going to kill yourself?

My heart is pounding in my forehead as I envision guys drooling over my photo. Then I picture clumps of my classmates scattered up and down the school hallway, passing around cell phones and ogling my nipples. I hold my hands over my chest at the thought.

Maybe I can convince Mom I need to be homeschooled. *Yeah, right. Like that would ever happen.* I might as well just face the masses before things get any worse.

TerriAngel445: Blaze? What are you going to do?

TerriAngel445: Blaze?

TerriAngel445: You are seriously freaking me out!

TerriAngel445: BLAZE!!

Blazefire22: I'll be in tomorrow. Hopefully things won't be too weird.

TerriAngel445: Pick me up on your way, I'll walk in with you

Blazefire22: I'll be fine.

TerriAngel445: Trust me, your gonna need the moral support

Blazefire22: That bad, huh?

TerriAngel445: That bad. You should probably stay offline.

Blazefire22: K. See you in the morning. Thanx

TerriAngel445: no thanx necesary. We'll get through this

Blazefire22: K

I can't resist the urge to check out FriendsPlace. While there's no actual copy of my photo posted there, there is much discussion of it, plus a few links to the site Terri was talking about. I try to do damage control, writing to folks and asking them to remove the links and threatening the Hot or Not people with a lawsuit if they don't take my picture down. Being officially declared "hot" for my photo doesn't make any of this okay.

The online buzz is going strong with comments like "It's always the quiet ones who are the biggest freaks," and "I never even noticed her before, but I'd sure hit that."

One girl claims I constantly park in the cornfields to have sex in my minivan, and it was only a matter of time before everyone found out what a slut I am.

It's like my photo gave everyone permission to make up lies about me, and since everything's online and anonymous they can fabricate whatever they want.

For Mom and Josh's sakes I pretend everything's just fine as we eat yet another burned casserole, but every time I blink my eyes I can see the hateful stream of vile remarks. Like pixilated knives stabbing me in the heart.

"Do you need to stay home tomorrow?" When I open my eyes, Mom is watching me with concern.

I straighten up. Suck in a deep breath. "No. I'll be fine."

I hope.

• • •

When I pull up to Terri's house the next morning, I honk lightly and shift Superturd into reverse. When Amanda appears with Terri at the front doorway I debate peeling backward out of the driveway.

"No way!" I coast the minivan away from my traitor friends.

"Wait!" Terri lunges for the doorknob. "She feels awful and has some good ideas for damage control."

"What's going on?" Josh asks from the backseat.

I give Terri a meaningful glare. "Absolutely nothing, Bro. Nothing at all."

"Is Amanda seeing Mark now?" he whispers to me.

I swing on him. "What makes you think that?"

He slumps down in his seat. "Nothing, I just figured…" He trails off, and I glare at Amanda through my window. Josh is right to suspect she'd go after Mark. Of course, she's welcome to have him at this point.

Amanda offers, "My mom would execute me if she knew I rode in a car with a seventeen-year-old driver." This fact actually holds some appeal.

I still don't trust her, but I point my thumb at the sliding back door. "Hop in. But Terri gets shotgun and we're not talking until we get to school." I glance at Josh to imply, *No nipple-shot talk in front of my baby brother.*

Terri and Amanda obediently climb into Superturd, and I blot out my thoughts with the blasting stereo. I'm not looking forward to what's waiting for me at school, but it does feel good to have my friends with me. Even if they are evil mutant friends who've ruined my life and turned me into some slutty Internet porn star.

● ● ●

After dropping Josh off at the middle school, I drive across the street, pull into the parking lot, cut the engine, and swivel in my seat to face Amanda. "So, what's this great idea you have for damage control?"

Amanda leans forward. "I am so sorry, Blaze," she pleads. I roll my eyes, and she promises, "I'll make it up to you, really. But for right now we just need to focus on getting you through this social tragedy."

"We tried to tell people yesterday that photo wasn't even you," says Terri. "But nobody was buying it."

"I tested out the lie that you were secretly doing some modeling and the picture is from a photoshoot," says Amanda.

"Seriously?" I say. "Did anybody believe you?"

"Sorry, no. Too bad we don't live in New York or California or someplace where models actually live."

"So now you want to blame this mess on geography?" I shoot. "You would make a great spin doctor, Amanda."

She adds hopefully, "Did you see how everyone voted 'hot' on that one site?"

"So you didn't even bother trying out the truth on anyone?" I ask. "You didn't admit to one single person that you took the photo and sent it to Mark with my phone?"

Amanda's eyes are wide. "Well, I didn't see how it would help to drag me into—"

"It's getting late," Terri cuts her off. "The biggest problem is, too many witnesses saw you stalking Mark a few weeks ago. Everyone knows you were into him. So now we just need to ride things out until everyone gets bored with sharing that photo."

Amanda adds, "People will eventually realize there is a difference between a girl like you who made one mistake, and someone like Catherine Wiggan, who is a career-slut destined for eternal slut-hood."

"Do people really think I'm like her?"

"Oh, yeah." The girls nod in unison. "You need to be prepared."

"We'll stay close by you," says Amanda. "Just act like everything is completely normal. If they smell guilt they'll tear you apart in there."

I chuckle, "I hardly think…"

"You weren't here yesterday," Terri says. "You don't know! It's like you're a serial killer with folks saying stuff like, 'I always knew there was something off about her.'"

"Oh my god!" I say. "The online shit was bad enough. I'm going home until this thing blows over."

Amanda puts her hand on my arm. "Everyone will just believe the lies more," she says. "You need to get in there and look innocent." She pulls my collar closed, which makes me feel a bit Amish. Which is probably a good look for me right about now.

"We'll be right here with you," says Terri.

"Seeing everyone the first time will be the worst of it," says

Amanda. "But once people realize you're acting totally normal, they'll find other stuff to focus on."

I look toward the school and see a trio of junior girls by the front door leaning into each other as they stare at Superturd. One of them points in our direction, and the three of them move into a tight whisper-huddle.

Terri takes me by the shoulders and forces me to look her in the eyes. "Just act normal," she commands.

Act normal, got it.

Pushing away the urge to drive home and crawl back underneath the covers for the next month or so, I force myself to exit the minivan. Marching between Amanda and Terri, I head toward my accusers.

Just act normal. How bad can this possibly be?

• • •

It is worse.

Worse than I imagined. And I have a pretty damn good imagination.

When we walk into the school, a large cluster of students turn to stare as if I'm Nightcrawler, straight from the freak show. I instinctively turn to head back out the door, but Terri and Amanda are right there, grabbing my arms so I can't escape. If only I had Nightcrawler's ability to teleport.

"Act normal," Amanda commands in my ear, and it becomes my mantra for the day. *Act normal.*

When two girls in my first period class start laughing and pointing the moment I walk in the door, I act normal.

When I stop to get a drink at the water fountain after third period and a girl who has never spoken to me before hisses "*Slut!*" in my ear, I act normal.

When guys proposition me throughout the day with invitations to suck their dicks, sit on their faces, and ride their cocks, I act normal.

I'm so focused on acting normal I become an android, completely closed off from feeling anything the whole hellish day. Not everybody seems aware of my Internet infamy. And some folks just give me pitying looks, or even wordless hugs, but those are worse in some ways. Those tempt me to feel something.

It isn't until later, when I'm home safe in my room that I allow myself to experience feelings. And there are a *lot* of them. Each clomping me over the head: Misery. Disgust. Anger. Sadness. Outrage. Shame.

The shame feels the worst.

I'm on my bed, balled up, with my arms and legs tucked in. It's as if I've absorbed every sneer and insult and become every awful thing said about me. *I am now Su-per Slut.* Maybe if I hadn't skipped school yesterday the impact wouldn't be so forceful, but as I lay on top of my bedspread, I feel like I just had the piss beat out of me.

Mark is such an ass. I punch the bed in fury. The one time I spotted him between classes, he gave me a sorrowful look and mouthed the words, "I'm sorry." I gave him the finger before storming away.

"Dinnertime!" Mom calls up the stairs. I draw a deep breath, pick myself up off the bed, and head down toward the kitchen. I command myself, *Just keep acting normal.*

• • •

It's as if I've entered some parallel high school reality. Like I'm trapped inside one of the *What if... ?* series of Marvel comics where imaginary storylines explore variations of mainstream reality. The various multiverses don't affect the main Marvel Universe (aka Earth 616) so it's okay to break characters' status quo, and major heroes often end up getting killed. I'm stuck in a bizarre issue entitled *What if... Everyone Decides Blaze Is a Whore?*

The comic includes a panel showing Terri and Amanda standing on either side of me as we enter the lunchroom. The double-page spread of the entire cafeteria is shown from over my shoulder as everyone stops to point and stare. Including the lunch ladies. Next, there's the classic scene of me eating my peanut butter sandwich while perched on the toilet looking pitiful.

A series of panels depict insulting words gaining mass as a crumpled wad of paper soars toward me in slow motion. The close-up drawing of the crumpled paper bouncing off my head leads to a close-up drawing of a laser pointer circling my breasts, which leads to a close-up drawing of a hand grabbing at my ass as I walk down the hallway.

A page divided into four vertical panels shows me day after day with my head dipping lower. I pile on layers of clothes so butt pinchers will only get a handful of loose cotton. Words penetrate where fingers can't, and I'm filled with fear that the weird girl in my gym class will make good on her threat to "nail that bitch" between classes. My alternate reality *What if... ?* comic shows a close-up of a bead of sweat on my temple as the class bell screams, *Brrrriiinng!*

The images grow more scribbled and disturbed and my features more distraught as I'm followed by the whispered words: "Slutbag." "Skank." "Ho." I start to wonder how this issue is going to play out. It definitely doesn't have one of those choose-your-own endings because if it did, I'd choose to end it all now.

• • •

"Hey, slut! Why don't you just do us all a favor and go kill yourself?"

It's not the first time I've gotten this suggestion. In fact, it's the reason I finally deleted my FriendsPlace account. But it is the first time someone's saying it in person.

"Cut Blaze a break, would you?" A male voice rises to my defense. "Go give somebody else a hard time, she's had enough."

I turn to thank my rescuer but stop when I see who it is.

Mark.

It's as if I have my very own arch nemesis standing right in front of me. Except that I have no energy left to make him pay, pay, pay for his horrible misdeeds.

"You won." I turn and stride away, but Mark catches up quickly. He puts an arm around my shoulders and I allow him to steer me to the dimly lit banks of the eighth-grade lockers.

"What the hell do you want?" He's wearing his stupid Kick Some Grass! T-shirt, and in my mind it morphs into the more fitting "I'm An Ass!"

"I'm so sorry." Mark reaches to embrace me, but I shove him away.

"I just wanted you to like me. To be my boyfriend," I say. "You were the first guy I ever had sex with, and you turned around and screwed me all over again with that photo."

"Blaze, I feel so bad about all of this. Stu's girlfriend talked me into doing it after that comic you drew. Mark the Shark was such a big hit, and I was just so mad at you. I had no idea the photo would go viral before I had a chance to take it down."

Viral? My photo is now "viral"? I am never going online ever again. Mark looks absolutely miserable. He is still so good looking it's almost breathtaking to have him stare at me like this. He takes my hand. "I really wish I could take it all back, Blaze."

I stand there. Seeing him. Really, clearly seeing him. Dating him would've been sentencing myself to an ego beating wrapped in a long, boring stream of sports-themed movies. I can't believe I ever thought he'd rescue me from my lame soccer mom life. Like some boyfriend superhero. What a crock of shit.

I just shake my head as I move to walk away.

"Hey, Blaze." I turn and he gazes into my eyes with gamma-ray intensity. "Maybe I can take you to the movies sometime? You know, make it up to you?"

I erect a force field to refract the influence of his grey eyes on my heart. I think I'll skip another battle round with the Shark. I think of Quentin and tell Mark honestly, "You don't deserve my time."

I can't believe I ever obsessed over waiting for him to call or send me a text or email. And boy, do I miss those days of having an empty inbox. Before I deleted my account, mine was stuffed with accusations. Oh yes, and offers. I've gotten plenty of squicky offers. Plus, for some reason folks seem to think I enjoy receiving links to porn sites. I suppose they figure I might want to start a book club with all the other sluts and whores.

I think of the kick-butt gang of prostitutes in Frank Miller's neo-noir comic *Sin City* that Quentin showed me and can't help but give a little smile. Quentin has been texting me, asking when we can hang out.

But I can't see him in person.

There's no way I can hide what's happening to me if I see him in person. When I look in the mirror I see the horror of it all etched in my face. Maybe it's better to have him wonder what happened to me rather than risk him ever finding out the truth.

• • •

Thankfully, my pornographic debut has yet to make the leap to the middle school. I figure it will only be a matter of time before some big brother or sister introduces my disgrace to Josh's classmates. I watch him, waiting for a sign that he knows and dreading how bad it will be when he finds out. But so far he seems to be watching me as carefully as I'm watching him.

Amanda and Terri stop telling me to act normal, and our conversations are reduced to them asking me, "How are you doing?"

My hope that things will just blow over at school eventually dies, and I realize I'm stuck in this continuity of *What if… the Blazing Goddess Can't Survive Her Senior Year?* There's no going back to Earth 616.

"It sucks, huh?" says a girl's soft voice.

I nod in agreement without even looking up. There's no need to clarify what she's referring to. By now, my social shift has become legend at our small school.

When I see who's talking, I understood why she sounds so friendly. Catherine Wiggan. Of course. My infamous predecessor as the school slut.

"Well, you must be happy." I drop my head back down and turn away.

"Why on earth would I be happy?" Catherine touches my arm so I face her.

"I just figured people are so busy calling me names now, they're not bothering you anymore."

She gives a tight smile. "I wish."

"Yeah, well, thanks a bunch." I pull my arm away and move to go.

"No, wait. I just mean I wish there was some way to go back to being anything other than a… slut."

"You've been a slut since the eighth grade," I say, which isn't being mean because it's just the simple truth. "Nobody will treat you differently unless you start acting differently."

Catherine gives me a half-sneer. "Blaze, do you know why people call me a slut?"

I shrug, not wanting to say the reason out loud.

"Go ahead. It's okay, you can say it." Catherine gives my shoulder a light shove, and it's more than I can take. Getting abused by random people for two weeks has been bad enough. I don't need this whore pushing me around.

"I'm not like you!" I say. "You screwed the entire junior varsity basketball team in the locker room the summer before eighth grade! And you've been with almost every guy in the school since then. Including Mr. Arturro."

Catherine closes her eyes against my accusation. "God. I hate the Internet," she says under her breath. Shaking her head, she gives me a direct gaze. "Blaze. I'm a virgin."

She smiles at my wide-eyed reaction. "My only crime was growing big boobs too soon and having Missy Henkel's boyfriend notice them. I didn't even like him, but he wouldn't stop coming on to me until finally Missy started that awful rumor about the basketball team."

She's lying. I cross my arms. "So why didn't the basketball players admit it was a lie?"

She shrugs. "Maybe they liked everyone thinking they'd had sex with me? Either way, they just stayed quiet and let Missy's rumor do its damage."

"Missy left our school in tenth grade. The truth would've come out by now." I can't believe Catherine is honestly trying to convince me she's a virgin.

She crosses her arms back at me. "I read online that *you* got caught giving some guy a blow job in the back of the comic book store at the mall." Her words knock the wind out of me. "Is *that* true?"

"No! That's totally not true!" I nearly shout. "Who the hell…" The thought of Quentin getting dragged into my nightmare is too much.

"Welcome to the dark side, Blaze." She raises an eyebrow.

I think of all the awful things I've heard about her over the years. I picture the comment threads and message boards. The mystery handle called @wiggantheslut who would post blurbs about her sexual exploits. Looking around the hallway, I can practically see the endless whispers weaving through the crowd like the Red Ghost. I believed every story without the slightest doubt, I realize. It was easy to imagine her with all those boys, letting them squeeze her huge juggs.

"If you're so virginal, why don't you at least dress…" I gesture to her V-neck tee that shows more than a hint of cleavage.

"What? Like a nun? When you have big boobs, you either end up looking matronly or sexy." She shrugs. "I wore turtlenecks for a while, but I got teased just as much, so I made a decision to dress how I wanted to and not let the haters win."

They won, all right. But as she holds my gaze, I realize there has never been any actual evidence that Catherine is a slutbag. I've never seen her out with a single guy, let alone hordes of them the way everyone says. Come to think of it, she does get pretty good grades for a skank-ho, and she hasn't even had a bathing suit photo posted online, let alone one of her wearing sexy lingerie.

Looking at hard evidence alone, I'm the only slut standing here.

"Why didn't you deny the rumors?" I ask.

"I did. At first. It just made me seem more guilty. If you want my advice, just ignore everything as best you can. Fighting back just makes things worse." I feel my inner-resolve gasp its final breath at her words.

"What am I supposed to do?" I plead with my unexpected mentor.

"Just do what I'm doing. Stay offline as much as possible. Hang in till graduation and then move as far away from this town as you possibly can. I'm cutting my hair, changing my name, and starting my life over at a SUNY school in Upstate New York." As she turns to go, I consider her hunched posture and realize all these years of being taunted have clearly branded her in a way no magical haircut will ever erase.

"Wait." Why had I believed the stories about her so easily? My mind whirrs with all the times I've heard ugly things about her.

And each time I was the one saying them.

Tears sting my eyes. "Catherine, I am so sorry," I say, but I know it isn't nearly enough. "I had no idea."

"Yeah, nobody does."

I give her a pleading look. "How do you deal with it? I feel like everyone hates me."

"That's because they do," Catherine answers brightly. "I guess some people just need someone to hate on and whether we have big boobs or blonde hair or just make bad choices, we end up fitting the bill."

"Does it get easier?"

She looks at me a moment before answering. "I just got doused with a bottle of water this morning as people chanted, 'wet T-shirt!'" She pulls on the front of her now-dry shirt, obviously still pained. "But, hey, at least now *you* believe I'm not a slut. That's a start."

I nod, but guilt slithers down my throat and blocks any reply as Catherine walks away. Why didn't I ever stand up for her? That's what the Blazing Goddess would've done. She would've fought for Catherine, and now it's too late for me to help her.

Now I can't even help myself.

• • •

My new profile looks something like this:

Real Name
Super-Slut, aka Slutbag, aka Skank, aka Ho
Secret Identity
(that is so super-well hidden it may never surface again)
The Blazing Goddess

Occupation: Giving folks something to blog about
Marital Status: Apparently, busy screwing everybody in sight
Group Affiliation: Orgies? Sure! Does 'em all the time
Known Superhuman Powers: Once had the ability to turn invisible, but this power was lost after her infamous battle with Mark the Shark. Currently able to turn others into whores by association, which explains her present isolation.
Base of Operations: Hiding in mouse-sized bedroom
Origin: One photo
Warnings: Careful, better not look her in the eye, or your reputation may be forever mutated

Comments: Hey, guys, no need to waste time talking to her like a regular human female. Just go right ahead and gesture to your crotch while making disgusting sucking sounds, because she's just dying to jump on your junk. And nobody should bother with, say, asking her for her side of the story, since she's obviously too much of a slutbag-skank-ho to deserve her say. Or your sympathy.

Rounding the hallway corner, I see Terri and Amanda, aka the helpful collaborators of Super Slut's origin story. I hug my books tightly to my chest and duck back to wait for them to pass. I'm letting them off the hook.

After all, how much can I ask of friendships founded on the convenience of living a bike-ride away?

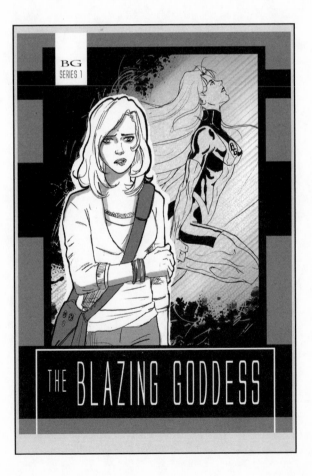

Chapter Fifteen

I think of Suicide.

No, not doing it. The character from the early nineties. He's a guy with a death wish who gets suckered by Mephisto, just like Johnny Blaze did. Suckering saps is apparently some sort of hobby with the guy, but then Mephisto is also known as the devil, Satan, Lucifer, Beelzebub, and the Lord of Evil (place of birth: Hell), so you know he's got a rep to protect.

Apparently he also has an overdeveloped sense of irony, since he went ahead and made Suicide immortal. Even when the poor guy gets burned down to just a skeleton he's painfully regenerated to full health.

I picture the comic cover with Ghost Rider giving Zodiak the penance stare as Suicide stands by in a rage shouting "Don't kill him! Kill me!" I understand that now. The desire to make all the pain and shame stop happening. To just want everything to go away.

I get that.

If it wasn't for how much Josh depends on me, I might even consider ending it all. Just to get a little peace. But Lord knows I wouldn't beg someone else to kill me, like Suicide. And I refuse to become some tragic chick who gets bullied into hanging herself. No, I know just what I'd do. I'd park in a cornfield with a hose running from Superturd's tailpipe to the window. That's how I'd go. If I was the sort of person to do that sort of thing. Which thank goodness I'm not, because that guy Suicide may be portrayed as some sort of reluctant hero, but really he comes off as more whiny and sad than anything else. It doesn't help that he's stuck wearing some wacky fishnet disco outfit as he tries to get Ghost Rider to kill him. What an idiot.

Everybody knows Ghost Rider won't spill innocent blood.

• • •

"On your way to the comic store to give some more sexual favors?"

"Wha—?" The cutting comment axes through my thoughts as I'm walking toward Sector Comics! My last small corner of unspoiled reality.

I'm even more surprised when I see my accuser. It's the red-haired girl who was nice enough to turn the lights off on my minivan back when I used to be awesome. My fan. But her open admiration is gone. In fact, I barely recognize her with the sneer she's wearing.

I look around. "Do you live at this mall or something?"

"I heard you got caught having sex with the comic book guy in the back of his store," she says, ignoring my question.

"What are you talking about?" I say. "I have a job there. Sort of."

"What kind of job?" she shoots back. "A blow job? Why didn't you tell me you were such a slut?"

"I'm not a…" my sentence trails off as I watch the girl turn to go. *I guess my photo has gone totally viral if even she—*

"What kind of person does that sort of thing?" She pops back into my face.

"I…" She has me completely rattled.

"You acted like you were so innocent in that comic you drew and put online, and meanwhile I saw the photo you sent. You trapped that guy into having sex with you and then you called him a shark."

"I never sent that photo," I start, but she just scoffs and strides away muttering "whore," under her breath. My Small Town Infamy has officially come back to bite me in the ass. After giving myself a moment to regain my composure, I command my feet to move toward Sector Comics!

"Lo! She returns!" Quentin greets cheerfully when I walk through the arched entryway. He runs a hand through his adorably messy hair, looking genuinely happy to see me. *Maybe he heard the rumor I'm here to give him a blow job.* "I thought you forgot about us."

I shake my head no as I pull the most recent comics he loaned me out of my messenger bag and place them on the glass counter between us. "I just came to return these." I glance nervously toward the door.

"Oh, okay." He reaches for the small stack. "So, what did you think of the storyline? I know you hate it when the resolution comes completely out of nowhere."

He's inviting me to enter a discussion, but I carefully keep my hair between us. "Story was okay." I shrug. "Art was better than the plot deserved."

"So, how would you compare these to the old school ones you're in love with?"

At the word *love*, I glance at him. He smiles, and I stare at the dimple under his mouth a moment before dropping my gaze. "Really, they're too different to compare at all." Which I know is not the reaction he's looking for. Nor is it the one I want to give, since I actually have some strong opinions about the way comics have clearly evolved over the years. But I'm afraid more banter will just create more rumors.

He looks at me. "Well, I've got some other issues picked out that you should read next. And there's another bin in the back that's ready for organizing." He lifts my chin to force me to look him in the eye. "You know, you can't just disappear on us like that."

My heart aches to settle into our routine, standing side-by-side sorting comics while discussing some small nuance of one character or another. Even more than that, I long to show him my most recent sketches. I've had plenty of time to draw lately, and the ugly tone of my newest work has an interesting feel that I think is fairly unique. But honestly, I can't give in. I have to get the hell out of Sector Comics! before someone else sees me and makes up a new batch of rumors. Or worse, decides to come in and show Quentin that awful picture of me.

I finally look at him. *Damn, he's cute,* I think as his brown eyes search my face. "I'm sorry. I can't be here." Quentin's brow furrows with concern. Which hurts. He's a really nice guy as long as you're not an underage customer. And I think there could've been something special between us. "I've got to go."

"When can I tell Stan you'll be back?" he asks in a rush. He clearly wants me to stay as much as I need to go. I turn and give him a sorrowful look, ready to break the news that I'm not coming back.

"Wait. A. Minute." Quentin's face suddenly brightens. "I know who you are!"

Oh, God, No! I nearly scream, "It's not me!" I telepathically will him to believe the photo is of some other slut.

"Yes, it's definitely you." He seems oddly happy, and I just continue shaking my head no.

"Just now I saw it so clearly," he says. "You stood in that same doorway looking back at me about five years ago. I can't believe we've been hanging out all this time and I didn't realize it was you."

What? I'm so focused on denying the sext it takes time for me to realize he's talking about the very first time we met when we were young.

"Your dad had an epic battle of the minds with the guy who used to work here." Quentin confirms, and I release the breath I hadn't noticed I was holding. "I've got to tell you, Blaze, your dad was like a huge hero to me that day. It was the first time I realized I might be able to actually do this." He gestures around the shop. "I mean, okay, I don't own the place yet, but I'm doing well enough with my website. Stan and I are discussing how we can best combine our businesses."

I cringe at the thought of him online, but he obviously hasn't come across my photo yet. He's still busy verbally worshiping my dad.

"It was your dad giving words to an opinion I had that made me see I can trust my instincts. He annihilated the other guy's arguments. It was awesome."

Quentin is smiling at me adoringly, and that flirty dimple underneath his lip is practically daring me to walk over and kiss it. I run my hand wistfully over the button-covered front of my messenger bag. I'd love to stay. But I know I need to get the hell out of here before the lies about me and Quentin get even worse. It would feel too awful to open myself to him, only to be rejected when he eventually finds out about my nasty reputation.

"Yeah, my dad's pretty great. I'll tell him you said hi." I turn to go.

"Wait, no." He looks perplexed. Leaning down so his elbows are on the glass counter he looks up at me. "I'm interested in your opinions, not your dad's. He just inspired me, that's all. I really, really enjoy talking to you."

With his messy hair and pleading eyes, he's too freaking cute for me to handle right now. I need to escape his magnetic field. "I've got to go."

I flee, ignoring Quentin's earnest, "Blaze?" that lands on my back.

When I reach Superturd I notice for the first time how much my pink flame job has faded from the sun. It's fitting, since I haven't bothered putting KoolAid in my hair for a few weeks, and it's mostly back to blonde with just a twinge of pink. Not to mention how faded my whole life seems right now. At least everything is all matchy-matchy.

• • •

Making my way down the hall at school the next day I seem to be inspiring pseudo-Tourette symptoms in random people. "Slutbag!" "Skank!" "Ho!"

"Hey, slut! Where's my *Daredevil?*"

It's the last person I can imagine verbally abusing me, and yet here he is. My ex-worshipper. Ryan.

Others glance at us as they pass by, and Ryan's pleased look tells me he's making a play for whatever public attention he can get. I could challenge him, and odds are he'd back down. But really, I just want everyone to go back to ignoring me.

"Oh, um, hi, Ryan," I say feebly, but his jaw stays set. Thankfully the comic is still in my messenger bag, although at this point it's way beyond 'near mint' and deep into 'fine.' I see Ryan lick his lips and glance around the crowded hallway as I pull the *Daredevil* out and silently hand it to him.

I turn to go, but instead of just letting me move on with my miserable life, Ryan actually raises the comic over his head. "Well, thanks a bunch! Now it's got your skanky germs all over it!" He slams it to the ground.

The *Slap!* it makes on the tiled floor makes me flinch.

Laughter springs up in patches as I stare at the crumpled comic. I look at the boy who once groveled for a single moment of my attention. The only reason he even bought the comic in the first place was to have a reason to talk to me. I search Ryan's face for some sign of remorse, but he seems delighted at hurting me.

"In fact…" He glances about. "Why don't you suck my dick, Blaze. You know you've always wanted it."

I turn and run.

As my ears ring with Ryan's words, I head directly to the

parking lot and the safety of the Flaming Superturd of Doom. I'm breathless by the time I reach her, but as I yank open the door, something catches my eye that makes me stop and stare. On the driver's side. Right in the middle of a swirling pink flame.

SLUT!

Someone has keyed the word into the side of my minivan. I feel like I've been physically violated. *Who would deface poor innocent Superturd?* Looking around to see if I'm being watched, I dive into the back, slamming the door behind me. It's nearly winter, but unseasonably warm, and the sun has been beating on Superturd all day. I'm so tired I flop onto the floor, which, I can tell you, is a considerable health risk. The carpet smells like it's harboring a locker room's worth of bacteria. I lie, numbly staring at the crumpled white food bags stuffed under the seat.

The horrific exchange with Ryan replays over and over in my mind. His cruel words are carved into me as deeply as the word *SLUT!* Eventually, I must doze off, because the next thing I know Josh is leaning over me with concern in his voice. "Blaze? You okay?"

I pop up as if he's just shocked me with a cattle-prod. "Yup!" I say brightly, "everything's great." Climbing into the driver's seat, I start Superturd and try to pretend I didn't just spend the last two hours of the school day lying facedown in toxic brown fibers.

"Why did somebody key 'SLUT' into the side of the van?" Josh asks, and I curse myself for not turning it around in the parking space when I had the chance. Of course he saw the crude vandalism when he approached from my side. *Stupid*, I chide myself.

I shrug. "Maybe Superturd has been making time with a conversion van or two." But Josh is busy staring at my face.

"Why is your cheek all red?"

My hand flies up to the side of my face that was nuzzled deep in the science experiment carpet a moment ago. It feels hot, and a brief glance in the rearview mirror shows a speckled pink rash running from cheek to chin.

Sigh.

"Just having one of those days," I tell Josh and turn up the radio full blast to blot out my memory of it.

When we get home, Josh takes advantage of the nice weather, staying in the front yard to kick his soccer ball around. I storm directly into the house.

My car has been vandalized. I'm a complete social pariah. I've been forced to abandon my chances with Quentin. And now my cheek is starting to itch. I toss my messenger bag on the couch, fling my head back, and scream loudly, as if there's a string of capital As rising out of my mouth: "*AAAAAAAAAAA!*"

It feels so good I take a deep breath and am just about to let loose again when the house phone gives a loud *BRIIIING!* I pick it up and blurt an angry, "Hello!" into the receiver.

"Oh, my! Blaze? What are you doing home so early?" It's

Mema Sissy's smooth voice. "I'm calling to wish your mother a happy Name Day."

I bang my temple with the phone. "Mom's still at work, Mema," I say with zero-percent patience in my voice.

"Oh, I am getting a bit forgetful in my old age," says Mema. "I thought she might be home by now."

"I can tell her you called," I offer.

"Hmmm, yes. So tell me, how is that boy Mark you're dating?"

A bit forgetful my butt.

"We were never really dating, Mema."

"I don't know, dear, I already have his Name Day down in my calendar to call you, April twenty-fifth." I can hear her dachshunds barking in the background as Mema goes on. "Mark has always been one of my favorite saints. Most people like Peter for his enthusiasm or John for writing so beautifully, but I'm a Mark fan all the way. In fact, maybe if I'd named your father Mark instead of Michael he wouldn't have turned out to be such a deadbeat."

"Mark and I have totally broken up," I interrupt before she can start ranting about Dad. "And this Mark is definitely *not* a saint."

"Did you know the winged lion is St. Mark's symbol? So majestic! I really regret not giving that name to your awful father..."

I can't take it anymore. I totally lose it on my Mema Sissy. I start with, "Listen here! I know you believe all this crap about names and saints is somehow meaningful..." and it just gets worse from there. By the time Josh walks in the front door, I'm saying some very unholy things into the phone.

His eyes widen as he flings his backpack on the couch. "Who are you talking to?" he mouths, which shuts me up pretty quick.

I stand, holding the receiver out toward him helplessly. "It's, um… Mema?" I squeak.

He stifles a laugh and takes the phone. Pressing it to his ear he says, "Oh my God, Mema, I am *so* sorry! Blaze is taking serious medication for a cold right now and…"

His end of the conversation dissolves into penitent 'yes's and 'sorry's. Until finally he ends with, "I understand, Mema, I'll tell her."

As soon as the phone disconnects, Josh morphs from mild to hysterical as I clap both hands over my mouth. "I can't believe I just let loose on Mema like that," I say. "I'm definitely going to hell."

"It's okay," Josh says. "I'll just be her favorite grandchild for a while." He tips his chin up and frames his smiling face with jazz hands.

The two of us start laughing, and I'm filled with gratitude that Josh doesn't have a clue what's happening to me over at the high school. I know time is shrinking before the rumors reach his grade, but I'm determined to keep him in the dark as long as possible.

When he finally stops laughing, Josh meets my eyes. "You doing okay, sis?"

"Fine." I shrug. "I'm just on the rag and took it out on Mema."

"Ugh! Blaze!" Josh crosses his wrists in front of his face to block my sharing. "Way, way, WAY too much information."

"Well, you asked," I say. "Are you sure you don't want to know details? Like for instance the tampons I use are—"

Josh jams his fingers into his ears and runs from the room loudly singing, "La! La! La! La! La!"

Maybe I should try that technique at school the next time someone calls me a slut, I think, heading for the garage for some paint to cover up the ugly word.

Fortunately, I saved the leftover pink paint from Superturd's flame job and so I cover over *SLUT!* without a problem. Well, other than the fact that there's now one bright pink patch on an otherwise faded pink flame that, if you look at it from the right angle in the sunlight, still says *SLUT!*

With a sigh I put the pink paint away in the garage as in my head I chant, *La! La! La! La! La! La!*

• • •

"Please send Blaze to Principal Hoovlen's office."

The monotoned static voice comes over the loud speaker during biology lab. When I stand up to go, some smartass in the back of the room gives a fake **cough* "whore,"* which gets a few laughs. The whole class is so juvenile and stupid I wonder why I even bother feeling sad as I clutch my books to my chest and barrel out the door.

I just need to ignore them, I think as I make my way toward the school office. *Keep my head down and pretend I'm someplace else.* Surely things can't get any worse.

When I get to the principal's office, the door is propped open and the secretary has her usual classical music blaring out of her computer. Her mild pleasantness tightens as she leads me to Principal Hoovlen's inner sanctum. I walk through the door, and that's when I see it. Physical proof that things can *always* get worse. A leg clad in light blue hospital scrubs. And not just any leg. Mom's leg. *I should just kill myself now and be done with it.*

Mom's back is toward the door, and I avert my eyes as I sink into the chair beside her. I know immediately she's here about the sext and that the evil bald dictator sitting at his desk in front of us is the one who called her in behind my back.

I glance at Principal Hoovlen. He's a total NASCAR fanatic, which is kind of a joke around the school, but he's actually pretty well-liked for a principal. A lot of the football players think he's some sort of chum because he used to be a coach, but I've always been intimidated by him.

It seems as if Mom is too, since she hides her reaction while he tells her about my "situation." To his credit, he manages to avoid using the words "slut," "whore," and "skank-ho." Apparently someone came to him after witnessing my exchange with Ryan. Mr. Hoovlen doesn't have all the details right, but he conveys the theme fairly well. Basically, I've been getting bullied and as he says, "We take this sort of thing very seriously these days."

When he finishes Mom's debriefing, he leans back in his chair, crosses his legs, and interlaces his hands over his knee.

We wait silently for Mom's reaction. She sits erect, eyes closed, chin raised, breathing shallowly. With a final slow, deep breath she seems to pull herself together.

"Do you have a copy of this photo?" Mom asks him calmly.

Principal Hoovlen straightens. "I don't think the indecent photo of your daughter is of consequence at this point, the other students seem to—"

Mom puts her hand out to me. For a moment, I think she's breaking me out due to lack of evidence, but she commands, "Give me your cell phone." I stare at her empty palm. "Right now, Blaze!"

My superhero buttons rattle gently in the silent office as I dig through my messenger bag. I find my phone and hand it over.

At first I think this is just step one of grounding me from all present and future technological devices, but when she turns it on and starts scrolling around I nearly lunge to snatch it back. I should've pretended I lost it or it was stolen or even that I crushed it underneath Superturd's back tire. Anything but let her get a hold of it, because I quickly realize what she's looking for. And it doesn't take long for her to find it either. *Curse that damned photo!*

I can tell the moment she catches sight of it because she sucks in her breath so sharply Principal Hoovlen actually flinches. Mom must've taken in all the air from the room too, because I suddenly can't breathe. A glance at Mr. Hoovlen confirms the sudden scarcity of oxygen.

Mom closes her eyes as she places the phone on the edge of the desk. I reach over and shut it off without looking at the devastating image. I curse myself for not erasing it. *I will definitely be crushing this thing under Superturd's back tire*, I promise as I toss the phone back in my bag.

When Mom opens her eyes they dart quickly to Principal Hoovlen. She draws in another slow, deep breath, nearly suffocating us all. She smoothes the front of her scrub top and places her hands on her lap.

"What do you have to say for yourself, young lady?" she says calmly, which is such an oddball thing to say it makes me realize she's actually concerned about Principal Hoovlen's impression of her mothering skills. She must be feeling judged, because the real Mom would go supernova over that photo.

"I didn't take it."

"Well, you sure looked happy enough to have it taken. Where did you even get that ridiculous underwear?"

"The girls and I were just messing around at the mall." I had been dreading her reaction, but now she's annoying me with her phoniness. "I *do* buy underwear, you know."

Mom glances toward Principal Hoovlen. "Don't you get fresh

with me, miss. I should be at the hospital right now." Mom's eyes dart back and forth. In a low conspiring growl she asks. "What the hell is going on with you, Blaze? First the pink hair and the minivan. Now this awful photo? And what happened on the phone with Mema Sissy? Don't you know we need her to keep paying your gas card? Do you want to ruin everything?" She leans back and widens her eyes at me. "Blaze. Are you pregnant?"

Principal Hoovlen gives a panicked squeak and I sit blinking at her a few moments before I feel it bubbling up from inside. Laughter. I must've snapped, because I can't help it. I start laughing hysterically. "No, Mom, I'm not pregnant." I spit on the *p* sound. "And I have the pink pee stick to prove it." Principal Hoovlen and Mom just sit there, helpless bystanders, as I come completely unhinged.

"Do you think this is some sort of sick joke?" Mom asks. I shake my head and try to look as serious as possible while wiping my eyes and breaking into giggles again and again.

"I hardly think your principal would waste his time if this wasn't very serious, Blaze." She turns to Mr. Hoovlen. "This is all because of her father, you know. He left us nearly five years ago. Took off to New York to pursue some silly dream..."

Anger squashes my laughter. I was bad at suppressing my giggles, but I'm even worse at suppressing my rage. "Would you mind *shutting up* about Dad?" I say to her.

The sound of typing from the next room stops, and everything goes still. Mom just stares at me a few moments. She shifts sideways in her seat and smiles apologetically to my mute principal.

But I'm not finished yet. I've had too much pressure piled on me for far too long. Mema's the one who was always harping on me to find my voice. Now it's time for me to use it.

"I am SO sick of you blaming him for everything." I hear my words, but it feels like it's someone else yelling. "God forbid anyone makes a mistake in your world. Do you have any idea how hard things have been for me?"

"Hard for you?" She finally forgets about pretending to be the perfect mother. "I'm the one who got stuck with all the work while that bastard runs around New York doing whatever he pleases!"

Mr. Hoovlen has the good taste to look completely mortified for the both of us.

"What thanks do I get? You're always acting as if your father is going to swoop in and rescue you," Mom says. "Like he's some sort of hero—"

"This. Is not. About. Dad." I stab her with my words. "I don't blame him for leaving you and Mema. Nobody is perfect enough for you two, ever. God forbid anyone show they're human or make a mistake. I'd leave too, if I could. As a matter of fact..."

With that, I stand up, fling my messenger bag over my shoulder, and storm out of the office.

"Blaze, wait!" Mom calls after me. "Come back here and discuss this."

But I'm already out into the hallway. The secretary's annoying classical music fades as I move away.

I turn back and see Mom standing in the office doorway. She looks deflated in her hospital scrubs, and I'm ashamed to be the one who knocked the wind out of her. She looks from me to the principal, as if deciding how she's supposed to act. Like she needs some sort of instructions to tell her what she should do. A How to Be a Mother manual.

I turn to my right and kick open the emergency exit doors. The alarm blares in protest and begins echoing throughout the school as I march across the student lot toward Superturd.

I need to put an end to this once and for all.

Chapter Sixteen

Whoosh! I'm doing it. I'm taking flight!

I drive well over the speed limit with a map printout lying face-up on the seat beside me. It has a thick yellow line tracing its way across Pennsylvania and into New York City. I'm going to see my dad.

Superturd's back cargo area is loaded with the boxes of comics. I'm headed to his apartment. Dad was a hero to Quentin, and now it's time for him to be a hero to me. It's my turn. I just know he'll be able to help.

I tried to call, but he didn't pick up and I didn't trust myself to leave a message without spilling my guts all over his voicemail. I went ahead and mapped out directions to the address I was supposed to ship the comics to. Now I'm zooming east along Route 80 and glad to be off the winding back roads that led to the interstate. According to Mapquest, the trip to New York will take about six and a half hours, but I really don't want to get to my dad's place in the middle of the night. Before I left, I grabbed my gas card plus all the money I've hoarded over soccer mom season. Of course, I've pretty much spent all my comic book store earnings using my employee discount on comics, but I should be covered if I get sleepy and need to stop at a hotel.

I'm so sick of feeling beaten down, and I'm sure Dad knows exactly what I'm going through. After all, if Mom and Mema were at all tech-savvy, they'd have set up an anti-Dad website to get the whole Internet hating him years ago.

I long to blast the radio, but each time I find a song that fits my mood it dissolves into static before it's even half over. I keep a couple of mix CDs in the van, but I've listened to them each about a million times, and besides, I need an entirely new playlist to capture my dark mood.

Finally, I turn the static-maker off and drive along in silence.

Superturd has never felt so quiet and empty. The interstate's exit signs are spaced miles apart and I find myself hypnotized by the long stretch of blacktop in front of me.

Maybe I can just move in with Dad. He must be doing pretty well by now with all the acting jobs he's been getting. I look down at the address. 162 West Sixty-Fourth Street. Apartment 4-F. I glance up, checking the boxes of comics in my rearview mirror. I'm really coming through for him, getting him his collection on time. That has to count for something, right?

I promise myself I won't have any expectations whatsoever. I'll just show up and see where things lead. I take in the broad sky above the passing mountains and feel hopeful about what I'll find in New York. *Who says you can't run away from your troubles?*

My phone buzzes, and I think it's Mom calling yet again. She's been leaving a series of messages that have gradually gone from angry to worried to officially freaked out. But a glance tells me it's actually a helpful classmate texting to tell me I'm a stupid-ho-bag-slut for setting off the fire alarms.

I reach over and turn the static-maker back on.

• • •

The carnage along Interstate 80 can get to be a bit much after a while. Amid the strips of discarded tire rubber, there's a virtual zoo of dead creatures. I pass one dead skunk, three deer, a groundhog of some sort, four opossums, and a completely mangled raccoon. It's like a morbid game of Cows. As I pass a graveyard visible from the highway, I can't help but think, *Ha, Blaze, everything's dead.*

An ocean of striped cornfields flows by, and the hillsides grow increasingly more scarred by brown power-line paths. I near the half-way point, and the billboards grow more vivid and common.

My stomach growls a complaint since I've eaten nothing but pretzels all day. I shove the empty pretzel bag under my seat, then exit at the next green sign displaying a grid of fast food logos.

Pulling up to the pumps, I hold my breath as I swipe my gas card. I wait for alarms to sound, but the screen just asks me to "please select fuel grade." Apparently Mema isn't actually vindictive enough to mess with my gas card. After filling Superturd with gas, I hit a fast-food drive-through so I won't have to talk to anyone other than the crazy-distorted voice-in-a-box that takes my order. I unpack my Arby's Limited Time Offer BBQ Beef and Cheese and arrange it carefully on my lap before pulling back onto the interstate. Driving with one hand, I shove the sandwich into my mouth with the other. It feels good to be doing something so normal. Eating and driving. Anyone watching might mistake me for a regular girl.

I pass a long car with a back window filled with sun-bleached stuffed animals that I find oddly depressing. The elderly couple driving the car looks somber, although I imagine they must be headed someplace enjoyable. Even if it's only to go bore their grandchildren with a complete history of Christian saints.

For a while I follow close behind a Winnebago, reading the mess of bumper stickers papering the back. There's a large map of the United States covered with colored-in state-stickers, presumably marking all the states they've been to. So far, they've been everywhere except North Dakota and Mississippi. Before today, my map would have only had Pennsylvania and Ohio colored in. And, well, it would still only have Pennsylvania and Ohio colored in, but at least I'm way over to the right-hand side of Pennsylvania for the first time. And if things go as planned, I'll be adding New Jersey and New York to my 'been to' states by tomorrow. It might still look pretty lame on a big ol' chart with only four states colored in, but who the heck needs a stupid braggy map like that anyway?

Annoyed, I speed by the Winnebago and continue on, passing more trucks in the left-hand lane. My mind wanders with the open road, and I wonder if truckers have some sort of social hierarchy. Like, does a guy hauling a pile of logs mock a fellow who drives a truck for Bunce's Bakery? I picture some big, burly guy taunting the poor baked-goods driver, saying, "What'cha hauling there buddy?" The burly guys shifts to a high-pitched girlie voice and mocks, "Cookies?" And the cookie driver hangs his head in shame. Maybe real life is actually like one giant high school experience.

As I contemplate that depressing thought, I slowly overtake a silver truck with purple mud-flaps. The mud-flaps have a silver horseshoe on each side, hanging luck side up. The sides of the truck are so reflective, it's like a giant, rolling mirror-cube. As I pass it going uphill I look over and see the reflection of my minivan, with its faded pink flamejob and the bright pink spot covering up the word *SLUT!*

And reflected from the driver's window, I see myself. Unwashed pinkish hair thrown back into a ponytail. I swipe at what must be a glop of BBQ sauce on my chin and look again. My face is bare and exposed and innocent.

I look so much younger than I feel.

And I am sad for the beaten-down girl reflected back at me.

The marble of regret lodged deep under my ribs shifts with the first sob that comes out. I cry with restraint at first, but the sound of my own sobs is so pathetic that before long, I just break down and go with it—driving and crying as loud as I can. I cry for the humiliating picture and all the shame it has caused me. I cry for all the dirty looks and words flung at me by my classmates. And worse, the faceless mob online with their pitchfork comments. People who don't even know me. Who couldn't hope to know me.

I wail, not caring who can see me or possibly even hear me if their radios are off. I'm almost sound-barrier loud. As I cry, that painful marble dislodges and floats free in my chest for a few moments before it catches again and hangs on until another sob dislodges it.

My face gets numb from my crying, and yet I keep right on going.

I weep for literally miles and miles.

Finally, I'm spent and striving to push more tears out. I let out a wail and then wait for the silence to build again. Wail and wait. Wail and wait. Until a wide-mouthed wail morphs itself into a yawn and I drive in peace for a time.

The calm after all the crying feels good.

I just want to erase everything, like Galactus erasing a planet. I want to erase giving Mark a ride home and going out on our pathetic "dates," and I want to erase ever wondering about what lay under his soccer shorts. Turns out, my fear of penises/peni is not completely unfounded. It starts seeming slightly hilarious that I managed to go from *Su-per Virgin Girl!* to *Su-per Slut!* in under three minutes. All I'd wanted was for Mark to keep playing with my tatas.

I give an involuntary nose-laugh. *Who the hell gives it up in the back of a smelly minivan for a little tata tickling?* I say "tata tickling," out loud and then giggle at how funny that sounds. I say it again, "tata tickling." I start laughing so hard I switch back to sobbing.

This goes on, back and forth, tears and laughter, until finally, I'm so light-headed I decide I should probably pull over and take a break from driving. I pull into the next rest stop and park behind the squat, tan building, far removed from the other cars.

Josh has sent me a text letting me know he knows about the photo and asking how I'm doing. I think of calling him, but I don't have anything comforting I can tell him at the moment. Instead, I send a text to Mom saying I'm staying at Amanda's for a few days and I'm really sorry. Mom calls immediately. *Does she not understand the purpose of a text is to avoid a phone call?*

"Hello?" I say cautiously.

"Oh my god, Blaze, I've been so worried about you!" From the sound of her voice, she's telling the truth.

"I'm fine," I lie. "Just having a sleepover at Amanda's"

"Good for you, sweetheart. You should do more fun things

with your friends." I look at my phone, wondering if there's a tracer on it of some sort.

"Um, okay? I will?"

In one big rush, Mom explains how she and my principal talked about what I've been going through. Mr. Hoovlen helped Mom see that I've been really hurting and need her support. Apparently those NASCAR-types run deep, because Mom sounds as if she's been handed a clue. "We'll have a long talk when you get home," she says, and I can't help but feel a little hopeful by the time we get off the phone. But still think, *if I come home*, as I hang up. It may be best for everyone if I just start a fresh life with Dad.

I can imagine the Blazing Goddess taking on the world with her base of operations in Manhattan. *If it's good enough for Spider-Man, it's good enough for me.*

Reclining my seat, I suddenly feel like I've been hit with a ray-gun and am nearly paralyzed with exhaustion. Driving for such a long time is tiring, but it's the complete emotional meltdown that really took it out of me.

● ● ●

Tap!
Tap!
Tap!

At the sound of keys tapping on my front windshield, I nearly pee all over the front seat of the minivan. I'm having an awful nightmare, and I go from sleeping to wide awake and terrified in about zero-point-two seconds.

Tap!

Tap!

Tap!

When I see it isn't the giant mob of pixilated protestors with chainsaws from my nightmare, I still don't relax all that much.

It's morning, and a middle-aged man peers through my windshield. His graying goatee widens into a smile as he sees I'm awake. He tips his John Deere baseball cap up and calls, "Hello!" as if he knows me or something. I instinctively cover my neck with my hands and shake my head no.

"It's okay!" his voice is muffled through the glass. "Everyone's been looking for you!"

I try to gauge just how crazy he is.

He calls over to his far left, "I found her, sweetie, she's okay!"

Great, and he has a friend. I squint to see if his friend is real or imaginary.

"Oh, thank goodness." A shrill voice floats through the closed windows. *Oh goodie. The friend's real.* I sit up to take a peek at who's been looking for me. A woman joins the man standing in front of my minivan, and she looks so happy to see me I wonder if I actually made friends with these people in my sleep. She wears her hair in a bun and has a big butterfly tattoo on the side of her neck, but in a classy way. She waves to me with long fingers that each sport huge silver rings. The couple's genuine happiness at seeing me finally convinces me to turn the key partway in the ignition so I can roll my window down just a crack.

Together, they scurry over to peer through the opening, like I'm a zoo animal they're admiring. "I'm sorry, but do I know you?" I croak. My face feels like I'm wearing a too-small mask from all my vigorous crying last night.

They look at each other and laugh. "Well, of course not, darlin'," says the woman, prompting me to open the window more, since anyone who calls me "darlin'" can't possibly be life-threatening.

The guy announces, "We-all been keepin' an eye on you since we saw you having such a rough time back there around mile-marker 225 or so."

I blink at the two of them, thinking *who the hell's "we-all"?* but just ask politely, "Who's been watching me?" I glance in my rearview mirror, picturing Uatu the Watcher tucked in one of those boxes.

"Oh, don't you worry none." The man chuckles. "We keep an eye out for four-wheelers who might need a hand. Boy, when we saw the way you was crying yesterday, we kept close tabs on you all the way, well, to here, I suppose. You disappeared around seven last night and channel nineteen's been buzzing ever since with everybody working to get an eyeball on you."

"Channel nineteen?"

"On the CB." The woman smiles. "My handle's Butterfly, and this here's Maniac. The two of us wanted to make sure you were safe. Seemed to us you were *extremely* upset."

"Yeah, well… I'm, uh, dealing with some stuff?" I don't know what to tell my self-appointed guardians, and it's a little over-whelming to think of channel nineteen "buzzing" over me. I've been getting enough unwanted attention on the World Wide Web and don't really need my own radio channel.

"We circled around a few times, then spent the night over by the truck stop in Hazleton off exit 262," says Maniac. "We got a tip early this morning from a fellow on his way to New Jersey. He'd spotted your flamin' four-wheeler at this here rest stop. And sure enough, here you are." He grins as if finding me is incredibly meaningful.

"Sure is an interesting paint job for a minivan," says Butterfly. "Did you do it yourself?"

I nod, trying to get my bearings. The fury that prompted my current pilgrimage has been dampened considerably by all the crying. I wonder if Josh is on the bus to school right now and how he and the boys are reacting to my mortifying photo and fall from grace.

"So, where you headed, darlin'?"

"Oh, God," I start, and that's all it takes for me to unload my whole story on the both of them. As I talk, they lean their faces to my window and listen quietly. A few times Maniac starts saying something, but Butterfly bumps his shoulder with hers and he stops. I keep going. I show them the copy of *The Blazing Goddess vs. Mark the Shark* I have tucked in my messenger bag and it makes them ooh and ahh appreciatively.

When I tell them about getting harassed by my schoolmates, my voice falters and their eyes gloss with tears. Then I explain what comment threads are, and they look perplexed but shake their heads with pity. I finish by putting my head on the steering wheel in despair, but Superturd rejects my self-pity by sounding the horn loudly. My head shoots back up, and the two of them leap back, with Maniac's arm instinctively shielding Butterfly.

"Sorry," I say meekly, and the three of us laugh together.

Butterfly suggests we move our little discussion on to the next exit so we can eat breakfast. "You've got a lot more driving to do," she says.

"We'll jump in the rig, and you can follow us," says Maniac. "There's a real good truck stop up ahead." He looks at Butterfly. "Tuggy's okay with you?"

At her nod, the two of them leave to get their truck, and it isn't until they drive past, sounding the air horn for me to follow, that I realize they're driving the shiny mirrored truck. The one that started me crying. As I follow my own reflection to Tuggy's, I stare at the purple horseshoe mud-flaps and hope I'm a better judge of middle-aged trucker couples than I am of boyfriends.

They could be nuts, I think as I get off the exit behind them, *and I could be about to disappear.*

I feel oddly okay with that.

• • •

"I called off the search party," Maniac says as we sit down at a chunky wooden table in Tuggy's. "We had lots of folks lookin' for ya."

"Sorry." I've decided they're not planning to kidnap me.

"No worries," says Butterfly. "We can be a little over-protective I know."

"We like to think of ourselves as highway guardians," says Maniac. "Channel nineteen is blowing up with fellas glad to hear you're okay."

As I eat "the best egg and pancake breakfast in the northeast" the two of them tell me all about themselves and their mission as sentinel truckers.

"My younger sister disappeared off this highway sixteen years ago." Butterfly gently strokes her neck tattoo as she explains how they may never know whether her sister ran into foul play or disappeared on purpose to get a fresh start. Butterfly has dedicated the past sixteen years first to looking for her sister and then to keeping an eye on women traveling alone. Of course, this had meant she, herself, was oftentimes a woman traveling alone, until she and Maniac met on the CB.

"Channel nineteen," Maniac smiles.

"At first I didn't trust him at all," she says. "Still not sure I do, and we've been married going on nine years now." He gives her a quick rib-tickle and she squirms and laughs in a way that makes her seem young.

"We met by accident, talking while driving side-by-side one night, until he looked over and saw my lips moving."

"And they were the prettiest lips I've ever seen too." Maniac looks at her like he still can't believe she's his.

"Now we mainly drive up and down the east coast, always keeping an eye out for solo travelers," Butterfly says. "Plus we try to grab a load heading west at least every few months or so..."

"To see my daughter, Dorothy," Maniac cuts in, smiling as he stabs his eggs. "That girl has become one of the great loves of my life." I can't help but be impressed by this man's capacity to love. He uses the handle of his fork to pick at the grease caked in the cracks of his palm as he explains that his daughter was estranged for many years.

"Dorothy's mother poisoned the poor girl against her own father." Butterfly looks angry as she says, "*Crazy-Bitch*," under her breath.

"That's what we call my ex-wife," says Maniac, grinning. "Crazy-Bitch."

The two of them explain how his ex-wife tried to turn Dorothy against him, but she eventually saw through her mother's lies.

"Crazy-Bitch always did love running the truth through a meat grinder." Maniac frowns.

Butterfly lays a hand on the side of his goatee. "But then, without Crazy-Bitch, we wouldn't have Dorothy."

"We wouldn't have our Dorothy," he agrees. "She is such a joy." The two of them smile at each other, making me nauseous over how beautiful both of their awful, messy lives have turned out for them. Suddenly, I'm not in the mood for the eggs on my plate and I'm nervous about seeing my father.

When I look up, Butterfly's watching me. As if she's read my mind she says, "You know, Blaze, your Daddy will be lucky if he gets to know you better. Not being in your life has been *his* loss."

"Maybe he's been waiting for a chance to spend some time with you," adds Maniac. "Give him that chance. You never know what can happen."

"Right," I say, trying to look optimistic. "You never know."

"There you go." Butterfly practically explodes with happiness over the idea that the two of them helped me. "Now, I've got something special for you." She reaches into her enormous quilted bag and pulls out a scroll of blue velvet. When she unrolls it, I see it's actually a portable jewelry display holding rows of silver rings in square velvet slots. She traces her finger across a row of thick rings. "Here it is," she pinches one of them up and holds it for me to see. "I knew this was yours just as soon as I heard your name. Not that your car's paintjob hadn't already put it to mind. See there." She slides the ring smoothly onto the middle finger of my right hand, "Perfect fit."

I look down at my finger and have to grin. The ring is more of a finger-cuff, really, since the thick silver runs the whole way up to my knuckle. Twisting flames are carved all around, and it couldn't be more perfect if I'd designed it myself. "It's beautiful," I say, "but I can't." I start pulling it off my finger half-heartedly, protesting "It's too nice," but am relieved when they stop me.

"That there is a Butterfly Original," says Maniac. "There's no taking it off your finger once she's set it there."

"It's a gift, from my hands to yours," she says firmly. "I probably give away more of these things than I sell, but trust me, when I do sell one or two, I make more than enough to pay for all my charity."

I smile at her briefly, but I can't take my eyes off the ring for long. There's a silhouette of a bird in the very center of the flames that I didn't even notice at first. A phoenix. As I study the ring, Butterfly explains what I already know about the bird rising out of the flames. "It comes from Greek mythology," she says, "but I've given the symbol my own twist. In my experience, sometimes the only way folks can manage to become the person they're meant, is to have destiny fling them straight into the fire."

"You've clearly got yourself in a fiery 'nough situation," nods Maniac. "Couldn't help but notice the profanity on the side of your van."

Butterfly holds my hand with the ring on it and looks me in the eye. "I was known as a slut back in high school."

I look at the plump middle-aged woman facing me and have to work to stifle a giggle.

"It's okay, you can laugh," she smiles. "See, I never allowed what folks thought of me to change who I am. Let 'em call me a slut. Didn't make me act like one. Now, my sister, on the other hand." Butterfly looks at her hands. "She allowed her bad reputation to carry her down a dark path. Figured she might as well be what she was accused of." She shakes her head sadly.

"I'm so sorry," I say and she nods.

"Don't let getting called names change you into something you're not," she says.

"Yes, ma'am," I say.

"And every time you look at this ring." Butterfly holds up my hand. "I want you to remember who you are, Blaze. Fire is a powerful element. No matter how beaten down or how stuck you may feel, you have the power to rise up anew."

I smile weakly, thinking how much I want to believe her. Maniac sits nodding and looking back and forth between us. "Well now," he says, "speaking of rising up, I know it's still morning, but this place has an apple crisp that is to die for."

I grin in spite of myself and give my awesome new ring a spin around my finger. "I'm in!"

"There's our girl," says Butterfly, and all I can say is Maniac sure does know his apple crisp, because it's absolutely delicious.

Who knows? I think as the cinnamony sweetness hugs my tongue. *Maybe Dad and I will turn out to be like Maniac and his daughter, Dorothy.* Our relationship wasn't even completely severed for fourteen years like theirs was.

As I give Maniac and Butterfly each a solid hug goodbye and thank them earnestly, Butterfly whispers in my ear, "Those of us that must rise above our circumstances know what we're made of deep down. Don't you let anybody make you forget what you're made of, sweetheart."

Which would be really helpful advice if I were made of something solid, like maybe Colossus's organic steel, or the Thing's orange stone, or even Iceman's ice. But I'm pretty sure that way deep down, all I'm made of is Fluffernutter.

Chapter Seventeen

I still haven't been able to reach Dad, but once I'm back on the road I try dialing him again with my story all set in my head. I'll tell him Mom and I discussed it and decided this was a good opportunity for me to check out the city, since I'm thinking of maybe going to college in New York. It's a complete and total fabrication, of course. My college applications have been side-tracked by hopelessness and sit in an untouched stack under my bed. But I also know he won't call Mom to check out my story. One of those side benefits of having parents who loathe each other.

"Hey there, kiddo, what's shaking?" Dad says when my call goes through.

"Oh, hey there, Dad, I—"

"I know, I know. You must've gotten the phone message I left yesterday about needing those comics for the Javits Center today."

Wrong. "I—"

"And," he interrupts, "Since they're not here, I assume you want to apologize for not getting them overnighted yesterday."

"Actually, I—"

He sighs loudly. "Yeah. It's okay, really. I mean, I was sort of counting on them being here for Comic-Con, but that's sure not happening. I'm actually dressed already and working my way into character."

"Oh, I didn't know…"

"That's right, sweetie!" His tone brightens as he apparently forgives me for letting him down. "I've got a great gig playing a new character! The Red Cardinal! How cool is that?"

"So, you'll be like a priest who wears one of those big, tall hat thingies?"

"What? No, I'm not playing a Catholic cardinal, I'm the *Red* Cardinal. He's a brand new superhero character!" Dad sounds so excited my resolve falters. *He doesn't have time to rescue me.*

I try to sound glad for him, "Wow, Dad! Congratulations. I haven't heard of him, but he must be pretty great if they're making a movie about him."

"No, no. Not a movie. Well, that is, not a movie *yet*." Dad laughs. "I've been working hard on this role and, hey, you never know who might see me at the Con. All sorts of producers and directors show up at these things, and this is exactly the sort of role that could get me discovered."

"So you're working—"

"At Comic-Con today! Over at the Javits Center. Isn't that great? So listen, sweetie. I've really gotta go. I can't very well show up there and be in character as 'Blaze's dad,' can I?" He laughs again. "Just try to pop those boxes off to me whenever you get a chance, okay?"

I look in my rearview mirror at the boxes of comics and try to imagine how much it would cost to ship them. I can picture myself handing over two giant white sacks with big black dollar signs printed on the sides. As I'm distracted, my dad must finish talking and hang up, because by the time I try to explain that I'm on my way to bring him the comics in person, he's gone.

Well, nice talking to you too, Dad. It certainly isn't the first time I've had a one-sided conversation with him, but this is the first time it really matters.

I mentally scroll through my options as I continue driving east on Route 80. Of course, I could try to call him back, but my first instinct is to turn my minivan around at the next exit and go back to face my rotten life. But then, the next exit doesn't come up for another twenty miles, and in the meantime I rub my phoenix ring and think of Butterfly's encouragement. I keep hearing Dad's voice saying "the Jarvis Center" over and over until I know just what to do.

• • •

"Excuse me, how do I get to the Jarvis Center?"

I've survived the trip through the filthy, white-bricked Lincoln Tunnel and find myself driving along the crowded streets of Manhattan. They should really have more caution signs warning that you're entering New York City and maybe post a few tips on how to not drive into anyone. I telepathically command Superturd to suck in her bumpers as I creep along 42nd Street with a sea of other cars.

I reach down to massage my right calf. Traffic has built steadily since I passed through New Jersey, and I've been pumping the gas and brake so much my muscles are cramping up. My directions show me how to get to my dad's place, but he'll be long gone by now. I need to find the Jarvis Center.

I have no idea if I should be headed uptown or downtown or even which direction is uptown or downtown. The sound of horns honking is constant, and I'm hit with the smell of charcoal. I hope nothing's on fire, because we're all pretty much packed between the buildings with no place to run.

The people of Manhattan seem glossy and mint-out-of-the-box, many of them wearing business suits with their hair slicked back. Both male and female. The official city color seems to be head-to-toe black, but there are plenty of dissenters who display their individuality by dressing like freaks. I grip the steering wheel at ten and two, taking in the crazy outfits accessorized with a plethora of chains, piercings, and mohawks. Every hair color imaginable is represented within five city blocks. I've seen old ladies with blue hair, but never bright green before. My pink is quite unremarkable all of a sudden. I'm clearly not in Butler anymore.

I try asking a few pedestrians for directions, but they mostly look at me like I'm crazy or something. Like, pedestrians and drivers don't speak to each other in this city, despite being the two main ingredients, with a few cyclists sprinkled in for flavor. Flavor of *crazy*, that is. Because one thing's for sure—the protective buffer of my minivan is my only comfort right now. I vow to never wish Superturd into anything small and cool and carjack-worthy ever again.

No wonder so many superheroes hang out in Manhattan. It's a savage concrete wonderland with more people packed on one sidewalk than there are in my entire high school. It's only too easy to imagine costumed heroes standing on the skyscrapers and swinging between the buildings on either side of me.

And I'm keeping an eye out because, boy, could I use a super-hero about now.

"Excuse me, how do I get to the Jarvis Center?" I repeat over and over, feeling like I may end up trapped here in endless traffic for all eternity. Everyone seems to be in a hurry to get somewhere important. I feel the most lost I've ever felt.

I finally manage to get a nice-looking couple on the side-walk to respond to my question. Unfortunately, their answer is to laugh and clap each other on the back as they tell me with Swedish accents that they're tourists too. Apparently they're flattered to have some teenager in a minivan from the sticks mistake them for New Yorkers.

As I continue down 42nd Street, I see marquees for movies-turned-musicals, and the traffic grows steadily even tighter. Following my Mapquest printout, I make a right onto 10th Avenue. Mapquest has no idea where Jarvis is, but nobody else seems to want to help me. I inch my way down the center lane as cars, cabs, and buses continually cut in front of me. Looking up, I spot a woman on top of a red double-decker bus snapping a picture of my minivan's paintjob. Which I might find completely hilarious under different circumstances.

A few blocks later, my first real New Yorker finally speaks to me.

I call out to a taxi driver for what feels like the zillionth time. "Where is the Jarvis Center?!"

The cabbie looks over and smiles at me. Nodding, he calls back, " هل أستطيع مساعدتك؟ "

Great.

"You mean *Javits*." A voice floats from my other side. I turn to my left, and above my window is a young man leaning from the cab of a big black semi. "You're Butterfly and Maniac's girl!" He seems pleased to see me. "I recognized the flame job on your van. Nice. Those two had everybody within range looking for you last night." He's tan and good-looking, with teeth that crowd a bit in the front. "Heard the news this morning they called off the hounds, but it's still good to see you're okay."

The kindest fellow in Manhattan has me follow him toward the Javits Center, which, as it turns out, is back in the direction I came from. He gestures where I'm to turn right, and I wave my thanks. He honks his booming horn in response, and for a split second I have the image of myself as a trucker, meeting nice people and seeing all the states from the cab of a semi. I could even get one of those big maps and fill in all the colored stickers as I visit every state.

But I still have something I have to do before I resort to a life of trucking. I need to find my dad.

• • •

Finding him may be an even bigger super-challenge than finding the Javits Center.

The moment I see the giant glass Mecca, I start feeling overwhelmed. Huge red banners proclaim "COMIC-CON," and people flow inward from every side. It's as if they're being sucked off the streets by a giant vacuum. I drive past the building and finally find a parking spot seven blocks beyond. I read and re-read the cryptic coded parking signs before finally deciding that since it's not between 2 a.m. and 6 a.m. on a Monday, Wednesday, or Friday, and it's not between midnight and 3 a.m. on a Tuesday,

Thursday, or Saturday, it might be okay to leave the minivan for one-hour parking. Maybe. And unless the No Standing During Emergency, Snow Route sign is invoked, which seems unlikely considering the warmish day we're having, I feel about fifty-fifty that Superturd won't get towed. *Good enough for me.*

I walk toward Javits with the massive flow of happy Comic-Con goers. There's an electricity flowing through the clumps of people wearing superhero T-shirts and *Star Wars* T-shirts and T-shirts with snarky sayings like *You read my T-shirt; that's enough social interaction for today*. I'm entering an utter mob scene. I can't help but feel a little bit excited.

My eyes widen as I step onto the tiled floor of the four-story-high glassed-in entryway. I take a program from a giant bin by the door that's filled to the top. As I casually read it over, my inner geek-girl does a funky dance in my chest. *Happy*, is all I can think as I scan the list of exhibitors. Besides all the major comic book publishers, there are movie giveaways, book signings, and a number of young celebrities popping by. There's even a section where artists can have their artwork evaluated. I touch my messenger bag and think of the copy of *The Blazing Goddess vs. Mark the Shark* tucked neatly inside. Pushing that spark of hope down, I think, *just gotta find Dad.*

I follow the crowd to another bin labeled "Badge Holders" and take out one of the red ribbons covered with sponsor names clipped to an empty plastic pocket. It's apparently designed to hold the colorful cards I see a number of people waving gleefully. I place it around my neck and step onto the line marked "Didn't Order Badges Online." Considering the throng of people moving across the giant hall, the line isn't very long. I soon discover why. Comic-Con has totally sold out and they aren't selling any more entry badges.

"Should've ordered online, babe," says the guy behind the counter. "Or at least gotten here by six a.m. to wait in line." He's wearing a T-shirt with a *POW!* design that says "Comic-Con Staff" on it. "Cool bag, though." He points to my superhero button collection, and then he's finished with our conversation. But I can't be. I have to get into that exhibit hall and find my father. If I try waiting at the doors and hoping to spot him, my minivan filled with precious comics will get towed for sure. Thinking fast, I reach into my "cool" messenger bag.

"Do you know where Butler, Pennsylvania is?"

The guy looks annoyed I'm still here, despite his claim that he likes my bag.

"Well, let me tell you," I rush on. "It is very far away. Very far. And I drove here through the night just to meet some publishers and get my work evaluated."

I open my comic to face him, and he leans in, taking in the pages as I leaf through a few of them. "These aren't bad," he says, placing his palm on a layout that shows *The Blazing Goddess* displaying ample flexibility. "She seems cool, what's her story?"

"Oh, she's just this character I've been playing around with…" and with that the two of us are discussing comics and super powers and such until finally he opens a drawer behind the counter and holds up one of the shiny square badges. It nearly has a radioactive nimbus around it.

"You don't know how lucky you are my buddy got pink eye," he says sternly. "He was still gonna come, dressed as Nick Fury, but his moms caught him and wouldn't let him leave the house." He hands me the entrance ticket to paradise.

"Thank-you-thank-you-thank-you!" I say. "And thank your buddy with the pink eye."

"Would you sign this for me?" he gestures to the copy of *The Blazing Goddess* still on the counter. And since I don't want to seem ungrateful, I sign over the only copy I have with me.

"Good luck in there, and don't be forgetting this face. I wanna see myself in one of your comics one day." He swirls his hand around his face and gives me a hammy pose. "It'll be cool if you can make me into some totally twisted evil dude."

"You got it!" I grin from ear to ear as I place the precious card in the plastic holder and join the gleeful, geeky throng headed to the huge, three-story escalators. Stormtroopers stand on either side, and I barely resist the urge to give one of them a hug as I pass through.

A guy dressed in head-to-toe camo rides up the escalator beside me, and as we ascend to the giant exhibit floor, my mouth falls open. "Holy Shit," is G.I. Joe's assessment and I have no choice but to agree. *Holy Shit.*

The space stretching out in front of us is huge and bright and chock-filled-to-the-top with awesomeness. Colorful figures fight for my attention, and I can practically feel my pupils enlarge to anime size as I try to take it all in. The enormous space opens three stories high and is so jam-packed with glorious geeks I can barely see the blue carpet. I wish Quentin was here with me.

Comic-Con makes the rest of Manhattan seem like bingo night at the Butler VFW. Regularly dressed people like me are just background noise to the costumed characters punctuating the crowd. Three caped vampires argue with frothing fangs, as a team of very realistic-looking Ghostbusters stomp by. I stand, frozen with awe, as a bald black man floats smoothly past, his creepy orange contact lenses boring through me. He's followed by Super Mario, who wears a red cap and blue overalls and carries a blow-up mallet slung over his shoulder. You barely even notice that Super Mario looks more Asian than Italian.

A shove from behind makes me look up in time to watch a huge green Hulk stalk by with a papier-mâché head and light-up purple eyes. A small mob suddenly lunges to help a girl in a homemade plastic cat suit who drops her cell phone. "Can somebody please get that?" she calls out, "I can't bend over!" I admire her courage—wearing little more than a skin-tight quilted hefty bag out in public. I'll tell you what though, despite her less than ideal figure, she struts away totally working that hefty bag. This is an alternate reality I never want to leave.

Impulsively, I hold out my cell phone, give a huge, geeky grin and take my picture with Comic-Con in the background. I send it to Quentin with the text "Guess where I am??" My phone rings almost immediately. After a pause I answer, hold it out toward the roaring crowd and ask, "You hear that?"

"I cannot believe you didn't invite me!" Quentin shouts.

"Sorry! It was very last minute. I just jumped in my minivan and drove. To be honest, I didn't even know this was where I was headed until I got here."

"Blaze… been meaning to… you…" I'm having a hard time hearing him. "Do… like… ?"

"What?" I can't make out what he's saying over the din of excited con goers, but I think he asked me something about limes.

Finally, he practically screams into the receiver, "I asked if you like the taste of limes!"

Moving into a corner, I face the wall and jam a finger in my ear so I can hear him better. "Did you just ask me if I like limes?"

He laughs. "It's my nerdy attempt to ask you out. I promised myself if I heard from you again I was going for it." He goes on in a rush, "There's this classic old comic where the Swamp Thing and his girlfriend Abigal Arcane kiss and she says he tastes like limes…"

"Swamp Thing? More DC? Really?" There's a long pause on

the phone before I take a breath and add, "Sounds like there's still a lot you can teach me."

I can hear his smile through the phone. "DC comics guide, at your service."

"Quentin, this probably isn't the best way to do this, but I have something I have to tell you." With that, I spill everything about the sext photo and getting harassed and even about *The Blazing Goddess vs. Mark the Shark* being a revenge comic.

It turns out he had that last part figured out all along. "I just took it as a warning to take things slow and to never double-cross you."

I laugh, feeling lighter than I have in a long time. "So it doesn't bother you that people are all talking about me?"

"Haven't you ever heard the line, 'Great minds discuss ideas, average minds discuss events, and small minds discuss people'?" His voice deepens on the other end. "Blaze, don't let a bunch of small minds make you question who you are."

I blush and smile. "But what sort of minds discuss comics?"

"The very best kind, of course." Looking around at the freaks, nerds, and superheroes surrounding me I can't help but agree.

"Thank you. I'm sorry I didn't just tell you what was going on."

"I'm glad you finally did. So… would it be awful if I searched around online for that photo of you?"

"Quentin!"

"Totally kidding, I promise. But I do happen to have some

mad hacking skills and might be able to help you get some of the posts and things taken down. But only if you promise me one thing."

"What," I say cautiously.

"Promise me next year we're going to Comic-Con together."

"I can hardly wait." We say our goodbyes, and I grin at my phone for a moment after we hang up. A text immediately comes through from Quentin.

When can we get together for a little lime-tasting?

I write back:

Let it go, Swamp Thing.

Then I add:

But face it, tiger… you just hit the jackpot!

Of course Quentin freaks out over that because he knows those are Mary Jane Watson's first words to Spider-Man. *Yes, we shall be the greatest nerd fancouple of all time.*

Just then, two Jedi knights angle their way through the mix, their glowing green lightsabers held up in front of them as they chant together: "Stay on target. Stay on target."

Okay, right! "*Stay on target,*" I think. *Red Cardinal. Look for the color red. I must focus on finding Dad, and he will be wearing lots of red.*

My eyes are drawn to the giant red Marvel section, and I automatically move toward it. *Spidey is red. And Iron Man, Captain America, and Thor all have red.* I continue working my way through the crowd, approaching the Marvel banners arranged like a floating square above the section. *The Marvel booth has red carpet,* I notice. And my heart starts beating faster as I see some of my favorite heroes walking around on the Marvel red carpet, posing for pictures with fans.

I can't resist the urge to run up and give the Amazing Spider-Man a huge hug. It's a really great moment for me.

Finally Spidey unhooks my arms from around his neck and eases them gently between us and I realize I've been hanging on him inappropriately. But I just stay there anyway, staring into his large, white, tear-shaped eyes. Even with his face completely covered, I can sense he's uncomfortable with my level of familiarity.

Thinking fast, I pull out my cell phone and click the camera key. "Excuse me, would you take our picture?" I ask the closest fanboy. With a renewed sense of purpose, Spider-Man puts his arm around me and shoots out an invisible web with his other hand. I put one hand on his chest and lean in for a moment, then rethink my pose. Widening my stance, I place my fists on each hip, and channel my best Blazing Goddess. I feel like I've just had a brush with destiny.

The fanboy hands me back my phone, and I turn my head in time to see him. My dad. Except that I can't exactly see his face. It's covered with an enormous red-feathered head. *The Red Cardinal.*

To borrow a phrase from G.I. Joe, "Holy Shit."

• • •

There is really no way to overstate the size of the Red Cardinal's head. I watch from the safety of the next aisle as my dad waves to folks on their way to the Marvel booth and tries to hand them what appear to be handfuls of red feathers. The people are mostly ignoring him.

Only Dad's cleft chin is exposed. The rest of him is covered in feathers from head to toe. Literally. Giant red feather-coated head to red feather-coated boots. The costume must've cost a lot of money to design and construct. The head itself is a work of garish art with an exaggerated red crest sticking up like a wicked cowlick on radioactive steroids. Huge orange glass eyes stare from where my dad's ears should be, and the orange cone of a beak emanates from his forehead. The black around the cardinal beak comes down as far as the bridge of my dad's nose, and his eyes must be painted with black makeup because every time he blinks they disappear entirely.

I look around, my mind whirring with embarrassment for my father. My eye catches a chubby make-shift Captain America holding a shopping bag with rolled-up posters sticking out. The guy has mini-wings on either side of his head, and his blue Lycra-clad gut is hanging over red and white striped briefs. Yet, my dad is still the guy's equal in the public humiliation department.

A loud "Wheeet! Wheeet! Wheeet!" birdcall rings out, and when I realize it is coming from the Red Cardinal, I decide my only course of action is to flee Comic-Con before he spots me.

So, of course, that's right when the Red Cardinal spots me.

The only part of his face that I can see grins widely as he motions with his red-feathered wing for me to come over. I paste on a fake smile.

He gives a few more piercing, "Wheeet! Wheeets," as I draw closer, and he shifts excitedly from feathered boot to feathered boot when I reach him. I instantly forgive him for looking so embarrassing.

"Blaze! My God." He's so happy I decide the giant red head looming over us isn't even all that bad. "What are you doing here? I can't believe it."

I just stand, basking in the glow of how thrilled he is to see me.

He hands me a feather, explaining, "This is just one of the promotions the team came up with to get a little buzz going for the Red Cardinal. If things go well here today, they're sending me to the San Diego con! Isn't that great?"

I take the red feather and twirl it between my fingers, smiling up at him. I can't wait to ask about spending time together and wonder how soon the Red Cardinal will be able to take a break.

He licks his lips in excitement. *See, I knew Dad would be here for me.* He asks, "So, where are the comics?"

The red feather drops from my fingertips.

"Whoa, don't want to lose that, Pigeon." He scrambles to catch the floating feather with his clumsy wing-arms. "You're going to want a little memento one day when I'm starring in my first movie role as the Red Cardinal." He says "the Red Cardinal" like an announcer declaring something important. "I've finally learned how to really open myself up to success, and good things are starting to flow toward me now. Here you go."

He's handing me another feather, and I'm not sure if he managed to somehow catch the one I dropped, or if he's just giving me a new one from the pouch at his waist. I see egg grenades lined up along his belt and know for sure there will never be a movie based on the Red Cardinal, starring my dad or anyone else. It's a bad idea, and if Dad knew anything about superheroes, he'd know it too.

I look up into his eager eyes, coated in black paint, and he repeats, "The comics, Blaze?" as if I maybe didn't hear him. *He was never going to rescue me.*

I feel something in my mind snap.

I envision jumping up and punching that stupid red head. I want to knock the damned thing off and make Dad look at the truth. Standing right in front of him. His daughter is here, and she needs to be seen. But he may as well be looking out of those stupid, useless, orange glass eyes.

I fixate on the left one. Big dome of glass. Pupil staring blindly. *Stupid bird.*

"Blaze, sweetie?" Dad sounds concerned, but I can't look away, I can only envision the deep pleasure that would be hauling off and punching the Red Cardinal directly in that eye. *Thwack!* I hate the fact that Mema and Mom were right about him all along. My hand balls into a fist without me telling it to as I continue staring at the dead glass eye. I feel a berserker wrath rising up and…

"Hey! I didn't know you brought Josh!" The Red Cardinal's nonsensical outburst jolts me from my trance.

I turn slowly in the direction he's looking. "Wow, you brought the whole crew," he exclaims, and sure enough, there they are.

Walking toward us through the crowd. The shabbiest-looking team of superheroes I've ever seen. My cretins.

Ajay wears gloves and a towel-cape over one shoulder that declares "Florida Is for Lovers." Andrew has a red bandana mask tied around his head with eye-holes cut out. Dylan has on a white wig and a shiny silver catsuit, and Josh, bless him, has on a rather authentic-looking Superman suit. "Hey, sis." He is the most heroic-looking thing I've ever seen. "They were letting kids with costumes in for five bucks. We would've been over here sooner, but we had to drag Ajay away from the Nintendo section."

"Wha—? How?" I'm completely confused. "What did you do? Fly here?"

Josh fingers his cape. "Yeah, sure, 'like a bird!'" He panto-mimes flying like Superman and laughs. "More like a 'speeding locomotive.'"

"You boys took the train?" I'm ready to throw a full-on fit. "Do your parents know—"

"You mean the boys aren't here with you?" The Red Cardinal asks me stupidly.

"Oh, they're here with me all right…"

"Relax, sis, everything's cool. We took the train right into Penn Station."

"That's just up the road," confirms the annoying red bird at my back. "Good to see you, Josh." He offers Josh a feather.

Josh ignores it. "I heard Dad's message about Comic-Con and just knew you'd show up here. Mom thinks I'm sleeping over at Ajay's house."

"More asking for forgiveness, not permission?" I ask, and Josh nods sheepishly.

"We got here faster than you did driving," says Andrew. He adjusts his mask by sticking his fingers in the eyeholes and pulling up.

"It seemed way longer, though, since I forgot to bring my charger." Ajay glances back at the three-story Nintendo banner. "Once I lost power, there was nothing to do but count cows."

"I won." Josh raises his hands in victory just as a busty girl wearing a slave Princess Leia coat-hanger bikini walks by and smiles at him. Andrew has to physically restrain Dylan from chasing after her, but regardless, the boys are obligated to observe a moment of silent worship, which is when the stupid Red Cardinal decides to chirp in.

"So, Blaze, I really need to get back to work here." He's still trying to hand red feathers out to random people. "But if you could get me those comics, that would be awesome."

Josh's gaze abandons Princess Leia to look me in the eyes. I roll mine.

I finger my new ring. I know Butterfly had her own meaning attached to it, but as soon as I saw the hidden bird, for me, it was all about the Phoenix Force. The nexus of all psionic energy, the Phoenix Force bonds with its host and wields almost limitless power. With Jean Grey it embodied everything from the powerful White Phoenix of the Crown to the Dark Phoenix, a seriously kick-ass villain. I rub my ring with my left hand. *Today I think she's feeling a little dark.*

Josh is still watching me, so I give him a small wink. "Sure, Dad." I smile up at the giant bird. "They're all packed up in the back of Supertu… er, they're in the back of the minivan and ready to go."

"Wow, Blaze, that's so great!" Dad is happy. "I had hoped I'd be able to get a good price for them here at Comic-Con, and the

Red Cardinal guys gave me a thumbs up to display them at their table." He nods his giant red bird head. "Looks like everything's gonna work out just super."

"Looks that way," I agree, smiling. I spin around and call, "Come on, boys. Help me get our dad his comics, will ya?"

To the Red Cardinal I say, "We'll meet you out front in twenty minutes or so, okay?"

His smile is wide. "Wow, kid. Thanks. I don't know what I'd do without you."

"I know, I know." I snatch another feather from his outstretched hand and head out the doors, my adolescent pseudo-superheroes falling in behind me.

Chapter Eighteen

Twenty minutes later, the boys and I are standing out in front, facing the Javits Center doors. Together, we've moved the boxes from the back of my (*not towed!*) minivan to where they are now, piled up on the sidewalk in front of us. The boys stand, two on either side of me, their homemade costumes hanging limp from the strain of our activity. Ajay seems to be breathing a little heavy, and I toss him his inhaler from the inner pocket of my messenger bag. He gives me a nod, pulling his glove up tighter, and opens his mouth wide for a quick squirt.

By the time my dad comes out, pushing a handcart to collect the boxes, a bit of my fury has faded. I no longer feel the unquenchable urge to punch him in the big orange eye. He looks so ridiculous trying to maneuver the glass door with the rolling cart and that stupid giant bird head—I almost feel sorry for him. Josh must sense my weakness, because he puts his hand on my arm and channels his Superman strength to me.

Our dad makes his way toward us, his red bird head nodding.

I'm incredibly calm as I turn to one of the exiled smokers standing nearby. "Hey, buddy, got a light?"

The heart-attack-waiting-to-happen sizes me up, shrugs, and hands over a plastic lighter. I quickly roll up the flier I'm holding in my hand, light it, and hold it out over the boxes piled at our feet.

Dad pauses, tilts the handcart to stand on its own, and stares at us. Even with his face obscured by the giant bird head, I can see he's confused.

"Hey, Dad!" I call. "You maybe should've thought more carefully about what you decided to name me. I've grown into a wildfire that won't be put out." In my peripheral vision, I see a crowd is gathering. "You wanted your precious comics. So here they are."

With that, I lower my torch and light the corners of the top box. Dad stands motionless as the boys on either side of me quickly pull out their fliers and start lighting and spreading, lighting and spreading the fire. Before anyone can make a move to stop us, we have the entire stack of boxes burning.

Once the fire's going, I flick the feather dad gave me into it before pulling the inventory list out of my messenger bag. I begin reading loudly, "*Fantastic Four*, 1961, issue numbers one through sixteen! *Fantastic Four*, 1981, issues two-three-five through two-five-one…"

The crowd around us gasps in horror and heart-attack-to-go

guy nearly flings his body onto the burning boxes. Luckily, a younger guy holds him back, because the fire is really going by now and his burning corpse would've smelled pretty rank.

"*The Amazing Spider-Man*, 1978, issue numbers one-seven-six through one-nine-six." I continue reading my list to the *Argh!*'s and *No!*'s and even occasional screams from the crowd when I read off some of the particularly rare and expensive items. "*Tales of Suspense* number thirty-nine!" I call out and hear a loud whimper, meaning that at least somebody realizes it's the very first appearance of Iron Man. When I glance up at my dad, I see that he's using the handcart to hold himself and his enormous red bird costume upright. Reaching up slowly, he pulls the cardinal head back like a giant hood, revealing his hair, all sweaty and plastered to his head. His blackened eyes are closed.

When I picture how he looks in that moment, when we turn and leave him there like that, with those boxes still burning, I like to think my dad feels remorse.

I hope that underneath all those phony red feathers, he's mourning more than his burning comic collection. I hope he's mourning me and Josh and all that was and can never be again. I hope he regrets letting go of everything that he should have held on to.

I take my brother's hand as we walk away from the blazing fire in slow motion. It's about time we rescued ourselves.

• • •

"You know, Blaze." Dylan pauses before climbing into the back of Superturd. "I thought your pose in that photo was rather tasteful."

"That photo shall never be spoken of in this minivan! Ever!" I command.

He holds up his hands. "I barely even looked, honest."

"Right," I say, "and my beauty mark is…"

"Directly underneath your right nipple," Dylan recites, then winces. "Honestly, Blaze, I still respect you."

Josh shoves Dylan shaved-head first into Superturd and says to me, "What I don't get is, why is it okay for models to show everything they've got?" He gestures to a towering billboard that features an underwear model with swirling hair. "But when a regular girl does the same thing, she's suddenly accused of being a slut. Seems unfair, don't you think?"

I look up at the girl in the ad. Her exaggerated pose makes it seem as if she thinks her breasts are her source of power. "Who knows?" I say. "Maybe she gets called a slut too. At least my picture isn't five stories high in the middle of Manhattan." I think about how exposed that must make her feel and decide my little cell phone photo circulating around Butler may not be the absolute end of my life after all.

It hurts like hell to be gossiped about, but I've come to realize that what other people think of me is honestly none of my business.

As Josh and I climb into the front, I ask him, "So how on earth did you even know I was here?"

"Mom mentioned something about you staying at Amanda's. I know you hate Amanda and her mom doesn't like you, so that had to be a lie." Josh rubs the back of his neck. "Then I heard Dad's message on the machine about needing his damn comics for Comic-Con, so I checked the basement, saw the comics were gone, and knew right away where to find you."

"But how did you pay for train tickets?"

Josh grins. "I stashed a handful of dad's comics away a long time ago. Sort of an emergency fund. Quentin gave me a good price for them."

"I'm sure he ripped you off." I laugh.

"He said to have you call him."

I blush. "Yeah, we already talked."

Superturd immediately erupts with sing-song teasing. "Ooooh, Blaze and Quentin..."

I nod and laugh at the taunts, not really minding all that much. "All right, enough, enough. I still can't believe you guys just showed up."

Andrew says, "We followed the flow of folks to Comic-Con and bought our costumes along the way."

Ajay flips his towel cape behind him. "Four bucks from a homeless guy selling stuff. Instead of a yard sale, it was a shopping cart sale."

The other boys start reciting what they paid for their make-shift costumes, but I just keep staring at Josh.

"So you came to rescue your poor humiliated sis, huh?" I say.

"Well, someone had to do it." He shrugs.

"How'd you know Dad wouldn't come through for me?"

Josh looks me in the eye. "If you haven't noticed, Blaze, our dad is sort of an asshole."

"I guess so," I say. "But how is it you're so okay with that?"

"I think it's because I never really needed him." Josh shrugs, then says meaningfully, "I've always had you."

I put my hands over my face. "I'm so sorry about that stupid photo!"

"Are you kidding?" Josh says. "Coach is a jerkwad! You didn't do anything wrong."

"Don't worry, Blaze, we got him for you," says Ajay.

I let my hands drop, open my eyes wide and scan around the van at the four of them. Everything is quiet a moment, and I calmly ask, "What do you mean you *got him*?"

The boys all look away, except Ajay, who tells me, "As soon as we found out he's the one who posted the photo, we went out to the student lot and slashed the tires of his pickup."

I wince. "How many tires did you slash?"

"All four of them." Dylan grins.

Josh adds, "We each got to do one."

"Guys!" I picture the risk they took just to get revenge on

Mark. They totally stuck up for me. My heart swells with gratitude, and I realize love is the best superpower anyone could wish for. And it's one I already have.

"That is so wrong," I say, but I can't keep the laughter out of my voice.

The boys look relieved as I picture Mark stuck with four flat tires trying to get a ride. *If a girl drives him, I hope she has read my comic.*

A new issue of *The Blazing Goddess* has been forming in my mind. It features a villain called the Gossip Monger, who turns people into cyborgs who believe everything they hear. The Blazing Goddess has to defeat him while defending the kids who are targeted by the mindless robots. I may need to include a vigilante gang of thirteen-year-old soccer players wearing crude superhero costumes and distributing justice. And of course I'll want my own Comic Book Guy sidekick, armed with a plethora of snarky catchphrases. Thinking of Quentin gives me glow-in-the-dark insides. I rub my new ring with my thumb and think of how much work it's going to take for me to rise like a phoenix out of the burning mess of my life. I'll probably have to face horrible insults every day until graduation. My thoughts must show on my face, because Josh puts his hand on my back.

"Hey, Blaze," he says, "everything's going to work out just fine."

And you know what? Maybe it's the Superman suit, or maybe Josh just has some sort of telekinetic mutant powers or something, because hearing him say it, I actually believe it's true. Things will work out just fine.

I give my brother a small smile, start up the van, roll down the window, and weave my way into the traffic crawling down 11th Avenue.

"Hey, Blaze," Dylan calls from the back as I merge into the heavy flow of cars. "Do you think if I send in this coupon they'll still send me these X-ray glasses?"

"Why, Dylan?" Andrew teases. "You want to come back here and see what Spider-Man is packing underneath his costume?"

"Hey, pass a few of those up here," Josh calls to the back.

"I have to admit," Ajay says, "these *Iron Man* issues from the nineteen-eighties are pretty addictive." In my rearview mirror, I see him grab another handful of comics off the giant mound in the back.

Oh, but wait.

Did you actually think we burned all those comics? Seriously?

When the boys and I went back to get the boxes, they helped me quickly empty them into the back of Superturd. Then we filled the empty boxes with stacks of the Comic-Con programs from the bins. All that burned were a bunch of programs, because, hey, my Dad may be a total asshole, but he did have a kickass collection of comics.

"Read up, boys!" I call back to my minivan-full of Superhero Cretins. "We've got a long drive home."

Acknowledgments

Special thanks to Superagent Ammi-Joan Paquette for believing in me and for smashing through force fields of rejection with grace and determination. To Aubrey Poole, my fantastic editor who soars above and beyond and to all of the incredible folks at Sourcebooks. Thank you so much for giving Blaze the chance to fly. Special thanks to Anne Cain for expressing Blaze's awesome talent with her own. And to Derry Wilkens for helping Blaze soar far and wide.

To the remarkable EMLA GANGOs, Verla's fearless Blueboarders and my cosmic critique buddies Alison Ashley Formento, Amanda Coppedge, Shana Silver, Kristen Spina and Michelle Castrofilippo. You folks fill this writing adventure with infinite goodness, wisdom, and laughter.

To Mom, thank you for raising me to love books and for giving me mustard seed faith (even when it nearly landed me in clown college). And thank you, Paw, for your awesome sense of humor and generosity. To Gerry, mentor extraordinaire and owner of the most amazing comic collection on the planet. To super-galactic siblings: Jenna, the wolf-whisperer, and Zach, the baby-wrangler. (I'm still waiting for a waterpik rematch.) To besties, Donna and Dorene, and to my extended legion of family and friends. Thank you all for your support, prayers and inspiration.

Most of all I want to thank the people who put up with my catch-phrase, *"Just a minute,"* as I worked on this book. Trinity, my Sweetie 3.14... and Aidan, my trampoline champion. Remember, "Cromptons never quit." And especially and always to The Best Mate. Brett, you can be pretty funny—just not as funny as me. Thank you for making the journey such a blast.

About the Author

When she was seventeen, Laurie Boyle Crompton painted her first car hot pink using forty cans of spraypaint. The paint dried a bit drippy, but the car looked great when it was flying down the back roads of Butler, Pennsylvania, where she grew up. Laurie now lives near New York City but she loves to visit the mountains and maintains a secret identity in New Paltz, New York, where she and her family can often be found crawling over rocks or tromping through the forest. You can visit her at www.lboylecrompton.com or read more about girls and comics at www.gofangirl.com. *Blaze* is Laurie's first novel.